BIDDLEBORN

A Fantasy World Attacks

Sheila Stowers

Cover design by Vila Design

Published by Van Rye Publishing, LLC
Ann Arbor, MI
www.vanryepublishing.com

ISBN: 978-1-957906-02-7 (paperback)
ISBN: 978-1-957906-03-4 (ebook)
Library of Congress Control Number: 2022936673

Dedication

For my twin sister, who has always been my biggest fan.

Contents

Chapter 1	1
Chapter 2	12
Chapter 3	20
Chapter 4	28
Chapter 5	35
Chapter 6	43
Chapter 7	49
Chapter 8	55
Chapter 9	60
Chapter 10	68
Chapter 11	76
Chapter 12	85
Chapter 13	91
Chapter 14	98
Chapter 15	105
Chapter 16	110
Chapter 17	116
Chapter 18	123
Chapter 19	128
Chapter 20	136
Chapter 21	143
Chapter 22	151
Chapter 23	167
Chapter 24	175
Chapter 25	184

Chapter 26 191
Chapter 27 198
Chapter 28 203
Chapter 29 211
Chapter 30 222
Chapter 31 229
Chapter 32 237
Chapter 33 245
Chapter 34 253
Chapter 35 257

About the Author 263

Chapter 1

MALEVOLENT EYES GLOWED in the darkness. They followed the man as he peeled the plastic wrapper from a slice of cheese. They followed the cheese as it was placed on the sandwich the man was artfully designing with piles of turkey and ham, and then they remembered that the real focus was the man. *Focus on the man, not the cheese—forget the cheese. Forget the piles and piles of turkey and ham. When the man is dead, he'll drop the whole sandwich. Oh, yes, oh, yes, oh, yes!*

A fit of ecstatic quivers shook the being. But with every ounce of power in his evil little soul, he pulled himself together. This was his chance.

Sandwich perfected and resting on a plate, the man flipped off the kitchen light and moved toward the basement stairs. Sounds of football rose from below, as well as the smell of beer and other terrible odors that permeated the lower level, where the man spent most of his time. Noisy things and the smell of sweat, dirt, and metallic things wafted up.

When the man is dead, the noises will stop. Oh, yes, oh, yes, oh, yes! The being moved through the unlit kitchen, slipped past the man, and took up a position on the darkened staircase. The man was not wearing the hateful boots. If he had been, this would be too frightful a plan. But his feet were bare and not likely to cause too much hurt.

There was a confused collision in the dark. The being bounced down a step as the man yelled, "Oof!" and tumbled over him. The man continued to tumble down, down, down, with his sandwich flying into the darkness, hitting before the man finished his noisy—so noisy—slide.

Then, there was the final wump and silence. Oh, the blessed silence and the smell of cheese with piles and piles of turkey and ham. The being was delighted.

* * *

Seventeen-year-old Artie McClintock poured chocolate milk on his Cheerios, grabbed a spoon from the dish drainer, and leaned against the kitchen counter, eating. "Okay, when was the Norman Conquest?" his best friend, Meridian Page, asked while slumped at the table, a stack of notecards in front of her.

"How about you ask in reverse. Give me the year, and I'll tell you what happened," Artie suggested.

Meridian shuffled the cards. "1066?"

"Uh . . . the first printing press."

"No. It was the first year of the Norman Conquest!"

"I feel like you just cheated."

"It can't be cheating. This isn't a game."

"Okay, Meridian. Maybe 'cheating' is the wrong word. But it was definitely trickery of some kind. Which is practically cheating."

Meridian rolled her eyes and reshuffled the deck as Artie's mom stepped through the kitchen doorway, carrying a small green backpack and a bug-eyed Chihuahua. Artie frowned at the dog, then blinked at his mom. "Dear God, why? What is that thing doing in our house, Mom?" Artie asked.

Belinda McClintock set the dog on the floor, then pulled a food dish out of the bag. Next, she pulled out a box of dog food, a water dish, a small rubber bone, and some bacon-shaped dog treats. She lined all these items up on the kitchen counter as the dog sniffed around while shivering.

"I told Mrs. O'Dell we'd keep Twinkie while she's at the hospital with Raymond," Belinda informed her son.

"What happened to Mr. O'Dell?" asked Meridian.

"Dude got drunk and fell down his basement stairs," Artie replied.

"No one said he was drunk," Belinda corrected him.

"He's always drunk, Mom."

Artie's mom shook her head at his response, set the food dish on the floor, and shook food into it. "Don't be late for school."

"It's not even possible," Artie said.

"Nope. We've tried," Meridian agreed. Still, she quickly gathered up the flash cards and shoved them into her purse.

Artie took a step toward the door, which was also a step toward the dog, which exploded in a series of psychotic growls and snarls and then full-on barking. Artie stepped back. The dog's bark subsided back into a low growl, with a bit of a quiver thrown in for emphasis.

"Good lord, what have you done to that poor thing?" Meridian asked.

"Nothing. That stupid little mutt has just always hated me," Artie said. "It knows I know how to do an exorcism."

"No, you don't," Meridian shot back.

"I *might*."

Belinda picked up Twinkie. "Go to school, you two." She carried the dog from the room.

Meridian grabbed her purse. Artie grabbed a package of Oreos from the pantry, and the two headed out the door, with the sound of doggie growls fading behind them.

* * *

Dale Kirchner moved among the fetal pigs, heading toward the front of the classroom. This was his favorite week of the school year. The pigs lay on their silver trays, smelling faintly of formaldehyde, just waiting for scalpel-bearing students to start peeling back their flesh. Dale smiled under his mustache as he turned toward his desk.

Tap tap tap.

Dale's eyes narrowed. He looked around the room.

Tap tap tap.

It was Daisy, his Burmese Python. Tap tap tap. She tapped her tail on the glass of her enclosure, looking at Dale with an intensity normally reserved for feeding time. She slid up along the glass, poking her nose at the lid.

"You wouldn't want to eat one of these pigs, baby girl," Dale told the snake. She bopped her nose on the glass. Her dance had become frantic, like a child needing to pee. "What's wrong with you, girl?" Dale wondered out loud. Behind him, a fetal pig opened an eye.

* * *

Meridian was disturbed to find a strange, bearded man standing outside her American Literature classroom. She hated substitute teachers. In truth, she hated any deviation from her normal routine. She headed toward her seat, which was halfway to the back on the side closest to the door, where she sat in every classroom.

A dark-haired girl with too much makeup and a lot of black clothing was sitting in Meridian's spot. Meridian froze. Jazz Miller grabbed her arm and steered her to the back of the room, depositing her into Josh Spangler's seat. Spangler the Strangler, who was standing halfway across the room, talking loudly to Chad "Cheese Fry" Davenport, yelled, "Hey! No!" But Jazz flipped him off, and that was the end of it.

"New girl took your seat," Jazz informed Meridian, pointing out the obvious.

"Uh-huh."

"How rude."

"Yup."

"You want I should whack her?"

"Shut up."

The bell rang, prompting The Strangler to plop down next to Meridian, taking the seat that was usually reserved for Norma Bellows. Norma was an invisible student who almost never came to class. A Norma Bellows sighting was akin to finding a four-leaf clover, and the students at Biddleborn High had declared it a reliable token of good luck.

The substitute teacher entered the room. “Your assignment is on the board,” he announced. “Shut up, and don’t bother me.”

“What happened to Ms. Gershwin?” asked The Strangler.

“None of your business,” the substitute replied.

“She finally run off with that carnie?”

“No, she had an accident with a hairdryer.”

The class pondered that for a moment. Then, a general buzz of conversation erupted. “You think she tried to kill herself?” Jazz stage whispered to The Strangler and Meridian.

“No,” said Meridian. “It probably really was an accident, whatever it was. Like that time last semester when she swallowed that chain of paperclips during *The Crucible*.”

“I remember the paperclips, but what the heck is a ‘crucible’?” The Strangler asked.

“We spent six weeks reading it aloud,” Meridian reminded him.

The Strangler shook his head. “Doesn’t even sound familiar.”

“You think the new girl tried to kill Ms. Gershwin?” asked Jazz, pulling the conversation back to the current excitement.

“Yes. Definitely,” said The Strangler.

* * *

“I think I’ve been adopted by Jazz Miller again,” Meridian said, opening her Diet Coke. Every day for the past three years, Meridian had eaten the same lunch: a yogurt, a banana, and a Diet Coke.

“He’ll get over it,” Artie said as he began to eat cafeteria pizza cut into squares.

"He touched my arm."

"I'm sure he didn't mean it. He probably just forgot."

Meridian opened her yogurt. "I don't need a babysitter."

"Of course not." Artie's right shoulder shrugged, which was a tell that he was lying.

"You think I do?"

"Almost never."

A squirrel ran past, clutching what appeared to be a candy bar in its teeth.

"If he does it to me again, you'll reprimand him for me, Artie?"

"I can tell him now if you want." Artie stood up and started to take a step, but The Strangler ran into him.

"Oh, sorry, man!" The Strangler said. He piled Artie's pizza back onto his plate and handed it to him. A leaf stuck to one slice. "You seen a squirrel with a candy bar?"

Meridian and Artie pointed. And The Strangler took off after the squirrel.

Artie sat back down and pulled the leaf off his pizza while inspecting the pizza for other dirt. Satisfied, he folded a piece and stuck it in his mouth. He chewed thoughtfully, with his cheeks puffed out, rodent-like. Meridian concentrated on her yogurt. Her focus shifted inward, and she slipped inside a daydream.

Warrior Princess Lanora was lost, deep in the woods of Detritus, the World of the Broken and Forgotten. The sun was going down, and the trees were full of shadows. Her hand gripped her sword. Shadows could be dangerous in Detritus. They worked for the Shadow King.

"We should go sit with the new girl," Artie suggested, nodding toward the girl who had taken Meridian's seat.

Meridian pulled herself out of her head and back into reality. "Why?"

"Because social media wants us to sit with the kids who are sitting alone. Haven't you seen the posts?"

"I'm not on social media. Besides, I don't like her. She took my seat in American Lit."

"How was she supposed to know it was your seat? Is your name on it?"

"Yes. It literally is. I wrote it on with a Sharpie, right across the back."

"She might be really cool. You could hang out with a girl for once—have sleepovers and go shopping. You could do each other's hair and talk about boys." Meridian just blinked at Artie. "Fine," he continued. "You stay here and eat your boring lunch. I'm going to go talk to her." Artie got up and walked across the quad, leaving his pizza and Meridian sitting on their bench.

Halfway to the new girl, Artie glanced back. Meridian was gone. And his pizza was being eaten by a squirrel.

* * *

The chainsaw roared to life in Carl's hands. Vibrations passed through him as he cut through the body of an oak tree that had fallen last spring. The vibrations always made him itch, but he kept cutting until the chainsaw sputtered, coughed, and died. "Dang it," he whispered.

Carl put the chainsaw down and wiped his forehead with his sleeve, leaving a streak of grease. It was time for a break anyway. Something crunched off to his left—a human sound. Carl looked, expecting to see his stepdaughter Meridian home from school a little early or Big Tom, his closest neighbor, come to borrow his reticulating saw again.

Instead, Carl saw nothing. The yard contained only its usual cast of characters: the old lawnmower, the new lawnmower, the old rocking chair with the broken back, a statue of St. Francis next to a dying yucca, the creepy-as-heck clown lamp Meridian and Artie set out near the woods, and three hens pecking at the ground. Carl couldn't see the goat pens from where he was standing—they were behind the toolshed. A cat slept on the woodpile.

The rooster was nowhere to be seen—a circumstance that always made Carl feel a little nervous. He paused, with his eyes roving back to the clown. He was certain it must be his imagination, but it really felt as if the clown were staring back, its painted eyes full of hatred. Carl shook his head. "I must be losing my mind," he said aloud.

* * *

There were shuffles and grunts, followed by a scream. The fetal pigs were alive somehow, and they were coming for Dale Kirchner. They were far more dexterous than they looked.

Dale ran toward the classroom door, but a pig jumped and flew at his shoulder. Another one climbed up his pant leg. "How?!" he yelled. But that was all he had time to say before sixteen fetal pigs were on him, biting with little, rubbery mouths that had far sharper teeth than they should have. Dale Kirchner's last coherent thought was, *What a stupid way to die.*

* * *

Artie got home early. Everyone had been sent home amidst secrecy and flashing lights. But the students always knew what was going on, as is the way of schools everywhere. Mr. Kirchner was dead, having been attacked by some wild animal or animals in his own classroom. Some were saying rats, which didn't surprise Artie in the least. Giant killer cockroaches wouldn't have surprised him either.

Artie leaned his bike against the garage and banged through the front door. His mom wouldn't be home for another two hours. It was time for a snack to ease the pain of the day. Artie would miss Mr. Kirchner. The man had been funny. Unintentionally funny, but still.

Artie had struck out with the new girl. He replayed the scenario as he opened the refrigerator. He had said, "Hey. I'm Artie," and held out his hand for a handshake, which he had believed was very suave and grown-up. Now, after the sting of rejection, he could see that maybe it wasn't suave at all. Pretentious, maybe. Dorky, maybe. The new girl had simply looked at Artie's hand, then looked away. She never even glanced at his face.

A pan of leftover spaghetti promised Artie pain relief and possibly some much-needed oblivion. He pulled it out and set it on the counter, kicking the refrigerator closed with his foot. He had no idea he was being watched. The little clicks on the kitchen tiles didn't register. Artie pulled a plate from the dish drainer by the sink. He grabbed a fork as the little clicks got closer.

As Artie began forking clumps of spaghetti onto his plate, the Chihuahua attacked. Twinkie bit Artie's ankle, growling like a bug-eyed demon. Artie yelped, dropping his fork, which hit the plate and bounced to the floor, losing its spaghetti as it fell. The spaghetti plopped onto the tile.

It was the spaghetti that saved Artie. Twinkie froze, quivering between his desire to kill Artie versus his desire for spaghetti. He lunged forward, toward the spaghetti, and Artie kicked out, punting the dog into the leg of the kitchen table. The dog cried out in un-dog-like rage. It was a cry that sounded as if it came from a much larger creature—a monster.

Artie threw the pan of spaghetti toward Twinkie and bolted toward his bedroom at the back of the house, expecting the dog to latch onto his ankle as he ran. But the spaghetti had distracted the dog, and Artie made it to his room, slamming the door shut behind him.

* * *

"You're early!" Elijah Schmidt, Meridian's boss and the owner of Biddleborn's only sci-fi bookstore, Galactic Books and Other Stuff, was setting up a chess set when she came in—early.

"I'm sometimes early," Meridian said.

"No. You're not. You arrive at exactly 3:58 every day."

"But my shift doesn't start until four. So . . . early."

"No. This isn't early. This is weird."

Meridian started to argue, then realized he was right. "Okay, okay. School got out early. It threw off my groove."

"Uh-oh. Not *the groove*—the rhythm in which you live your life. Beware the groove!" Elijah giggled as he teased her. But Meridian didn't laugh at all. "Since you're here, do you know how to set up a chess board?"

"I think so."

"Cool. I'm gonna take off. Carolyn has plants I'm supposed to pick up from The Wild Flower. The pieces are all labeled on the bottoms, so you know who's what. I think it's weird that they made the Millennium Falcon queen. And why does C-3PO get to be a rook? No one wants to go into battle with Threepio."

Meridian had no answer. Elijah's rambles never really required one anyway. She set her book bag down behind the counter and began setting up the *Star Wars* chess set, trying to remember if knights went on the outside, or was it the rooks?

"Call me if you need anything," Elijah said. "And may the Force be with you."

"Okay."

Meridian's favorite time of day was 5:00 a.m., when she went outside to commune with the chickens before they fully woke up. Her second favorite time of day was when she first got to work. It was orderly. She came in, Elijah prattled on about something, then he left. She would finish whatever task he had given her, then settle in behind the counter. At 6:30, the Dungeons and Dragons group would come in. They'd gather in the back and pretty much leave her alone. In general, it was a quiet job. Rowdy customers didn't shop at Galactic Books and Other Stuff.

Meridian flipped Darth Vader over. *Bishop. Bishop goes next to queen*. Then, her mind slipped away.

Lanora looked to see who had spoken. A skeleton turned its empty sockets toward her. The skeleton's ragged jaw moved as the whole bony assemblage leaned toward her. "I don't suppose you're looking for this," he said, holding up a golden key.

The bell over the door rang, pulling Meridian out of her head and back into reality. She glanced up. The substitute teacher from American Lit filled the doorway. He moved into the store, allowing the door to swing shut behind him. He stood still, looking around.

"May I help you find something?" Meridian had practiced this line a lot. She felt it came out smoothly this time, even though the man before her was a bit creepy. He paused, and Meridian got the distinct feeling he was checking to see if they were alone. Fear tingled along the back of her neck, and she considered running out into the street.

"You have to stop," the substitute said.

Briefly, Meridian thought he meant she had to stop thinking about escape. But then, she realized he couldn't have known what she was thinking . . . probably.

The teacher approached the counter. Meridian straightened and took a step backward. The man leaned his elbows on the counter and said, "You have to stop bleeding Detritus into your own reality. You're killing people in the *real* world!"

Chapter 2

THE MALEVOLENT BEING hurled himself at Artie's bedroom door. He was trembling in rage and covered in spaghetti sauce. The evil boy must not escape. He hurled himself at the door again, but his body bounced off it.

Twinkie used his teeth and claws, scratching at the hateful wood. *No time! No time to chew through the stupid, awful wood.* He was quivering so much that it was making it difficult for him to concentrate. Snarls and grunts poured out of his mouth. He could almost taste the boy's flesh. The spaghetti had been good, and his belly was so full. *But the boy! The boy must die!*

Twinkie's body started to convulse. His eyes rolled and turned black. A shadow, shaped like a hand, poured out of the dog's mouth and ears. It rapped on the door once, twice, three times. Then, it wrapped itself around the doorknob and began to twist.

Artie could hear the dog slamming against the door with far more force than should have been possible. "This is ridiculous," he muttered. "It's just a freaking Chihuahua!" The door shook on its frame.

Artie looked around for a weapon, wishing he were into baseball or hockey. "Lightsaber!" he yelled and started tearing through his closet. There it was, half-hidden by all the fallen clothes: the lightsaber that he had fallen in love with while visiting Meridian at Galactic Books. He had mowed lawns for a whole summer for that lightsaber. Artie wrapped his hand around the hilt of the lightsaber. "I am one with the

Force!" he convinced himself.

The door stopped shaking, and there was silence on the other side. Artie crept toward it, reaching out just as the doorknob began to turn. His chest tightened as he watched it turn. *No, it can't be the dog*, he thought. "Mom?"

The thing that pushed Artie's door open was not his mother. Instead, Twinkie stared at him with his bug-eyes aglow. Twinkie seemed . . . swollen—bigger. His right paw looked as if it had been stretched, with his toes elongated into stubby fingers. Stubby fingers with sharp claws. His face was puffy, and his muscles throbbed beneath his skin. The dog's mouth stretched into a malicious grin. His teeth seemed larger, too.

Artie was not an athlete, but he had spent hours in his garage, dueling with Cheese Fry Davenport. His nerdom, of which he was quite proud, had built his muscles. He raised his lightsaber and stepped into the attack.

The dog lunged, and Artie swung. The lightsaber's blade was made of polycarbonate, strong enough for dueling. Artie's swing glanced off the dog's shoulder. Twinkie yelped and spun, trying to bite the blade. Artie swung again, smacking him across the face this time, then sidestepped to put himself between dog and the door.

Twinkie roared. Artie stepped back, stunned. The dog's eyes rolled, showing red around the edges. He bared his teeth and jumped through the air.

Artie raised the blade too late. Twinkie's teeth clamped down on his arm. Artie screamed. Later, he would insist it was a manly scream. For now, he slammed his arm against the wall, but the dog held on. Artie slammed him again. Twinkie's grip loosened, and Artie shook him off. As the dog hit the floor, Artie ran, slamming the bedroom door behind him.

* * *

Jazz Miller and Cheese Fry Davenport were sitting in Jazz's truck in the Dairy Cream parking lot when they saw Norma Bellows walking toward a black Ford Focus. "Norma Bellows sighting!" Cheese Fry shouted. "Quick! Say something to her!"

Jazz Miller leaned out of his window. "Hi, Norma! Where ya been?" She ignored him, so Jazz got out of the truck in pursuit. "Norma! Wait up!" He ran to join her.

Norma busied herself with her car keys as she neared the Ford. "Seriously, how have you been?" Jazz continued. "We haven't seen you in a while." Norma turned and hissed at him. Jazz took a step backward. "Yeah, okay," he said as he took another step backward and she got in the car. "Right back at you!" he yelled as she backed out and drove away.

Cheese Fry came running up to Jazz. "Oh, man! Did you see that, Jazz?! That was epic!"

"Not epic. Just freaky."

"No, epic. Like, I'm gonna tell my grandkids someday about the time I saw Norma Bellows hiss at Jazz Miller."

"You might want to embellish the story a bit."

"Yeah. You're right. I'll say you hissed back." They stared at the spot where Norma Bellows had parked, then stared off in the direction she had gone. "This whole day has been weird."

"Yeah," Jazz agreed. "I think I need ice cream."

* * *

Meridian could feel her mouth hanging open, but she was momentarily at a loss as to how to close it. Her skin felt crawly, and all her energy was directed toward staying on her feet. "Huh?" she managed to say.

The substitute glowered at Meridian. "You don't even know who I am, do you?"

"Ms. Gershwin's sub."

The man rolled his eyes and opened his mouth to speak, but at that moment, the store's door flew open with a frantic ringing of the bell. Artie rushed in, his eyes wild. "I need your help!" he said. He was holding his right arm against his abdomen.

Meridian had never been so happy to see a friend dripping blood that she was going to have to clean up. She came around the counter with a roll of paper towels. "Great! Let's get this mess cleaned up." She kneeled down to wipe up the blood.

"No, that's—" Artie began.

"You're still dripping," Meridian said, interrupting him.

"We have to save my mom. That dog's going to kill her!"

"Good God!" exclaimed the substitute. "This whole world is doomed."

Meridian and Artie looked at the man. He looked down at the floor and muttered something unintelligible. "Hi, Mr. Gray," said Artie. "I was bitten by a dog. I don't suppose you can help? It's still in my house, and my mom has no idea that it's . . . rabid."

"You're on your own," Mr. Gray said as he turned away, his eyes falling on the *Star Wars* chess set Meridian had set up. "The rooks go on the outside." He picked up Han Solo, slipped him into his pocket, walked around Artie in the doorway, and left the store.

Meridian and Artie looked at each other. "You're a walking biohazard," Meridian said.

"Twinkie tried to kill me! He's possessed or an alien or something." Artie held up his arm as proof.

"Stop dripping on my floor."

"It's *Elijah's* floor, not yours. We have to save my mom. And kill the dog."

"Are you talking about that stupid Chihuahua?"

"He's no Chihuahua. He's a monster. I swear to you. Something's happened to him."

"Artie, I'm at work."

"You heard Mr. Gray. This whole world is doomed. We have to

save it."

"How do you even know his name?"

"He was Ms. Gershwin's sub. He wrote his name on the board."

"Okay. But I'm still at work. Can't you just call your mom and say, 'hey, Mom. Mrs. O'Dell's dog is a murderous alien. Don't go home'?"

"She'd never believe me."

"I don't believe you either."

"Can you call Elijah and tell him you're sick? Or having a family emergency?"

Meridian glared at Artie. But he *had* saved her from the creepy substitute. "I'll just tell him the truth—that my friend is having a mental health emergency and needs my help."

"Thank you!" Artie smiled, then winced. "And do you have a first aid kit around here?"

* * *

Carl stacked the last log on the woodpile. He was sweaty and tired, but the job was done. Something crawled across the wood. A spider. "Hey, fella," Carl said. He was feeling good—at peace with all of nature.

Another spider moved across the pile. And another. Suddenly, spiders poured out of the woodpile. Different species of spiders, but all big, as if they were swollen. Hundreds. Maybe thousands. They moved together—an army of terror, spilling onto the ground and heading toward Carl.

Carl ran.

* * *

Artie and Meridian pulled up to the curb outside Artie's house. They were in Meridian's car, an old silver Toyota that just wouldn't die. Artie would have been happy to own an ugly old Toyota. His main mode of transportation was a bicycle, which he had left in the break room at Galactic Books. They had stopped at McDonald's on the way.

Even a demon dog can't resist cheeseburgers—they hoped.

"Okay, let's go over the plan," Artie suggested.

"No."

"But we need to be prepared."

"It's a Chihuahua, Artie. I'm going to lure it into the bathroom with a cheeseburger and close the door."

"It can open doors. I saw it, Meridian. It literally turned a doorknob."

"With its stretched-out toes. Got it."

Artie touched Meridian's arm, and she flinched. "Listen, Meridian. You don't have to believe me. But I really, really need you to *pretend* you believe me. Can you do that?"

Meridian shook off his hand. "Yes. Just . . . no touchy."

Artie sighed. "Cool. So, here's the plan: we sneak into the garage, grab a tarp and a shovel—"

"We're not going to *hurt* it," Meridian interrupted.

"No, of course not," Artie confirmed. "So anyway, we grab a tarp and a shovel. We use the cheeseburgers to lure it close enough, then throw the tarp on it. We'll trap it underneath. And if you still think it's just a regular Chihuahua, we'll wrap it in the tarp and carry it to the bathroom. We'll lock it up and tell my mom it attacked me."

"And what's the shovel for?"

"For when you stop thinking it's just a regular dog."

The garage was quiet and free of possessed canines. Meridian grabbed the shovel. "I get the shovel; you get the tarp," she directed.

Artie looked around for the tarp. "I think it was . . . here." He pointed to a pile of paint cans sitting under the window. "Crap."

"What about that instead?" Meridian pointed to his mom's fishing gear. A large dip net hung on the wall.

"That might work, if he hasn't grown any more."

"Tell you what, if that dog has grown too big for the net, we'll hit it with the shovel."

"Deal." Artie grabbed the net.

Everything was quiet when they stepped inside. Meridian held the shovel in her right hand, the bag of cheeseburgers in her left hand. Artie walked ahead of her, gripping the net. They stopped just inside the kitchen door and listened.

"Okay. Open a cheeseburger," Artie instructed.

Meridian set the bag on the counter and reached inside. She pulled out a cheeseburger and crinkled the paper loudly as she unwrapped it. The smell and sounds were unmistakable. And they could hear the click click click of little feet heading down the hall. Meridian tossed the cheeseburger to the floor.

Twinkie stepped into the kitchen. He was a small, quivering Chihuahua. He crept to the cheeseburger, his ears pinned down and tail tucked, and began eating while keeping an eye on the humans who were watching his every move.

Meridian leaned the shovel against the wall, and Artie swung the net over the dog. The dog roared, his teeth as large as a lion's. His muscles pulsed and expanded, his skin stretching thin from the sudden growth. His eyes were laced through with red veins. He pulled the net out of Artie's hand and started shaking his head to free himself.

"Hit it, Meridian!" Artie cried out.

As Meridian grabbed the shovel, Artie threw the rest of the bag of cheeseburgers, hitting the dog in the face. The bag bounced off and slid across the floor. The dog ignored it, with his fury focused on Artie and Meridian.

Meridian swung the shovel. It thudded against the dog, who ignored it completely. His eyes were full of murder. He crouched, growling.

"Give me the shovel and get behind me," Artie said.

"I think we have to burn your house down."

"Seriously. Give me the shovel."

Meridian slowly stepped to the side and moved the shovel toward Artie. But the dog snarled and leaped before Artie could grab it. Meridian whirled the shovel toward Twinkie instead, catching him on the chin with the tip. He yelped and snapped.

"Open the door, Artie!"

Artie yanked open the door, pulling Meridian out with him as she slapped the dog repeatedly with the shovel. Then, Artie slammed the door closed, and Meridian sagged with relief. But Artie reminded her, "He can open doors. Run!"

Chapter 3

ZELDA GERSHWIN WAS HAPPY to be alive. Her scalp was sore, half of her hair had been shaved, and she had been nearly strangled, but she had survived. No one believed her story, though.

Zelda had been blowing her hair dry when the hairdryer began to suck instead of blow. It breathed her hair right in and pulled it tighter and tighter. She had unplugged the hairdryer, thinking that would take care of the problem. She figured she would be able to pull her hair out or cut it if necessary. But instead, she could smell her hair burning. *Oh, Lordy, Lordy.*

Then, the cord—the cord tried to kill her. Zelda had unplugged the hairdryer and dropped the cord. But the cord rose up like a snake and wrapped itself around her throat. She couldn't scream. She clawed at the cord and tried to get her fingers underneath it to remove it from her throat. But it was too tight, and the world grew fuzzy around the edges.

Zelda grabbed the hairdryer instead, and she slammed it against the sink. She could hear it crack, and the cord loosened a little. She slammed it again. But the hairdryer bit her hand. *Lord, help!*

Zelda had next grabbed a towel off the rack. She threw it over the hairdryer, wrapping it up as she would a cat she had to give a pill. The cord tightened around her throat as she hurled the hairdryer—towel and all—into the toilet. Zelda slammed the lid as the hairdryer thrashed. The cord was still wrapped around her throat, and the tension pulled her to her knees. She leaned her head on the toilet lid as she desperately tried to slip her fingers between the cord and her throat.

Can you drown a hairdryer? That was Zelda's last coherent thought before the world went black. Later, she awoke in an ambulance, surrounded by efficiency and concern. That was the previous night. Now, she sat up in her hospital bed, her grandmother Rose Marie by her side. Rose Marie had saved Zelda by cutting the cord.

Rose Marie was ninety years old and still always knew what to do. Zelda wasn't always grateful for this—some days, it was hard to live with, especially since Zelda herself was prone to indecision and, worse, bad decisions. Today, however, she would allow her grandmother to gloat a little about being a hero.

"I still don't know why you put it in the toilet," Rose Marie said.

"I told you. I was trying to drown it."

"Mmmmhmmmm."

Zelda's grandmother—and the doctors, and probably everyone else in Biddleborn—thought she had tried to kill herself. Zelda had to admit that made far more sense than her hairdryer coming to life and trying to strangle her. *It had to be possessed*, Zelda thought.

What if the thing that possessed her hairdryer were still out there? What if it possessed her IV? Or worse—what if she really *had* tried to kill herself? What if her own mind was the enemy? Zelda read a lot of books, so she was well aware of how strange the world really is.

* * *

Carl grabbed a half-full, five-gallon can of gasoline and set it in a wheelbarrow, next to a butane torch and two cans of wasp spray. He wiped a gloved hand across his forehead. Those spiders weren't like anything he'd ever seen. He pushed his load toward the woodpile, carefully scanning for spiders as he went and hoping fervently that they hadn't moved toward the house.

Carl heard a scratching sound behind him. He turned. It was the rooster, standing on one leg, giving Carl the evil eye. "Go on, you!" he told it. "I don't have time for your shenanigans today." He grabbed the gas can. "And you don't want no part of this." He carried the gas can toward the woodpile. The rooster followed at a distance.

The woodpile looked as if it were undulating, with the top layer of bark rippling like the brown surface of a lake. But Carl knew it was spiders. When he approached, they stilled. He could see them now, an army of spiders, turning as one to face him. So much evil glinting in so many eyes. But it was their intelligence that scared him most.

Carl opened the gas can and doused the grass between him and the spiders. He circled the woodpile, splashing. He splashed some on the wood, setting the spiders in motion. Some of them jumped onto the grass and headed toward him.

Carl tossed the gas can and grabbed the wasp spray and the butane torch. A spider crawled along the grass toward him—a fat fellow, the stuff of nightmares. Carl soaked it in wasp spray. More were coming. He sprayed them, then retreated a few steps and lit the torch. He sprayed the flame and set the yard on fire. The gasoline erupted, and the spiders screamed.

Then, two things happened at once: Meridian's car pulled into the driveway—*early*, thought Carl—and something crawled along Carl's arm. He looked down. Spiders! He started dancing, and something bit his leg, inside his jeans. He cussed and started stripping.

* * *

Miss Lindy's Diner had only one patron, a circumstance that was unusual at 6 p.m., even on a Monday. Belinda McClintock, Artie's mom and the owner of Miss Lindy's, brought the man a refill of coffee. He was a stranger, and strangers were rare in Biddleborn. "You want a warm-up?" she asked.

"Sure." He watched her pour coffee into his cup. "Thanks."

"You're welcome."

A small black kitten peeked out of the man's coat. He fed it a bite of bacon. "Sorry. I know I shouldn't have brought her inside, but I was afraid something would happen to her while I was eating. I found her in the parking lot."

"She's cute. And since you're the only customer, how about I get her a bowl of milk?"

"Actually, cats are lactose intolerant. They like milk, but they shouldn't have it. Besides, she got most of my bacon." The kitten climbed out of his coat and jumped onto the table. She headed for the man's plate.

"Let me get her some bacon of her own—and maybe a slice of ham."

When Belinda got back with a small plate piled too high with ham, bacon, and roast beef, the kitten was sitting on the man's shoulder, sniffing the man's beard. "I must have food in my beard," the man said.

"She seems to really like you. What are you going to name her?"

"Oh, I can't keep her. I'm staying in a motel. You want a kitten?"

"I can't."

"Why not?"

Belinda hesitated. *Why not, indeed?* she thought. "Well . . . I mean, I guess I've just never had a cat before."

"Cats just happen to people. And I think this one wants to happen to you."

"Yes. Yes, it does. Maybe I'm *meant* to take this kitten."

The man smiled. "Yes. I think maybe you are."

* * *

Meridian's stepfather had just started a striptease in the yard—the yard that he had set on fire. Meridian jumped out of her car and ran for the hose. But she wasn't sure which to spray first, Carl or the yard. She started with Carl.

Meridian couldn't see what was making Carl dance, but a blast of water would take care of it. She sprayed him down. He slapped at himself, shimmying in the spray. Finally, he stopped dancing and ran for the house.

Next, Meridian turned her attention to the raging inferno that had engulfed the woodpile. There was no saving the wood, but she could keep the fire from spreading to the house, the shed, the barn, and all the years of junk Carl had left piled here and there. *Come to think of it, maybe I should let the fire burn*, Meridian thought. But she didn't.

Spraying water from the hose all around the edges of the fire, Meridian soaked the grass. Fortunately, their yard was largely dirt due to the sheer number of trees, which somewhat helped contain the fire. But there was a fair amount of rotten leaves and other debris.

Artie came up beside Meridian, having grabbed the shovel they had used to fight the dog. He started beating the flames. Meridian put down the hose and ran to the shed to get a rake.

The rooster pranced over to Carl's clothing piled on the ground and scraped and inspected it. A spider fell out of the shirt. The rooster warbled, calling to his hens. They came running. These spiders would make a fine snack.

Carl came back outside, fully clothed, a can of wasp spray clutched in each hand. "Watch out for spiders!" he yelled. He started kicking leaves away from the edge of the fire, helping Meridian clear the perimeter so the fire would run out of things to burn.

"This is a gasoline fire," Meridian said. It was an accusation, not just a statement.

"Yup. Sure is."

"What on earth, Carl?"

"Spiders. Thousands of spiders. Big ones. Real big. And not all the same kind of spider. They were just pouring out of the wood, coming for me." He raised up a hand, still clutching the wasp spray. "I know how it sounds. But I swear they were working together, like an army. I ain't ever seen anything like it."

A hen ran by with a spider dangling from her beak. Two other hens were chasing her, trying to steal her treat.

"I don't think this fire's going anywhere," Meridian noted. "Artie and I need your help. Whatever . . . *happened* to your spiders also happened to a dog. The dog is in Artie's house, and we need to . . . deal with it . . . before his mom gets home."

Artie held up his bandaged arm. "It tried to kill me!"

Carl nodded. An hour ago, he would not have believed them. But now . . . "Okay. Artie, you know how to shoot a gun?"

* * *

"You sure you got this?" Belinda asked Marvin, a giant of a man who had been the cook at Miss Lindy's for the past nine years.

"Yes, ma'am. It's a ghost town in here tonight. Ain't no reason for both of us to stay. You take that kitten on home."

"Thank you, Marvin. You call me if you need anything."

Which is how Belinda McClintock ended up leaving work early and heading home, accompanied only by a small kitten and the naive belief that the world was still obeying the old laws of physics.

* * *

As soon as Zelda got home from the hospital, she started worrying about the appliances in her house. What if the stove decided to kill her? What if the refrigerator swallowed her in the middle of the night? And, oh Lord! They just got the garbage disposal fixed.

When Zelda's eyes roved through the kitchen and landed on the new knife set her grandmother had just purchased, she decided to go to bed. "Rose Marie, I'm going to go lay down," she said to her grandmother, who had accompanied her home. "Yell if you need anything. And please do me a favor?"

"What's that?" Rose Marie was not keen on doing anyone any favors.

Zelda hesitated. There was really no point in warning her grandmother about the garbage disposal, the kitchen knives, or the stove. Rose Marie was a born skeptic.

"Just . . . be safe."

* * *

Armed for war, Meridian, Artie, and Carl piled into Carl's truck and headed to Artie's house. "I'll go in first," Carl decided. "Artie, you cover the back door. Meridian, you take the side door."

Belinda's car was in the driveway. Artie jumped out of the truck before Carl had completely stopped. Carl yelled, "You stick to the plan!" But Artie didn't hear him.

* * *

Belinda carried the kitten into the house, intending to close her up in the bathroom while she went out to buy kitten supplies. Belinda had never owned a cat and knew little about them, but she knew she needed a litter box and cat food. And one of those "red dot" laser toys.

Belinda moved down the hall toward the bathroom, wondering what Twinkie would think of the kitten. Then, she heard movement coming from the kitchen. "Twinkie? Come meet somebody."

A dog stood at the head of the hallway, snarling. It was the same color as Twinkie, but that was where the similarity ended. This dog was massive, with a huge barrel chest and bulging muscles. Its eyes were red with hate.

The kitchen door slammed open. "Mom!" Artie yelled. Belinda's son was holding a handgun. Normally, Belinda would have been horrified to see a gun in her son's hand.

The dog looked back over its shoulder. It bared its teeth at Artie, almost like it was smiling—gloating. Artie pointed the gun.

The kitten squirmed in Belinda's hands, and the dog looked at it. He licked his chops.

Carl Davis, Meridian's stepfather, appeared behind Artie. He was holding a shotgun. At the end of the hall, Artie's bedroom door opened, and Meridian stepped out. She had a revolver in one hand, a machete in the other.

The dog jumped toward Belinda, who screamed. The kitten flew from her hands, landing on the dog's back. But it was no longer a kitten-sized kitten. It was a hulking panther, and it was roaring as it clung to the dog's flesh.

Chapter 4

AT NINETY YEARS OLD, Rose Marie looked frail. But woe to those who treated her as such. Rose Marie imagined that she was as strong as ever, which is why she insisted on mowing her own grass. Zelda tried mowing it sometimes, but bless her heart, she did such a terrible job. She needed to stick to teaching and hysterics.

Rose Marie, dressed in a monochromatic red sweatsuit, started the lawn mower. Although it was seventy-five degrees out, she was cold. She was always cold. The world was a cold place.

The lawnmower coughed. "Don't you dare die on me," Rose Marie scolded it.

"Sorry. I was just clearing my throat," the lawnmower answered.

Rose Marie fainted.

* * *

As the demon dog and hell kitten wrestled in the hallway, Meridian grabbed Belinda by the arm and pulled her down the hall, then into Artie's bedroom. She closed the door and pushed Belinda toward the window. "Is this the apocalypse?" Belinda asked as she climbed through her son's bedroom window.

"I guess so." Meridian crawled out after her.

"I never dreamed the apocalypse would start in my hallway."

They met Artie at Carl's truck. Belinda threw her arms around him. "Where's Carl?" Meridian asked.

"He said he was going to 'clean up.'"

"Whoa—he's not gonna hurt my kitten, is he?" Belinda asked.

Artie shrugged one shoulder. His mom put on her determined face and marched back toward the starting point of the apocalypse. "Mom! Wait!" Artie shouted after her.

* * *

As shadows pulsated around her, Norma Bellows lit a candle in the darkness. She could feel how thin the barrier between worlds was growing. Creatures were pressing through from the other side. Soon, it would be possible to slip through from here to there. She was ready.

But first, she would call forth another shadow. Norma Bellows opened the Biddleborn High School yearbook she had stolen from someone's locker at the beginning of the school year. She flipped through until she found the person she was looking for . . .

Jazz Miller.

Norma opened a safety pin and stuck the point into her index finger. A drop of blood bubbled up, and she wiped it across Jazz Miller's smiling face. Norma Bellows laughed.

* * *

Carl stood in Belinda's kitchen, his shotgun loaded and ready. Twinkie and the kitten were still locked in battle. The kitten had Twinkie pinned down. It looked as if the fight would soon be over, and Carl was ready to take care of the winner. "Don't you dare shoot my kitten!" Belinda shouted from behind him.

"That thing ain't a kitten anymore," Carl responded.

"She saved my life."

"Nah. She just saw an opportunity for a fight."

"Carl Davis! You give her a chance to prove she's all right before you shoot her. Maybe she's on our side." Belinda's hands were tucked into fists and resting on her hips.

The kitten had Twinkie by the throat and was shaking him. Twinkie was limp and smaller than he had been. The kitten dropped his body, which hit the floor as a Chihuahua once again.

Carl raised his shotgun. The kitten began cleaning her paws, getting smaller by the second. Belinda put a hand on Carl's shoulder. "Look at her," she said.

A tiny black kitten looked up at the humans. She hopped to Belinda and jumped. The kitten caught the hem of Belinda's skirt and tried to climb up her but fell.

Belinda scooped the kitten up. "What on earth am I supposed to tell Gracie O'Dell about her dog?"

* * *

The lawnmower mowed around Rose Marie's prone body, not really knowing what else to do. He hoped the woman wasn't dead. She seemed like a nice person. She took good care of her lawn equipment.

The lawnmower took pride in his work. As he was carefully edging around a clump of lilies, Rose Marie awoke. She pushed herself up and sat watching him for a moment. Being watched made the lawnmower nervous, especially since he knew the woman had mad grass-mowing skills. He really wanted to impress her.

Rose Marie was struggling to stand. The lawnmower rolled himself next to her. He was afraid to speak because of the effect it had last time, so he just stood there, hoping she would understand. And she did.

Rose Marie grabbed hold of the lawnmower's handle and pulled herself up. "Thank you," she said with as much dignity as she could muster, considering she had grass stains on her red monochromatic sweat suit and was talking to a lawnmower.

"You're welcome." Oops. He didn't mean to speak. The lawnmower tensed, waiting for Rose Marie to faint again.

But Rose Marie merely patted the lawnmower's handle and looked around at her backyard. "You'll want to leave the front yard for now. It wouldn't do to have you out there by yourself where everyone can see. Stay here inside the fence." She paused a moment, looking around. "I don't suppose the weed eater can also . . . run by itself?"

"No, ma'am. It's just a machine."

"Yes. Well. I'm going to go lie down for a bit." Rose Marie walked, a bit unsteadily, into the house.

* * *

Carl, Belinda, Artie, and Meridian gathered at Belinda's kitchen table. The kitten played at Belinda's feet. They had wrapped Twinkie's body in a black garbage bag. The plan was for Carl to take the dog and cremate it.

"What did the man look like, Belinda?" Meridian asked.

"He had dark hair, dark eyes, and a beard. He was sitting down, so I can't be sure, but he seemed tall. He said he was staying at a motel."

"Mr. Gray, probably," Artie said. "He was our sub today in English class."

"Anyway, he had just found the kitten in the parking lot. I'm sure he didn't know . . . what she can do."

Meridian opened her mouth to speak, then closed it.

"Well, I don't like any of this," Carl said. "I've got a rooster at home that tries to kill me at least once a week as is. What happens if he . . . mutates?"

"I'm not sure that's the correct word," Meridian said. "Mutants don't un-mutate."

"Dude, if only Mr. Kirchner hadn't been eaten by rats. He could have helped us," Artie pointed out.

They all stared at each other for a moment.

"What about the sheriff? We could call him," Belinda suggested.

"What would we say?" Carl asked. "That the animals are . . . on steroids? Could that be it? Like, some kinda extreme steroids?"

"It *was* a bit like roid rage," Artie said. "So, maybe? Maybe there's a . . . mad scientist around here? Or . . . kryptonite or something?"

"Ain't nobody going to believe us," Carl said with dejection. "Not with that dog being a little Chihuahua again."

"I'll tell Gracie he ran away," Belinda decided. "Slipped out of the house and ran off, probably looking for her."

"Yeah, that's a good idea," Carl agreed. "In the meantime, keep yourselves armed."

"What about school?" Artie asked.

"They ain't got metal detectors. Just don't get caught."

"What if next time, it's a whole herd of giant, angry cows? Or horses? What if a circus rolls through town and the elephants escape?" Artie asked.

"That's a good point," said Carl. "We need heavier artillery."

"We could turn your truck into a Vehicle of Destruction," Meridian suggested.

Carl nodded. "That ain't a bad idea."

* * *

Jazz Miller was feeling good. Heck, Jazz Miller was looking good, or so he would have told you. He was on his way to pick up Katie Sparks for a date. His truck was clean and sparkling. It smelled good. He smelled good. The world smelled good. Jazz cruised down Main Street, believing everything was fine in the universe. He was, of course, quite wrong.

Driving from one end of Biddleborn to the other takes eight minutes, or closer to nine if you get stopped by the streetlight in the center of town. One hand lazily beating time on the steering wheel, country music twanging from the speakers, Jazz pulled up in front of Katie's house at 6:59. He stopped the truck, debated getting out, then sent her a text that said, *I'm here*.

The house's front door opened, and Katie Sparks erupted from it, her father right behind her. Marty Sparks was the reason Jazz had sent a text rather than knock on the door. Jazz knew all the right moves to impress a girl's father, but Marty Sparks was unimpressible.

Katie rushed to the passenger side door. Her father yelled from the front stoop, "You get her home by ten, or else!"

Katie rolled her eyes and reached for the door handle. But the truck had other ideas. The locks clicked. Katie pulled up on the door handle. "It's locked," she said, staring at Jazz through the window.

"Sorry." Jazz hit the unlock button, but there was no sound. He pushed it several more times, refusing to believe it really wasn't going to work. "Locks are broken. Hang on." Jazz leaned across the seat to unlock Katie's door manually. But the truck shifted into drive and sped off across Biddleborn.

Jazz sat up, grabbing the steering wheel. He slammed on the brakes, but the brakes did not obey. For good measure, Jazz screamed loud and long. Once that was over, he pulled out his cell phone. *Who do you even call when your truck has gone mad and kidnapped you?* Jazz wondered. He called 911.

"911. What's the address of the emergency?"

"I'm in my truck! Driving on Brockmeier Road, heading toward . . . I'm heading out of town! And I can't . . . the truck won't stop. My brakes! They aren't working."

"Okay. How far down the road are you? What landmarks are nearby?"

"Uh . . . I just passed . . . Saint Stephen's Church. I'm outside of Biddleborn now, on the highway. Please help!"

"Okay. What kind of truck are you driving?"

"It's a red Dodge Ram. License plate is 707 UXC."

"Sir, the police are on their way."

"We're turning! The truck is turning. It just turned on Paulson Mine Road."

"The truck turned?"

"Yes, ma'am."

"Are you in the driver's seat? Or is someone else driving?"

"I don't know what's happening! Yes, I'm driving! I mean . . . I'm in the driver's seat, but the truck is driving itself! It . . . it won't let me steer!" Jazz was trying hard to avoid words like "haunted."

The truck swerved. Jazz grabbed the steering wheel, dropping his phone in the process. The speedometer climbed from fifty-five to seventy to seventy-five. Jazz looked for his phone. It had slid across to the passenger side floor. Intending to retrieve it, Jazz unbuckled his seatbelt. *Maybe I should call my mom, just in case*, he thought.

A siren screamed behind the truck. Jazz looked in the rearview mirror. Flashing lights! Both of Biddleborn's police cruisers were chasing him down.

The road heading toward the mine was narrow and twisting, with the double line down the center warning the reckless that this was not a good time to pass. A slow SUV puttered ahead of Jazz's truck. Jazz screamed as his truck flew around it on a particularly tight curve where many a Biddleborner had lost their life. He screamed even harder as a semi-truck barreled into view around the curve.

Chapter 5

MERIDIAN DIDN'T CRY when she heard about Jazz Miller's death. She felt like she should cry, but the tears wouldn't come. She hadn't cried since shortly after her mom's death, nine years before.

The house Meridian lived in was Carl's. It was an old farmhouse that had been in his family for years. Meridian's mom had married Carl after knowing him for only a few months, unaware that she had cancer and would soon be leaving her daughter in the care of a man who was practically a stranger to Meridian. As it turned out, Carl did all right as a single father—eventually. Things were really awkward between them for the first few years, though.

Now, Meridian sat in her bedroom, the loft at the top of the house. Her room was decorated in navy and white, but it was not a nautical motif. She hated boats. She sat in her window seat, looking out into the darkened yard. She had to work to see past her own reflection.

Jazz Miller. Meridian had known him forever, since before he went by Jazz, back in his Calvin days. That was before he decided he was cool.

But really, Jazz had always been cool, starting with the time he punched Ross Jacoby for throwing dirt at Meridian. And then later, in middle school, when he adopted her as part of his crowd. It hadn't worked out because Meridian didn't want to be popular, but it did cause everyone to stop picking on her. It was as if she became the weird cousin of Biddleborn's class of 2023—the person they didn't understand but felt protective toward.

Jazz Miller was underrated as a friend. Meridian leaned her head against the cool window, and her mind began to drift off.

The dungeon was cold but surprisingly dry. Lanora could hear rats skittering, and she flinched involuntarily at each sound. She huddled against the wall—she might as well; the chains on her wrists kept her from moving much farther out into the cell anyway.

A dead man was chained across from Lanora, his flesh having rotted long ago. He was bone and cloth now. She shuddered, looked away, and struggled against her chains once more.

"You may as well give up, my lady. You'll never get loose that way," a voice told Lanora. Surprised, she turned toward the voice, but all she saw was the man of bones. His skull had shifted, and his empty sockets were now looking at her.

"Did you . . . speak?" Lanora asked.

"Indeed, I did," the man of bones confirmed. "As this dungeon's oldest resident, I can assure you the chains are quite strong. You'll need cunning, not physical strength, to get out of this mess. Fortunately for you, I have quite a good deal of cunning." He grinned, or at least, Lanora imagined he did.

"Your help would be much appreciated. I have no doubt that the Cat Lord will reward you handsomely for rescuing me."

"Ha! I'd trust a bog wight before I'd trust the Cat Lord. I don't need a reward, my lady. Throwing the Shadow King's dungeons into a bit of chaos is all the reward I need."

"I'm Lady Lanora of the Sands. And who is my brave rescuer?"

"Sir Calvin, of the Thieves' Guild."

"Is that why you're in this dungeon?"

"Absolutely. I tried to pick the Shadow King's pocket. Only, turns out, he doesn't have pockets. Just a really nasty temper."

* * *

Artie and Meridian only had one class together: biology. Since their biology teacher was brutally murdered by small animals the day before, neither was surprised to have a substitute teacher. It was Mr. Gray.

Fetal pigs lay on trays, waiting to be sliced open. They were cold and rubbery. "Bleh," Artie said, looking at the pigs while taking his seat between Meridian and The Strangler.

Mr. Gray stood before them, a dry erase marker in his hand, the biology text open on the podium in front of him. "I'm going to be your biology teacher for the rest of the year," he announced. "Since there are only six weeks left, there'd be no point in hiring a real . . . anyone else. So, you're gonna want to take notes."

"Let's talk about . . ." Mr. Gray paused and glanced at the textbook before finishing with, "cells." He drew an oval on the board. "This is a cell." He added some squiggles inside the oval. "It runs on mitochondria, which, as everyone knows, is the powerhouse of the cell, rather like lithium. The whole thing operates according to three laws: hegemony, kinesthetics, and mitosis. Science, of course, is simply magic that's explained with . . . math. So, for instance, this cell is . . . approximately one-eighth of the width of your average blind shuffle, times several feet of . . . permeable tissue samples. When you add in tricyclics and repeat the sequence three times backward in a mirror . . ." Mr. Gray paused and glared at the students. "Well, take notes!"

Artie raised his hand. Mr. Gray frowned and called on him via raised eyebrow. "Er, Mr. Gray . . . will the tests come from the textbook or the, uh, notes?" Artie asked.

Mr. Gray hesitated a moment and glanced at the textbook as though the answer to Artie's question were written there. "Both."

"Oh God," muttered Artie. It was, in fact, a prayer.

"So, let's cut open these pigs," Mr. Gray directed. "Get going! Chop chop!"

Missy Reynolds, who hoped to be valedictorian one day, raised her hand. "What?" Mr. Gray snapped.

"We just . . . cut it open? Are we supposed to . . . label parts? Is there a worksheet?"

"No. Cut it open and explore. Look for the squishy bits. And watch out for any excess teeth."

Artie and Meridian were sharing a pig. "What are we going to name him?" Artie asked.

Meridian pulled a pair of safety glasses out of her backpack, put them on, and donned the nitrile gloves the substitute had laid out on every table. Then, she picked up her scalpel. She sliced along the pig's belly, then did a V-shape on the chest, like all the autopsies she had seen on television. "His name is John Doe," she said. "We have to weigh his organs and look at the contents of his stomach. And one of us should probably be talking into a tape recorder."

"I think the cause of death was being soaked in formaldehyde," Artie joked.

"I forgot to look for blunt force trauma." Meridian put down the scalpel and examined the outside of the pig.

Artie leaned over. "Hey!" he pointed to the pig's head. "Is that 'blunt force trauma'?"

"It looks like a thumbprint. Like someone squeezed his head. Probably postmortem."

"You watch too many crime shows, Meridian."

"Yes. Do you want to cut?" She offered Artie the scalpel.

"Nope. I'm happy to supervise. Besides, the person who carries safety glasses with her has definitely earned the right to use the scalpel."

Meridian resumed cutting. There were lots of squishy bits in the abdomen. She peeled back the skin and muscle. "Hey, look in the textbook and see if there's a picture. I don't know what I'm looking at."

"How about I Google it?"

"Yes. Ask the Great Google."

Artie found a picture on Google Images. It was a real fetal pig, not a drawing, splayed open. The greenish-gray organs were all a jumble, like an organic car engine, with words superimposed to identify the squishy bits. Artie took a screenshot and sent it to Meridian.

"Hey! Share that with me, too," The Strangler pleaded. Artie did.

Meridian picked up the dissecting scissors. She used them to point at an organ. "This is a kidney. And this . . ." she glanced at her cell phone, "is the colon. I'm going to cut the organs out. Go get me an extra tray. And see if you can find a scale."

"We don't really have to—" Meridian stopped Artie with a look. Artie sighed and hopped off his stool. Then, Mr. Gray wandered over. "I need an extra tray and a scale, Mr. Gray. Is that cool?" Artie asked.

"Sure. Go find them," Mr. Gray agreed.

Artie roamed off to start searching cabinets while Meridian concentrated on removing John Doe's organs, acutely aware that Mr. Gray was watching. Artie came back with a tray and a scale. Meridian transferred a kidney, the large intestine, and a couple of other organs to the new tray.

"What's that?" Artie pointed.

"That's the stomach, and this is the pancreas," Meridian responded. Mr. Gray had moved to another table. Meridian relaxed.

"The stomach looks . . . full."

Meridian poked at it. "Kind of weird, since he was fetal. Not like he was eating garbage from a trough."

"I don't think pig food is considered garbage."

"Whatever." Meridian picked up the stomach and snipped it open with the scissors. She emptied the contents onto the tray. They both stared at it.

"Is that . . .?" Artie began to ask.

It was the tip of a human finger.

* * *

Sheriff John E. Amory took off his hat and ran a hand through his thinning hair. He really needed a drink. He glanced at his watch. The

AA meeting at the Presbyterian church started at 6 p.m., and that night, he would definitely be there, front and center.

The sheriff turned to Mr. Mayfield, Biddleborn High School's principal for the past twenty-seven years. "I'm going to want to talk to the other teachers from this hall. In the meantime, this is a crime scene. No one comes in."

"No problem," Mr. Mayfield agreed. "We'll move Mr. Kirchner's classes to the library for now."

The fetal pigs were being sent to the crime lab in Springfield. Biddleborn wasn't big enough to do its own forensic analysis.

How on earth did pieces of Dale Kirchner end up in the stomachs of sixteen fetal pigs? Amory didn't know—couldn't even imagine, truth be told. He thought about the 911 call the Miller boy made before crashing head-on into a semi. Add to that Zelda Gershwin's insistence that her hairdryer had tried to strangle her, and it had been a week straight out of the X-Files.

The sheriff didn't know which he needed most: a drink, a psychiatrist, or a paranormal investigator. Maybe what he needed was a long vacation.

* * *

Zelda needed coffee. The school was abuzz with the news that either Mr. Kirchner was mauled by fetal pigs or his killer had a sick sense of humor. Most people favored the latter theory, but not Zelda.

The new substitute teacher, Mr. Gray, had been kicked out of his classroom by the ongoing investigation and had settled himself into the green chair Zelda normally used as her station when in the teachers' lounge. It was a scratchy avocado plaid from the early 70s that most other teachers avoided due to the texture and dubious smell, as if it had spent at least two decades in a damp basement.

"You were my sub yesterday, right?" Zelda asked.

"Ah. You're Mrs. Gershwin."

"*Ms.* Gershwin. But you can call me Zelda."

"Hi, Zelda. Robert Gray." He stood momentarily, leaving the green chair to shake her hand before resuming his place.

"It isn't always . . . crazy like this. Normally, Biddleborn High is pretty quiet. The most exciting thing that happened last year was some student let a hundred crickets loose in the cafeteria."

"Yes, well—"

"I mean 'tragic.' Sorry. 'Exciting' was a poor word choice."

Mr. Gray shrugged. "Today is a day these kids will remember for the rest of their lives. Some people would define that as 'exciting,'" he suggested.

"I suppose so," Zelda conceded. She poured coffee into her cup and added peppermint mocha creamer until it was more or less khaki-colored.

"How are you feeling?"

"Me? Oh . . . better." Her hand went to her throat briefly.

Mr. Gray started to speak again, then paused. Zelda lowered her hand and looked away. "Be careful," he finally said. "I fear the 'excitement' may be far from over."

Zelda sloshed a little coffee out of her cup. "Oh!" she exclaimed at the sight.

"Here, let me get that." Robert Gray got up to get some paper towels. Coffee was on the floor at Zelda's feet. He wiped it up, then threw the paper towels away. All of this gave Zelda time to process his words.

"I don't disagree with you, but why do you think the excitement may not be over?" Zelda asked.

"Because there's a cause of it, isn't there? And the cause has to be dealt with. Something in the universe is broken, and until it gets fixed, well . . ."

"Do you have any idea what's broken?"

Mr. Gray looked at Zelda with intense eyes and a sad smile. "I'm afraid my knowledge may not matter much," he said. Zelda raised her eyebrows and started to ask what he meant, but, as often happens in schools when the discussion actually gets good, the bell rang. "Well, time to go!" Mr. Gray noted, gathering up his briefcase.

"Okay. Well, I'll see you around, Robert."

"Probably."

* * *

Only the smallest shadows could slip through the tear. The Shadow King himself could not . . . *yet*. But he could feel the girl calling to him, and her calling frayed the edges of the hole. Soon, he would send his lieutenants through it. And not long after that, he would go himself, and then her world would be his!

Chapter 6

CARL'S NERVES WERE a bit jumpy as he went out to feed the goats. He had a can of wasp spray in his pocket, a nine-millimeter in his holster, and a hunting knife attached to his belt. He couldn't find his boot knife, though. Meridian was forever swiping it, so he assumed she probably had it. Today, he hoped that was the case as he would feel better knowing she was armed. Part of him had wanted her to stay home from school so he could keep an eye on her. But there were far more animals at home, so maybe she was safer at Biddleborn High.

The goats crowded the fence, hoping for treats. They looked like ordinary goats, with big bellies and bony butts. Most of them had floppy ears, except for the two Mini-LaManchas, whose ears looked like they had been cut mostly off, with the remaining pieces rolled tight to their heads. Carl scratched the side of Merlin's face. "Don't you kids go getting possessed on me, okay?"

Carl measured out a cup of beet pulp for each goat—seven cups in all. A little pulp remained in the bucket, and he dumped it on the ground for the chickens. But where *were* the chickens? He looked around, unaware that his hand was creeping toward his gun.

Off to Carl's right, the trees were thicker, and the woods was held together with patches of poison ivy and rambler rose. To his left, the back of the toolshed blocked most of his view. Not knowing the rooster's location always made Carl nervous, and now, that was even more true.

Carl scanned the tree line. The chickens never strayed far, but they sometimes gathered near the edge of the woods, near Meridian's creepy-as-heck clown statue. The clown statue that was now missing.

Carl stared at the spot where the broken lamp—in the shape of a creepy ceramic clown that Meridian and Artie dubbed the Guardian of the Woods—normally rested. It was about a foot high, mostly blue and red, with a manic grin painted on a face that had faded to gray. Its left hand, which once held a lamp, was broken—the handiwork of a long-gone dog who used to bulldoze through the house, creating carnage in his wake. Now, the spot where the clown kept watch over the farm was empty—just a bare spot in the grass.

Carl's hand pulled the gun from its holster. He turned in a slow circle. Maybe Meridian had moved the clown for some unknown reason. Maybe someone had stolen it—although he couldn't imagine why anyone in their right mind would want it. He tried to remember the last time he saw it but couldn't.

Behind Carl, the rooster crowed. He spun around. The rooster pulled one foot up, balancing like a flamingo. It regarded Carl from fifteen feet away. Carl was relieved to see it was no bigger than it had ever been.

"I don't guess you know what happened to the clown?" Carl asked the rooster. The rooster put its foot down. It flapped its wings, stretched its neck, and crowed. "Yeah, right back at you," Carl told it.

Circling far out of the rooster's way, Carl headed toward the house. The rooster watched him go. And so did . . . the clown.

* * *

The students in Zelda's seventh-hour class were busy reading or, in some cases, pretending to read *Animal Farm.* After they finished, they were to write five open-ended discussion questions each. She was hoping that the next day there would be a lively, student-led conversation.

Today, however, the classroom was quiet—almost *too* quiet. A collection of plants lined the windowsill: a star aloe, a fern, a peace lily left over from Zelda's grandfather's funeral, and an areca palm. Zelda could almost hear them thinking of water and warm, delicious sunshine and the way it sent strength flowing through their leaves and roots. The plants longed to be outside where the air moved of its own accord and the sunshine could touch them. They wanted the feeling of roots spreading through dirt, unstopped by clay pots. Zelda wanted to go outside, too. She wanted to bury her feet in the soil.

Dane Peterson's hand went up, breaking the spell. Then, without waiting for Zelda to call on him, he blurted out, "Can I go pee?"

Zelda's murmur of thoughts faded as she sighed and grabbed her pad of hall passes. She scribbled something that could have been Dane's name, signed something that barely looked like her own, and held the paper out for him to grab on his way out of the room. It never ceased being weird to Zelda that part of her job was literally giving children permission to pee.

The door had just closed on Dane Peterson when it reopened, this time to admit Norma Bellows. She approached the desk and handed a tardy slip to Ms. Gershwin before sliding into an empty seat. Zelda glanced at the tardy slip, then at the clock. The school day was almost over—there were not quite twenty minutes left. And then, it occurred to her. She checked her seating chart, flipping through the classes, and realized that Norma Bellows was supposed to be in her first-hour class, not her seventh hour.

Zelda frowned and sighed again. Teaching involves a lot of sighs—tired ones. Norma was the living embodiment of that dream where you haven't been to school in so long that you've forgotten where you're supposed to be. It would have been funny if the girl hadn't looked so pale and limp, like Lucy after Dracula started draining her.

There was no point, really, in making Norma leave. She had already missed so much school, and it was astonishing that she had bothered to show up at all. Zelda would wait and try to talk to her after class.

One by one, the students' attention drifted away from Norma Bellows and back to *Animal Farm.* Some of them—those who read faster and those who didn't read at all—put their books down, and some of them began to write questions for the next day. The others began packing away their belongings, ready to end the day.

"Don't forget to write your discussion questions before you leave," Zelda reminded the students. Half of the students who had started packing sighed loudly and started unpacking. They grabbed pens and started scribbling vague questions in their notebooks, like, *What do you think of the story?* and *Who's the main character?*

The plants stirred nervously as Zelda could see them thinking of crows and beetles, darkness and cold, and snow without warning. As for Norma Bellows, she was staring out the window. Her gaze was fixed beyond the plants, as if she, too, dreamed of being outside. *In the outer darkness.* Zelda flinched. That last thought she had didn't come from the plants! It was stronger, darker, and . . . corrupt.

Zelda's eyes met Norma's. The girl was looking at her with a faint, mocking smile. But then the bell rang, and the students rushed out, carrying Norma Bellows with them. Zelda made no attempt to stop her.

After the classroom was emptied of the last few stragglers, Zelda realized that Dane Peterson had never come back. His copy of *Animal Farm* was lying on his desk. And his open backpack was propped against his chair.

* * *

The rooster patrolled the perimeter, keeping one eye on his hens. They were scratching for bugs. Most of the spiders had been eaten. But not all of them.

The spiders were of less concern to the rooster than the evil he felt creeping through the woods, drifting among the trees, and weaving in and out of the daylight that filtered through the leaves and the shadows that trembled in the air. The rooster heard laughter and puffed out his feathers, ready.

* * *

At exactly 3:58 p.m., Meridian pushed open the door of Galactic Books and Other Stuff. Elijah was behind the counter, ringing up a purchase. The customer was an older woman wearing the largest, thickest glasses Meridian had ever seen. It was hard to look away from her, but Meridian worked her hardest not to stare. Meridian wondered if the glasses were fake. They made the woman look more like a caricature than a real person.

Fixing her eyes on the floor, Meridian made her way to the back of the store, beyond the door that said *Employees Only*. She hung her purse up on a hook below a handwritten sign that read *Meridian's Stuff. Touch it and you will be forever cursed.* The handwriting was Artie's.

Meridian went into the staff bathroom, washed her hands, then looked at her phone. It was 4:00. She pushed back through the Employees Only door and scanned the counter. Elijah saw her and tipped an imaginary hat. The old woman with the enormous glasses was gone.

Meridian slipped behind the counter as Elijah slid around it. "Hey, Meridian, we're missing Han Solo from the Danbury Mint chess set. If you have downtime tonight, see if you can find him."

"You mean *when* I have downtime."

"You gotta stop with that negative thinking."

"Uh-huh."

Elijah shook his booty while doing something that might have been the twist. He finished it up with jazz hands, tipped his hat again, and took a bow.

"I hope to never see that again," Meridian said sarcastically.

Elijah smiled and skipped away toward the break room. Meridian heard him mutter "Ow" as he opened the break room door. Belatedly, she rolled her eyes. Then, she settled in to one of her favorite silences: the quiet of an empty bookstore.

The shadows pulsated and swirled around Lanora and Calvin. Blindly, they ran through the king's forest. Darkness like bat wings beat against them. Suddenly, a black cat appeared, arching its back. "It's the Cat Lord's guard!" Lanora shouted.

"You have got to stop," Robert Gray said, standing in front of the counter. Meridian hadn't heard him come in.

Meridian glanced up at the bell over the door. "It didn't ring," she noted.

"No. Of course not."

Meridian had the sudden desire to look away and shuffle her feet. But she stood her ground and forced herself to make eye contact.

Mr. Gray leaned his elbows on the counter and sighed. "Look. I know you're not doing it deliberately. Or even consciously. But your . . . dissociations . . . have more power than you realize. You've let the Shadow King's forces slip through!"

Meridian blushed. "How did you . . ."

Mr. Gray leaned toward her, his gaze intense. "Because . . . I'm the Cat Lord, my lady."

Chapter 7

NORMA TWISTED THE SWING she sat on, then lifted her feet and let it unwind. This used to be one of her favorite activities, back when she and Meridian Page were best friends—before Jazz Miller stole Meridian away. *Jazz Miller deserved what he got*, Norma reminded herself. *But Artie McClintock deserves even worse.* And after all of Meridian's friends were dead, Norma would deliver her to the Shadow King.

An old woman in ridiculously enormous glasses was sitting on a bench at the far end of Clyde J. Anderson Park. The park consisted of a small patch of playground equipment, benches, and a mostly-unused bandstand nestled in the middle of Biddleborn, a block off of Main Street. The woman had an emerald snake draped across her shoulders. It hadn't been there a moment before.

The woman smiled and waved at Norma. It was a shadow smile. Norma, slick with fear, stood up from the swing and walked toward the woman.

* * *

"That's impossible," Meridian said.

Robert Gray smirked. "Impossible like a small dog turning into a Shadow Hound?"

"Oh God," Meridian whispered.

"Impossible like dead unborn pigs mauling a man to death? Like a truck suddenly becoming sentient and murdering its owner?"

Meridian folded her arms on the counter and cradled her head. "This isn't real," she murmured into her arms.

"My lady? Look at me."

Meridian did look. And Mr. Gray was now, suddenly, wearing a black, feathered cloak that hung to the floor. It was as if he had murdered thousands of crows and stitched their skins together. A sword was belted around his waist. The rest of his clothes—tunic, trousers, vest, and leather gloves—were straight out of Meridian's imagination of what characters in a fantasy story might wear. This was, indeed, the Cat Lord, just as she had always pictured him.

"Convinced?" the Cat Lord asked.

"I think so. Maybe convinced that I'm crazy. I'm not sure."

"Dog. Unborn pigs. Truck. Your English teacher's hairdryer."

"Yeah, okay."

Mr. Gray was suddenly wearing his substitute teacher's clothes again: jeans, a blue button-down shirt, and a gray blazer. It was as if he were teaching at a junior college instead of a high school.

"So, what am I supposed to do?" Meridian asked.

Mr. Gray sighed. "First off, you can stop calling us." Meridian opened her mouth to speak, but he cut her off with a wave of his hand. "You need to think about something else. Try to stay . . . present."

"I don't like to. It's . . . uncomfortable."

"I'll bet being mauled by fetal pigs was uncomfortable, too."

"You're saying *I* killed him."

"No. That's not what I'm saying. I'm saying you let things into this world, unintentionally. And I need your help to stop more from coming."

"Okay."

"Okay? Just like that?"

"Yes," Meridian confirmed. "Jazz Miller was my friend." The Cat Lord, a product of Meridian's imagination, patted her arm awkwardly. She looked at the place where he touched her. "I can't believe you're really real. What about Lanora? Calvin?"

"They aren't here."

"And I have to . . . *abandon* them?"

"For a time. Yes. Maybe not forever. We just need to seal the hole, as it were."

A noise from the back signaled Elijah's approach. Meridian and Mr. Gray both straightened, taking a step back from each other. Mr. Gray turned away and picked up a book. It was a copy of *Something Wicked This Way Comes.*

"Bradbury! Always the right choice!" Elijah said with more enthusiasm than was strictly necessary.

"Um . . . yes. Thank you." Mr. Gray forced himself to smile, but with only limited success.

"I can ring that up if you're ready," Meridian offered.

The Cat Lord looked at the book, then at Meridian. He passed the book across the counter. Meridian smiled. "He was asking about the *Star Wars* chess set, too," she said to Elijah.

Elijah's face brightened. "It's a great set, even with the missing bishop. Released by the Danbury Mint in 1994, it's handcrafted pewter. You could get a replacement Han Solo on eBay. I think they run about $30. I had the set priced at $800, but since it's no longer complete, I could let you have it for $600."

Mr. Gray looked at Elijah, then looked at the chess set. His fingers twitched. "Oh . . . I think . . . I'll have to think about it. Er . . . thanks." He gathered up his purchase and left the store. The bell over the door rang as he left.

"We have to find Han Solo," Elijah asserted.

"Maybe *you* could order one on eBay?"

"Do you think someone stole it?"

Meridian shrugged. "I guess."

Elijah frowned. "Glass display cabinet. That's what we need. Add that to our shopping list. That, and Han Solo."

Meridian made a note of both items.

* * *

As tends to be the case with lawnmowers, Mowey was parked in the shed. Rose Marie had asked him if he needed anything before she left him there—some oil perhaps, or a sandwich. Mowey had never actually eaten a sandwich, or anything else, for that matter. But he was willing to try. A sandwich sounded like a life-changing idea. If he could eat a sandwich, he could accomplish, well, just about anything.

Rose Marie had patted Mowey and gone inside to assemble his lunch. Mowey loved her already. As he settled in to wait, a shadow stirred behind him.

Cold crept along Mowey's handle. His blades felt tingly. Something was wrong. Darkness rolled toward him, spitting and growing until it filled the shed. Mowey, trembling, fought back a scream.

Something slimy touched Mowey's handle. "No!" he yelled, starting his engine. Sharp blades whirring beneath him, he flung himself at the shadow. He hit a wall of ice and evil, but he didn't stop. His blades chopped the air. Something snarled, and the shadow retreated.

Mowey, panting, turned off his engine. Rose Marie stood in the doorway, holding a sandwich on a plate. "Well, now. Wasn't that something?" she said.

Mowey rolled to her. "It isn't safe here."

"No, I suspect not," Rose Marie agreed. "Maybe you ought to come inside the house. I think we might be a bit safer if we stay together."

* * *

The young man's body was stuffed inside two different lockers—that is, the jumble of parts that once made up his body. It was the leaking fluids that led to the discovery. Sheriff John Amory stood back as the crime scene unit, most of them called in from Springfield, processed the scene. So far, they hadn't found the head.

"Aaaaaand, we've got a wallet," Jerry Benson announced. Fat and friendly, Jerry was the only crime scene officer who worked for the Biddleborn Police Department. Normally, his job revolved around investigating traffic accidents. This was his first time sifting through mutilated body parts found inside a set of high school lockers.

Sheriff Amory stepped toward Jerry, careful not to contaminate the scene. Using a gloved finger, Jerry flipped the wallet open. "Dane Peterson. You know him?" Jerry asked.

The sheriff cursed. "Yeah, that's Kenny and Julia Peterson's boy. They live out on Route 4. Good people."

"You think this is connected to the science teacher's death?"

"It'd be an uncomfortable coincidence if it weren't."

"So it would," Jerry agreed.

* * *

When Meridian got home from work, Carl was sitting on the couch, drinking a beer and watching *Dancing with the Stars*. He changed the channel as Meridian hung up her purse. "Too late. I already caught you," she teased him.

"You tell anyone, you're grounded for life."

Meridian went through the kitchen on her way upstairs, grabbing a chicken leg, a slice of cheese, and a cupcake—her usual supper—along the way. She carried her food up to her room. Carl's cat, Dionysius, followed Meridian by walking in front of her and rubbing against her leg.

Before stepping inside her bedroom, Meridian pulled the skin from her chicken leg and tossed it to the cat. She shut herself inside her room before he finished eating. It was her nightly ritual. Inside her room, Meridian settled into her window seat to eat her chicken-cheese-cupcake dinner. Between the cheese and cupcake, she pushed the window open.

Dionysius tapped on the door. "Go away!" Meridian yelled at him.

Lanora climbed the spiral stairs . . .

Meridian's thoughts trailed off, and she sighed. She had to focus. "Stay present," she reminded herself. She tore the bottom half of the cupcake off and pressed it down over the icing, making a cupcake sandwich, which she ate in three bites.

A giggle rose from outside, followed by manic footsteps. Meridian scurried out of her window seat and flipped off her bedroom light. Ducking low, she crept back and laid on her belly on the window seat. She moved the curtain aside and strained to see in the darkness. Each shadow raised suspicion.

The giggle came again, closer this time. Something was scuffling in the weeds below the window. Meridian slid to the floor and army crawled to her bedroom door. She sat on her butt, opened the door, and scooted out into the hall. Then, she ran downstairs.

Meridian practically fell into the living room. Breathing hard, she threw herself against the front door and turned the lock. "Carl!" she yelled.

Carl turned the volume down on the TV and looked at Meridian. "What's going on?" he asked.

"Monster! Outside!" Meridian ran through the kitchen and threw herself against the back door. Something moved beyond the door's glass window as she thumbed the lock.

Carl appeared in the kitchen doorway, a twelve-gauge shotgun in his hands. He grabbed his headlamp off the kitchen counter.

"No, no, no!" Meridian scolded him.

"That dog was able to be killed, and so were those spiders. Whatever this is, I'll take care of it," Carl said as he moved Meridian aside and unlocked the door. "Soon as I'm out, you lock this and keep it locked. You got your revolver?"

"In my purse."

"Good. Go get it. That machete, too, if you can get to it. If not, grab a knife." With that, Carl went out into the darkness.

Chapter 8

BECAUSE THE STUDENTS were banished from the science classroom and exiled to the library, Cheese Fry's new science teacher, Mr. Gray, had assigned them an essay in lieu of dissecting a frog. The essay prompt was, "Tell me what's inside a frog."

Cheese Fry wasn't sure what was inside a frog, but he was fairly certain that Mr. Gray didn't know, either. So, instead of looking it up, he decided to wing it. He opened to a blank sheet of notebook paper and began to write. *It's really dark inside of a frog*, he wrote. *But if you were to turn on a light inside one, you could see all kinds of things. It would probably be damp and warm.*

Cheese Fry smiled. This might be the best essay he had ever written. *Some frogs have regular guts, like hearts and gizzards, but most are just an empty hole where they store lots of bugs. Frogs eat bugs all day long, catching them with their really long, really sticky tongues. They especially like fireflies. Fireflies are spicy.*

The most famous frog is Kermit, and he's just full of stuffing, like cotton balls or something. Kermit doesn't eat bugs, I don't think. But I know he drinks tea because I've seen pictures.

Somewhere outside Cheese Fry's window, a frog was hopping across a neighbor's driveway. Shadows swirled around him. Deep inside, the frog was changing, hollowing out. A mile away, another frog was growing a gizzard.

Cheese Fry Davenport kept writing. And reality kept trying to keep up with him.

* * *

Meridian ran to the front door, where her purse waited on a hook. She pulled it down, dumped the contents on the floor, and snatched up the revolver she had been carrying with her, even to school. There was no time to get the machete, though—it was upstairs, next to her bed. She ran back to the kitchen and grabbed the knife she used for cleaning fish. It was thin and sharp.

Meridian stood in indecision for a moment. Carl told her to stay inside. Without Carl, she would be an orphan. She didn't even know how to pay bills. She trusted him, but this was all her fault. Whatever was giggling in the yard was out there because *she* had called it.

Carl was wearing the headlamp. Meridian pulled her cell phone out of her pocket, turned on the flashlight, then slipped it halfway into her pocket so the light was peeking out. Then, she went out into the darkness.

Carl's headlamp told Meridian that he was near the chicken coop. She could hear the chickens clucking frantically, the way they do when there's a possum in the coop, stealing their eggs. Meridian walked toward the coop, hoping Carl didn't get startled and shoot her. She was about to stage whisper, "Don't shoot me," when he spun around and pointed his shotgun in her direction. She froze, hands raised as if it were a stickup.

"Dadgum, Meridian! I told you to stay inside!"

"Yeah, well, I'm a rebel."

"You hear them chickens?"

"Yeah. Think it's in there?"

Carl took a deep breath. "Let's find out."

As quietly as he could, Carl slid the latch and pulled the coop door open. The rooster flew out in a flurry of wings and rage. Carl scurried backward, falling on his butt. Behind them, something giggled.

Meridian spun around, revolver ready. The light from her cell phone reflected on crazed eyes about a foot off the ground. Her clown lamp stood about ten feet away, its painted mouth open, revealing two rows of very sharp teeth.

Meridian and Carl both shot the clown, and it disappeared in a swirl of shadow and smoke. Rapid footsteps faded toward the house. "Dad-blast consorn fiddlesticks!" Carl shouted.

"I agree," Meridian said.

"Help me up."

Meridian grabbed Carl's arm and helped him to his feet. The rooster ran past them, clucking. He was headed toward the house. Meridian and Carl, fearing their guns were useless, followed the rooster, which was growing larger with every step.

* * *

"See how they do that? They use heated superglue to make the fingerprints show up."

Zelda heard her grandmother's voice from the den. At first, she assumed Rose Marie was on the phone. But then, she heard a male voice respond, "Oh! That's really neat." *Who on earth is visiting Rose Marie at this time of night?* Zelda wondered. She peeked through the doorway.

Rose Marie was alone, watching *Forensic Tales* on the TV. The push mower, normally stowed in the shed, was next to the couch. No one else was in the room.

Zelda stepped into the den, fearing her grandmother had come down with a sudden bout of dementia. "Why in the name of all that is holy is there a lawnmower in the house?" Zelda asked.

Rose Marie looked at Zelda, then slid her eyes over to the lawnmower. "Hi! I'm Mowey," it said.

Zelda sat down heavily on a chair. "Dear . . . God," she whispered.

* * *

Norma stood at the end of Blackbird Lane, where the road petered out to a dirt path leading to a field that, in the summer, would be full of corn. She wore enormous glasses that magnified her eyes. A large ditch ran between the road and field. Green water provided a place for frogs and snakes to hide from the human and her shadowy entourage.

With a decided lack of concern for her shoes, Norma stepped into the ditch and began to hum. Ripples formed where snakes swam around her. Stooping, she snatched up a cottonmouth and bit off its head.

Norma cackled with the voice of a very old woman. The air around her swirled dark with shadows. Raising her hands, with the headless snake still clutched in her left hand, Norma stepped into the darkness and disappeared.

* * *

Artie was studying a diagram of a frog's internal organs when he realized there was a buzzing sound somewhere in his room. He looked up, frowning. His eyes wandered as he looked suspiciously at each electronic device in turn.

Artie's air conditioning was provided by a window unit. He cocked his head toward it. There was a tower fan behind him. He rolled his chair in that direction and listened. His computer sat silently in front of him. Finally, he picked his cell phone up and held it to his ear.

The sound seemed to be coming from the ceiling. Artie looked up. His ceiling fan turned lazily. The buzzing didn't seem to be coming from there. It seemed louder.

A bubble moved through the ceiling as if something were crawling just under the paint. It looked like some sort of ceiling parasite moving through the sheetrock's skin. Artie watched it in fascination. It slid along to where the ceiling met the wall, then turned and began to move down through the wall as a bulge in the paint. It was about the size of a mouse, Artie thought.

This didn't seem possible, but reality had been a bit twisted lately.

Artie stood, grabbed his lightsaber, and moved toward his bedroom door. As he opened it, his mother's kitten, whom she had inexplicably named Pineapple, bounded into the room.

The kitten was growing as it leaped up to bat at the bulge. The thing behind the paint was also growing. It was now the size of a dinner plate. "Oh crap," Artie exclaimed when he saw this.

Suddenly, the wall burst open, and out poured inky dust that slid to the floor with a swooshing sound. The dust puddled like liquid on Artie's carpet. The kitten arched its back and hissed. It scampered toward Artie, jumped out with its claws, and climbed up his leg. He pulled it off when it got to his waist, and he hugged it with one arm.

The world fell away as the puddle spread. Artie ran into the hallway, then raced to the kitchen, the kitten growing heavy and wriggling in his arms. He dropped her halfway through the kitchen.

Pineapple hit the floor, then leaped onto the kitchen counter and used it as a springboard to hurl herself at Artie, knocking him backward. As the liquid shadows raced toward them like a wave, the boy and cat tumbled through the floor, through the veil of this world. They landed in a heap next to a castle made of silver sand.

Chapter 9

CARL SIGNALED MERIDIAN to stop running. "Shhh," he whispered. The farm was silent. "Turn off your light," he instructed while clicking off his headlamp.

Meridian fumbled with her cell phone, finally getting the flashlight turned off. Carl grabbed her arm and pulled her toward the house. He pressed his back against the wall and motioned for her to do the same. "You think he can see in the dark?" Meridian whispered.

"I don't know. What I do know is that we need a plan. We can't just blindly chase that . . . thing. It ain't flesh and blood, I don't think."

"Right. It's not a Velveteen Rabbit."

Carl was silent a moment in the darkness, puzzling that out. "You mean . . . it ain't real?"

"Right. It didn't turn into a real clown. But it's not a lamp anymore, either. It seems . . . ghostly."

From near the toolshed, the rooster, now five feet tall, crowed. All of Biddleborn surely heard him. "But we oughtta be able to shoot the rooster," Carl suggested.

"He was chasing the clown, though. So, I think he's on *our* side."

"That rooster ain't never been on our side."

"He might be our only hope."

Carl sighed. "Dagnabbit." A peal of high-pitched laughter rang out off to their left, amid the burned remains of the woodpile. "How do we kill a ghost?" Carl asked. There were more giggles, followed by the distinctive sound of a chainsaw roaring to life. "Run!" Carl shouted while pulling Meridian toward the driveway. "Truck!" he wheezed.

They ran blindly toward Carl's truck, both wishing they still had flashlights. Small footsteps and a whirring chainsaw were coming closer. The rooster flew, diving toward them. He landed between the humans and the ghost-clown, growing as his feet touched down.

The rooster was now twenty feet tall. He turned his eye toward the clown as he would a bug and bent down to peck at him. The clown squealed.

Carl and Meridian threw themselves toward Carl's truck, yanked open the doors, and piled inside. Carl fumbled for his keys. "We can never come home," Meridian said.

"Well, they ain't getting my house," Carl asserted. He pushed the key into the ignition, gave the truck gas, and turned. The truck sputtered to life, and Carl shifted into reverse.

"Where are we going?" Meridian asked.

"I dunno. Somewhere we can think. Maybe the McClintocks' house."

Meridian opened her mouth, then closed it. Mr. Gray—the Cat Lord—would probably be more useful than Artie and his mom, but she couldn't bring herself to say it. "Yeah. Okay," she reluctantly agreed. Carl's truck bounced over the roads as they sped toward Artie's house.

* * *

The sky above Artie was pink. He stared at it for a moment, then pushed himself up. Pineapple rubbed against him.

Artie was definitely not in his kitchen. He was on a beach, but the colors were wrong. Pink sky. Silver sand. The water was blue but too blue. It was a child's drawing of water.

And then there was the sandcastle. Artie reached out and touched it. It was solid, like rock. It was more a tower than a castle, jutting up ten stories into the pink of the sky. "Don't build your house upon the sand," he muttered, recalling the saying.

A giant crab dressed in armor came around the tower. "Hey! How'd you get out of the dungeon?" it asked. He ran at Artie, his sword drawn.

Artie was still sitting in the sand. He raised his hands and closed his eyes. This had to be a dream.

"Fritz! Tony! We have an escapee!" the crab bellowed.

Fritz and Tony, both giant crabs, joined the first soldier. They dragged Artie into the tower of the sandcastle, then dragged him down a dark, twisting staircase. Evidently, the tower went as far below the earth as it stuck up above.

Pineapple followed.

* * *

Zelda stared at the lawnmower, remembering how the hairdryer's cord felt around her neck. Just think what a lawnmower could do. "Rose Marie, we have to get out of here," she insisted.

"Don't be silly," Rose Marie responded. "We're watching *Forensic Tales*."

"Would you like some nachos?" Mowey asked. "Rose Marie made some. They're really good."

Zelda's eyes noticed the plate on the floor. The globs of cheese and tortilla crumbs testified to the lawnmower's words. "No, thank you," she whispered.

Rose Marie sighed, picked up the remote, and hit pause. "I invited Mowey inside because there seems to be some sort of demonic presence in the shed. He fought it off, for now, but I didn't want to leave him out there, in case it comes back. Oh, and I suppose you were right about the hairdryer trying to kill you." Then, Rose Marie hit play, and *Forensic Tales* came back to life.

"The hairdryer isn't still in the house, is it?" Mowey asked.

Zelda looked at Rose Marie. It hadn't occurred to her to ask, until now. "No," Rose Marie answered. "I threw it out. I assumed it was broken after what it did to Zelda's hair."

Zelda's hand touched what remained of her hair. The left side and most of the front had been shaved. She hid the damage with a scarf. Mowey didn't have eyes, but he rolled forward just a little, and Zelda imagined that if he did have eyes, they would have focused intently on her.

"Some souls are really just shadows. Their light died long ago," Mowey said.

Zelda blinked at him. "I don't understand. I mean, I understand that some people . . . and things . . . people and things with *souls* are evil. But how did my hairdryer have a soul at all? And you. How are you talking to me?"

"I'm not sure. One moment, I was in the Roanoke marketplace, and the next, I was here. I think your world is sucking souls in from Detritus. Normally, you know, it's the other way around. It's like the suction got reversed."

"Detritus?"

"It's the world I'm from."

"When you say 'world,' you don't mean planet, do you?"

"No. It's like, another reality, I guess."

"Of course it is. But . . . are you the same lawnmower we've had for the last few months?"

"Yes. I think so. But I'm also *not* the same. Before today, your lawnmower was just a machine."

"And what were you before you were our lawnmower?"

"I've always been a lawnmower."

"Are you two about finished?" Rose Marie asked. "You're interrupting my stories."

* * *

Sheriff Amory sat at his desk, wishing he could sneak a cigarette. But Geraldine was watching. Geraldine worked the front counter with so much efficiency it was terrifying.

The sheriff's desk was a mess of case notes. He had no system—or, perhaps, the lack of system *was* his system. He thought best in messy piles.

What did all three victims have in common? The high school. Amory was including Jazz Miller on the victim list for now. He couldn't explain the boy's death, so that made it suspect.

The sheriff scribbled a tangle of lines on a notepad. What if Zelda Gershwin *didn't* try to kill herself? What if she was the killer's first failed attempt? That would make two teachers and two students.

It seemed likely the killer had some connection to Biddleborn High School. But most people in town had graduated from the school, and many had children there. So, that wouldn't be much of a surprise or lead. Still, it was a start.

Another twist of lines encircled the first tangle. Amory hoped the killer wasn't a student. He hated arresting young people. But Mr. Mayfield had given him a list of students he thought capable—the outcasts and troublemakers. The list was short. Apparently, Jazz Miller's goal in life had been to befriend the outcasts and pull them into the fold. He had done a good job of it. Poor, sweet kid.

There were three names on the list: Michael Davenport, Norma Bellows, and Chance Wright. The sheriff glanced at Geraldine. She was still watching.

Two of the victims were teachers. Could the killer also be a teacher or some other staff member? A disgruntled janitor, perhaps? Possibly a substitute teacher?

Sheriff Amory watched enough television to know the stereotype of the small-town lawman who is always suspicious of any strangers riding through town. He tried not to be that guy, but the fact was that there was a stranger in town, and Amory did regard him with a considerable amount of suspicion. Underneath "Chance Wright," he wrote "Robert Gray."

In fact, Mr. Gray seemed to the sheriff like a great place to start his questioning. And on the way over to the Paradise Motel, where the substitute teacher was staying, he could smoke a cigarette or two.

* * *

Someone was beating on Belinda's kitchen door. Wondering why they didn't use the front door, she peeked out. Carl and Meridian, both heavily armed, were peeking in.

Belinda opened the door. "Come on in. From the looks of you, I'm guessing this is bad news."

"We've had a visitor. A . . . clown. A broken clown lamp that Meridian and Artie put out near our woods."

"I remember that lamp. It used to be Artie's."

"Yeah, well, now it's running through our woods, giggling like a maniac and threatening folks with a chainsaw. Oh, and our rooster is about twenty feet tall."

"Well. Sounds like an adventure!"

"I'm starting to hate adventure," Meridian said.

"So, I'd like to leave Meridian here for a bit," Carl continued. "That okay, Belinda?"

"Sure. What are you going to do?"

"No! You're not leaving me," Meridian protested.

Carl turned Meridian to face him. "Look. You stay here, put your heads together, and think. You're better at that than I am. I'm gonna go see your Uncle Franklin about some . . . heavier artillery."

"But you're coming back here before you go use the artillery, right?" Meridian asked.

"I'll call. If you've got a better plan by then, sure, I'll come back."

"Promise?"

"Promise." Carl patted Meridian's arm. "Okay. See you in a bit." With that, Carl left Meridian alone with Belinda.

"Artie's in his room, doing homework. Why don't you go get him while I fix supper?" Belinda suggested. "I'm sure we'll all think better with full bellies."

"Yes, ma'am," Meridian agreed. She went down the hall to Artie's room and knocked. "I'm coming in," she announced while pushing open the door.

Artie wasn't there.

* * *

The dungeon was dark, if it was, in fact, a dungeon. It felt dungeony—cool but dry and hollow. The giant crabs had clamped a shackle around Artie's ankle, secured to the wall by a thick chain.

Artie still wasn't sure whether any of this was real. It *felt* real, but part of his brain—the part that did his homework—told him it couldn't possibly be. It was illogical. *Shut up*, he told his brain. Twinkie's mutation was illogical, but that had been real. The world had stopped making sense.

"Hello there!" a voice said, startling Artie out of his thoughts. The voice sounded like Jazz Miller.

"Jazz?" *Is this some kind of afterlife?* Artie wondered. Artie went to Sunday school. So, he knew this wasn't heaven.

"My name is Calvin, of the Thieves' Guild. And this is Lady Lanora of the Sands."

"Hello," said a female voice. She sounded an awful lot like Meridian.

"Now I know I'm dreaming," Artie said.

"Ah, if only that were the case," Calvin continued. "You are, in fact, awake and imprisoned in the dungeon at Fowler's Keep."

"I'm not going to get my biology homework finished."

"My traitorous uncle has taken control of the Keep," said the voice that sounded like Meridian. "I'm sorry to say his hospitality is lacking somewhat."

"If only I had a flashl— Oh wait!" Artie said, interrupting himself and pulling out his cell phone. The screen lit up, dispelling the darkness enough for Artie to see that he definitely wasn't in his bed, dreaming. He turned on the phone's flashlight function and shined the light around the dungeon. And it really was a dungeon. Lady Lanora looked an awful lot like Meridian but prettier. And Calvin—

"You're a skeleton!" Artie exclaimed.

"Indeed, sir. It comes in handy."

"Does it?"

"Oh yes! For instance . . ." Calvin slipped his hands out of the shackles snapped around his wrists. He held his hands up and did Jazz Miller's signature move: jazz hands.

"So, how do we get out of here?" Artie asked.

"I'm glad you asked," Calvin responded, "because we have a plan."

Chapter 10

ZELDA WAS SETTLING DOWN in her bedroom with a cup of tea, trying to make sense of the world, with its talking lawnmowers, when the house started buzzing. She carefully set the tea aside. She was not going to panic. Zelda got up from her bed and moved quickly toward the door.

Black liquid poured out of the bedroom walls, and Zelda ran from the room. "Rose Marie!" she yelled. Heart beating fury in her chest, she stumble-ran to her grandmother's bedroom. "Grandma!" Zelda flung open her grandmother's bedroom door.

Rose Marie was smothering her bedside lamp with a pillow. "I . . . need . . . help!" she called out as the lamp struggled to free itself. "Get Mowey!"

Zelda ran from the room. The house buzzed around her. "Mowey!" she screamed. She ran toward the den, hoping that's where he was. She hoped her grandmother hadn't given the spare bedroom to a lawnmower!

Mowey rolled out of the kitchen as Zelda passed. "Did you call?" he asked.

"Rose Marie needs help!" Zelda ran back toward Rose Marie's bedroom, and Mowey rolled after her. By the time they reached the bedroom, the lamp had freed itself and was snapping at Rose Marie as she blocked it with the pillow.

"Oh, I see," Mowey said. "Back away, Rose Marie!" He started his engine, chopping up a rug in the process. "Sorry!"

Zelda pulled her grandmother out of the room as Mowey launched himself at the lamp. The walls bubbled around them. "We have to get out of here!" Zelda cried. "Mowey! Come on!"

Zelda pulled her grandmother toward the front door. The floor began to vibrate. "Run! Run! Run!" Rose Marie yelled. Rumbling raced toward them like a thunderstorm.

Mowey was charging down the hall, chopping shadows. "Run!" he yelled.

They ran.

* * *

Carl's brother, Franklin, was a man who could get things. And that is how Carl managed to pull back into his driveway armed with three hand grenades. Everything was quiet on the farm—a condition Carl found quite alarming.

Carl strapped on his head lamp and clicked it on. He turned his head, sending the beam across the junk piled here and there, the burned woodpile, the chicken coop, the toolshed, and the goat pens. Then, he guided the beam across the house. He saw no evil ceramic clown and no twenty-foot-tall rooster. It was too quiet, as if the night had been wrapped in foam.

"Rooster?" Carl called out, mostly to break the silence and make sure he hadn't gone deaf. Soft footsteps were coming at him. Turning toward the sound, he saw glowing eyes bouncing closer. It was Dionysius. "You don't need to be no part of this," Carl said to the cat.

There was a giggle off to Carl's right. The clown was near the goat pens. Carl needed it to come out in the open. He had no intention of blowing up any of the animals in his care. He also had no intention of leaving them to the mercies of a devil-clown. Not even the rooster, if he could help it.

Carl walked toward the goats with a grenade in his right hand, his left index finger ready to pull the pin. He had never thrown a grenade, although he had blown plenty of things up when he was younger. Every boy needs a hobby.

Carl stopped walking. *Make it come to me*, he thought. He turned, heading toward the house. He whistled to Dionysius, and the cat followed by walking in front of him.

There were fast footsteps off to Carl's right. A car door slammed. He spun around just as his truck started in the driveway. A lot of words competed to be the one to come out of his mouth, but the winner turned out to be a simple, "Oh."

The truck rumbled through the yard toward Carl. He pulled the pin and threw the grenade.

* * *

As a professional thief, Skeleton-Jazz had a substantial amount of lock-picking experience. Or so he said. Artie was starting to doubt Skeleton-Jazz had ever picked a lock in his life . . . or death. Of course, since this was all in Artie's imagination—he had decided he was probably in a coma—it was his fault for not imagining better skills for Jazz Miller's skeleton.

"Can't you do that any faster?" Artie asked. Gorgeous Meridian had been freed by the skeleton after what seemed like forever. Now, the skeleton was struggling with Artie's shackles.

"They've used magic pins, I think. They're a bit slithery," the Skeleton noted.

"'Slithery' as in . . . *things* that slither?" Artie asked.

"Yes, a bit like that."

"Well, if you don't hurry, the guards are going to catch us."

"And they'll surely throw us in a dungeon," Gorgeous Meridian added. She was carving something in the sand-rock wall—some part of their escape plan that Artie didn't understand.

Artie found Gorgeous Meridian very disturbing. What did her image say about his subconscious attitude toward his friend? Did he have a crush on her? Did he think she needed a makeover? He really didn't think he felt either of those things. So, why hadn't he imagined Meridian looking more like herself?

And if this was a dream, why didn't the act of critiquing the dream change it? Could Artie think his way to a different dream? He closed his eyes and pictured McDonald's.

"Got it!" Skeleton Jazz cried. Artie felt the shackles drop, and he opened his eyes. He was still in the dungeon, with not a cheeseburger in sight.

"I have the map finished," Gorgeous Meridian announced. "Now, we just have to get through this wall."

"How long is that going to take?" Artie asked. Even though this was just a really lifelike dream, he was getting worried.

"Not long at all," Gorgeous Meridian assured him. "By rights, these walls belong to me, so they'll obey my commands."

Artie had a flash of memory: playing a game they thought of as "bowling" in Meridian's room. They had knocked a hole in the wall, and they tried to hide it from Carl by covering it with posters, even though it was only a foot off the floor. If only walls obeyed their owners.

"Sure. That's a great plan," Artie said.

Gorgeous Meridian flashed him a dazzling smile—something the real Meridian would never do. Then, Gorgeous Meridian put her hands on the wall. "The two of you should memorize the map while I do this," she instructed.

"Um . . . okay," Artie agreed.

Skeleton Jazz motioned Artie over to the drawing Gorgeous Meridian had carved into the wall. "Let's see. We're here," Skeleton Jazz said, pointing to an incredibly well-drawn tower. In fact, the whole map looked like it had been drawn by a professional whose medium of choice was a wall made of sand.

Artie pointed to an X. "Is this where we're going? The 'Cat Lord's Cottage'?"

"Yes," Skeleton Jazz confirmed. "Lanora is convinced he can help her overthrow her uncle and reclaim her kingdom."

"Oh."

"He *can* help," Lanora insisted.

"Not the Deadly Forest again," Jazz Skeleton responded. "Couldn't we put something else here? How about Farmer Drumpkin's Field of Turnips?"

"If you prefer," Lanora said.

The skeleton rubbed out the forest, drew some turnips, and wrote, *Farmer Drumpkin's Field of Turnips.*

"I don't think maps work that way," Artie said.

"What do you mean?"

"You can't just draw what you want. You have to draw what's actually there."

"That's the most ridiculous thing I've ever heard."

Artie opened his mouth to argue, but then he realized he was talking to a skeleton. Maybe logic didn't apply.

A hole appeared in the wall beneath Lanora's hands. "Let's go. Quickly!" she said.

Artie admired the hole. "Was that some kind of magic?" he asked.

"No. It was science," Lanora answered.

* * *

The Cat Lord was restless. His room at the Paradise Motel was dank and drab and getting smaller by the minute, or so he would have sworn. Shadows were stirring. He could *feel* them. This world was changing. No—this world was *being* changed.

Mr. Gray, the Cat Lord, grabbed his room key, the motel notepad, a pen that sat by the phone, his sword, and his cloak. He went outside. The night was cool and dark.

The Paradise Motel was wedged between a gas station and a liquor store. Behind the commercial property was a narrow residential neighborhood that dwindled to fields and trees just three blocks north. With his feathered cloak pulled tight against the night air, Robert Gray walked north, toward the edge of Biddleborn.

Mr. Gray couldn't feel the girl. Normally, her thoughts pushed against his mind like waves against the shore. But tonight, the edges of his mind were all his own. "Edges." There was something in that, but he couldn't quite grasp it—the edge of an idea.

Stopping under the last streetlight he came to, Mr. Gray pulled out the motel stationery and pen. He needed the girl's house to be within walking distance. In the weak light, he drew a square on the stationery, labeling it *M.'s House*. Next, he drew a line that he labeled *The Edge* and some squares labeled simply *Houses*. Finally, he drew a square on which he wrote, *Motel*.

Mr. Gray looked at his map. It might work. If it *did* work, however, that certainly didn't bode well for this world. He followed his map to the edge of Biddleborn, just a few steps away. He stepped into the trees, walked a few paces, and arrived at Meridian's just in time to see a truck explode.

Debris flew, and Robert Gray ducked back into the trees. He could hear the bleating of frightened goats. A scared cat flew past, its feet barely touching the ground. It ran up a tree.

A high-pitched giggle erupted from the fire. The Cat Lord recognized the sound. It came from a shadow wight. Unsheathing his sword, the Cat Lord stepped into the yard. A man spun toward him with a grenade in his hand. In the form of Mr. Gray, the Cat Lord stopped walking and called out, "I'm here to help!"

"Watch out!" the man holding the grenade yelled as the shadow wight, in the form of a very short clown, came charging toward Mr. Gray. As it ran, it grew taller. By the time it reached Mr. Gray, it was taller than he was.

The Cat Lord dove at the shadow wight. Its fingers had elongated, sprouting sharp-looking talons, which it used as swords. It swiped at the

Cat Lord, its claws beating his sword away. The Cat Lord stepped back, took a breath, then danced forward, jabbing at the creature. It side-stepped, causing the blade to scratch its arm rather than pierce its body. And so, they continued, with thrusts and parries and slashes and jabs.

The Cat Lord was nimble on his feet but terribly lazy, so his sword-fighting consisted mostly of beating at his opponent until they were tired, then stabbing. His methods also included a lot of cheating.

The creature leaped at the Cat Lord. The Cat Lord raised his sword and whispered, "Fly!" His cloak burst into a thousand crows that swarmed the creature, ripping with beaks and claws. While the shadow wight frantically beat at the birds, the Cat Lord stepped in and stabbed the creature through the heart. It dissolved into sand and smoke.

The crows reassembled into a cloak, hovering in front of their master. The Cat Lord sheathed his sword and slipped his cloak back over his shoulders. "Are you Meridian's father?" he asked the man.

"Sure am. Carl Davis." He slipped the grenade into his pocket so they could shake hands.

"Robert Gray. I'm your daughter's science teacher."

"Science . . . teacher? Huh?" Carl looked at the man's cloak and sword. "Does that mean you have a scientific explanation for that thing you just killed?"

"Yes. Magic. Is Meridian home?"

"No. She's at a friend's house."

"We need to go there. Now. I believe she's in danger."

"Let's go. You can explain on the way." Carl looked at his burning truck. "We'll have to take your car."

"I walked."

"Meridian's car, then. Assuming she left me a key."

* * *

Cheese Fry Davenport couldn't sleep. Tomorrow was Jazz's funeral. Cheese Fry was pretty sure it would be closed casket. He had a hard time believing his friend was really gone.

Cheese Fry was supposed to speak at the funeral. But he didn't know what to say or if he would even be able to talk. His eyes burned with tears, and he wiped them away.

Flipping on his bedside lamp, Cheese Fry sat up. He figured he might as well write the eulogy since he couldn't sleep anyway. He grabbed his notebook, flipped past his frog essay, and found a blank page.

Jazz Miller was my best friend, Cheese Fry wrote. *We met in first grade, and he was always nice to me, even when other kids made fun of my glasses. He stood up for me. He stood up for everyone, all the time, even though he was born cool and could have been a jerk.*

Cheese Fry tapped his pencil against the page. His hand started moving while his brain became faraway static. He continued writing: *Jazz Miller came back from the dead to save the world from the Shadow King. Jazz Miller will save us all.*

Cheese Fry Davenport looked down at what he had written. He didn't know what the words meant, but they filled him with dread. Suddenly, he was cold and wanted nothing more than to crawl back into his bed and go to sleep.

Chapter 11

THE HOUSE WAS shaking and buzzing, and the floors were rolling like angry waves. Shadows poured like sand from the walls. Mowey was screaming like a tea kettle—high, shrill, and constant.

Zelda reached the front door, which frowned at her and said, "Don't you da—" as she grabbed it by the nose and twisted. She hoped the real world still existed on the other side, not this nightmare wonderland. She pulled her grandmother out with her, into the night.

Moths were beating against the porch light. And a frog hopped across the sidewalk. Zelda had no way of knowing he had undergone a change in anatomy. So, the night looked normal to her, except for the lawnmower who was desperately trying to catch his breath.

Rose Marie locked the front door. "Can't have burglars getting in while we're gone."

"I think they'd regret it," Zelda quipped.

"So, what happens now?" Mowey asked.

"I think it's time to go to the sheriff," Rose Marie suggested.

Something thumped against the front door from inside, making all of them jump.

"I don't have my car keys," Zelda moaned.

"I don't know that we should trust a car anyway," Rose Marie said.

"I don't even have my cell phone. Or proper clothes."

"I have a full tank of gasoline!" Mowey announced. They looked at him. "Well, it's something," he said.

"Let's get away from the house," Rose Marie insisted.

The trio started walking. "I guess we could ask to use a neighbor's phone," Zelda said. "What will we even say, though? Is the sheriff going to believe us? He didn't believe me about the hairdryer."

"We have a talking lawnmower. He'll either believe us or he'll check himself in to the mental hospital."

"I'm not sure *I* believe us," Zelda said while looking back at their house with its darkened windows, pale yellow siding, and front porch with flowers and a *Welcome to the Porch* sign. The house looked so cozy and normal, yet she knew she'd never feel safe there again. Her whole world felt violated.

Rose Marie, dressed in a flowered cotton nightgown, walked toward the Tillermans' house to the east. Zelda and Mowey followed. "Mowey, you should pretend to be a regular lawnmower for the next few minutes," Zelda whispered to him.

Rose Marie knocked on the door with three hard raps. They could hear footsteps and see lights coming on. Bobby Tillerman opened the door, taking in their appearance and the fact that they had brought a lawnmower with them. With the sort of dignity only a ninety-year-old woman could muster under such circumstances, Rose Marie said, "Good evening, Bobby. May we borrow your telephone?"

"Yeah, sure, come on in."

Rose Marie and Zelda followed Bobby into his house, leaving Mowey outside. Bobby Tillerman handed his cell phone to Rose Marie, who handed it to Zelda. "I have never figured out how to use one," Rose Marie said.

"Is everything all right?" Bobby asked.

"A little trouble at the house," Rose Marie responded. "I think we've got ourselves a poltergeist. It was always bound to happen."

"Ah," Bobby said.

"Call Geraldine," Rose Marie said to Zelda. "She'll know how to get the sheriff."

"No, I'm calling 911."

"Don't do that. Here, give me the phone," Rose Marie insisted. Zelda handed it over. Rose Marie dialed, then handed it back.

Zelda stepped away, giving herself a little privacy while she talked with Geraldine. After a couple of minutes of muffled, one-sided conversation, she handed Bobby's phone back to him. "Geraldine's going to send Sheriff Amory over to the house," she said.

"Well, I guess we better go wait outside for him," Rose Marie suggested. "Thank you for letting us use your phone, Bobby."

"No problem. Good luck with the poltergeists. I hear those things can be hard to get rid of."

"Worse than termites," Rose Marie said.

* * *

Meridian had not, in fact, left Carl a key to her car. "Dadgummit," he said.

"We'll walk," Robert Gray suggested, nodding in the direction from which he had come. "I have a map."

"I don't need a map to know it's nine miles into town."

"On my map, it's only about . . . twenty feet. I don't like walking very much."

"Your map is smoking crack because it's nine miles," Carl insisted. "We need a car. I'll call my brother Franklin to come get us."

"We don't have that kind of time. Trust me." Mr. Gray started walking toward the edge of the property. Carl ran after him, pulling out his cell phone.

It was late, but Carl was sure Franklin would be up. The phone rang twice before Franklin's voice said, "I hope you didn't blow yourself up."

"Nah. But I need a—" Carl stopped, seeing that they were already in Biddleborn. "Never mind," he said and hung up. Carl looked back over his shoulder, confused.

Mr. Gray pulled out his map. "Where's Meridian?"

"She's at her friend Artie's house."

"Ah, yes. The McClintock boy." Mr. Gray drew a house on the map and labeled it *Artie's House*. Then, he pocketed the pen. "This way," he said. Ten steps and they were at Belinda's door.

Carl looked over his shoulder again, even more confused. The street was where it should be. The whole town looked normal, if a bit menacing in the darkness. Carl knocked.

Belinda pulled the door open. "We can't find Artie!" she shouted, ushering them into the kitchen where Meridian sat drinking coffee. Meridian looked up when they entered, her eyes going from her stepfather to the Cat Lord.

"If the kitten is with him, he'll be fine," Mr. Gray told Belinda.

"I haven't seen her recently." Belinda looked around, then left the room, yelling, "Pineapple! Here, kitty, kitty!" She came back to the kitchen. "She must be with him. You're sure she'll keep him safe?"

"She took care of that dog all right," Carl said.

"But where could he be? Does something . . . *have* him?"

"You haven't told them anything, have you?" Mr. Gray asked Meridian. She shook her head, then stared resolutely at her coffee. Mr. Gray sighed. "I think it's time I told you all a little story," he began. "Please, have a seat."

"I think we all need coffee first," Belinda said.

"I could use a beer," Carl noted.

Belinda poured coffee for herself, Carl, and Mr. Gray. They gathered around the table. Mr. Gray steepled his fingers and said, "Sometimes, the stories we tell can reshape reality."

"No," Carl said. "Reality is time and space. We don't make it. It don't matter what kind of map you draw."

Mr. Gray nodded. "Yes, in *general*, that is true. However, in certain *particulars*, the stories we tell matter. If you shape the way people perceive an event, then eventually, those perceptions become reality because everyone starts living as if they're true. You follow?" Everyone nodded, although Carl's nod was rather grudging.

Mr. Gray continued. "So, let's imagine a place where, for reasons having to do with very small science intertwined with threads of magic, the fabric of reality is a bit . . . thin. It's like a really old T-shirt that you can see through. It's a small town where not much happens, so the children are especially adept at dreaming. They dream up whole worlds, and one of those worlds becomes a bit . . . solid. And the place where it presses against reality is one of the particularly thin spots. The story and reality start to bleed into each other. Does that make sense?"

"For something that makes no sense, yes, I suppose it does," Belinda said.

"Well, that's what is happening here. There are creatures from another world, a place called Detritus, that are bleeding through into Biddleborn."

"How do you know all this?" Carl asked.

"Because that's how *I* got here." Mr. Gray put down his coffee cup. The coat he was wearing was now a black cloak made of feathers.

Carl nodded. "Yeah, I guess that makes as much sense as anything."

"Do you know where Artie is?" Belinda asked.

"He's in Detritus," Meridian said. "It's all my fault."

"Of course it ain't your fault. How could it be?" Carl asked.

"Because it's *my* story."

* * *

The hole Lanora had created in the wall didn't open onto the beach where Artie had first awakened. Instead, it spilled them into the turnip patch. *Dreams are weird*, Artie thought, as he followed Calvin the Skeleton and Gorgeous Meridian through rows of what he assumed were turnips. Artie had no real experience with most vegetables.

Scarecrows in tattered black robes dotted the field. Artie counted ten of them. Their faces appeared to have been carved from pumpkins, then dried. Faint shadows stirred behind their eyes. "Psssst," Artie said to the others. "I think these scarecrows are watching us!"

"Most surely. That's their job," Calvin explained. "Let's try not to make them angry."

"Oh." Artie fixed his eyes on Gorgeous Meridian's back, then caught himself admiring her shape. He looked down instead. The turnips were covered with eyes, like some kind of biblical angel. Artie picked up his pace, just in case they also had teeth.

"Hey! You kids!" a voice bellowed.

"It's Farmer Drumpkin! Run faster!" Calvin yelled.

Artie risked a glance back. The farmer was dressed in overalls, had a red face, and was pointing a shotgun. That last detail was the part that concerned Artie the most. "He's got a gun!" he yelled as a shot rang out, making his observation a bit superfluous.

"Let me handle it," Calvin said, pushing Artie behind him. The skeleton started walking toward the farmer.

"What's he doing?" Artie shouted at Gorgeous Meridian.

"Whatever it is, just let him do it. He's already dead. Being shot won't hurt him." She grabbed Artie's arm, and they ran toward the edge of the field while the skeleton held out his arms and walked brazenly toward the choleric farmer.

The shotgun boomed. Artie glanced back and saw Calvin looking for his head. "Now that was rude," the skeleton muttered. He picked up his skull and dusted it off.

Artie wanted to point out that the shotgun blast should have shattered the skull, but he was running through a field of turnips that had eyes. And the skull in question belonged to a skeleton that walked and talked. And this was all a dream, no matter how real it felt.

The scarecrows opened their mouths and howled. All ten of them came down from their poles and fixed their sights on the trespassing trio.

"Calvin!" Gorgeous Meridian yelled. "The scarecrows!" Calvin bowed to the farmer, turned, and ran.

"Get 'em!" Farmer Drumpkin called to the scarecrows. He threw back his head and laughed maniacally.

Artie felt as if he were trapped inside a demented cartoon. The scarecrows came from all directions, penning them in. Everywhere the trio turned, a scarecrow was running toward them. "Someone has a plan, right?" Artie asked.

"We fight," the skeleton and Gorgeous Meridian spoke together.

"I wish I had my lightsaber." Something fell from Artie's hand. "My lightsaber! Ha! I love this dream!" He scooped it up and ran at the nearest scarecrow. In this dream, he was a Jedi. Artie smiled.

"He's gone mad," the skeleton said from behind Artie.

The first scarecrow was no match for Artie's blade, which cut through the scarecrow's tattered robe and whatever squooshy bits were tucked away beneath it. Artie whooped loudly and spun, arms outstretched in victory. His lightsaber had *cut through* something. He loved this dream!

Three scarecrows attacked, and Artie spun like a Jedi. He was strong and skilled, and he was *using the Force*! He sure hoped Gorgeous Meridian was watching.

Artie slashed and spun, spun and slashed. Three scarecrows fell. The remaining scarecrows gathered up their robes and ran. Artie threw back his head and laughed, rather like a cartoon character.

"He's gone mad!" Calvin repeated, a little louder this time.

* * *

Sheriff John Amory pulled up to the curb outside of the Gershwins' house. The night was quiet and a little cool, with a sky peppered with stars. The citizens of Biddleborn were, by and large, tucked up in their houses for the night. The sheriff got out of his car and walked to where Rose Marie and Zelda waited on the sidewalk.

Rose Marie was leaning on the handle of a push mower. "Good evening, Sheriff," she said. "Thank you for coming."

"Hello, Mrs. Gershwin, Zelda. What seems to be the trouble? Geraldine said you had someone in your house?"

"Not some*one*. It's more like some*thing*," Zelda corrected him.

The sheriff looked at her. "Some kind of animal?" he asked, hoping it was a raccoon and not another story about her hairdryer trying to kill her.

"More like a poltergeist, I think," Rose Marie said.

"Actually, they're, um . . . shadow wights," the lawnmower said.

"Oh, is that what they're called? How about that," Rose Marie said to the lawnmower.

"You didn't call me out at this time of night for a prank, did you?" Sheriff Amory asked Rose Marie.

"Not at all. You should have seen it. It's like the whole house was alive!"

"Uh-huh. And how do you do the trick with the lawnmower? Do you have a tape recorder or something hidden?"

"No, sir," Mowey said. "My name's Mowey. I'm really me. I mean, I'm really alive. And talking. And other stuff. I can dance! You wanna see?" The lawnmower began to dance while humming Michael Jackson's "Billy Jean." It's hard for lawnmowers to break dance, but Mowey tried his best.

Sheriff John Amory watched the Gershwins' lawnmower dance on their lawn in the pale April moonlight. He could feel some piece of the way he understood the world tilting sideways and crumbling away. It had been a long day. Now, it looked as if it might be a very long night. "Well. Okay. Let's go see this poltergeist," he finally submitted.

"*Shadow wights*," Mowey corrected.

"Yeah, whatever," Amory said, clicking on a flashlight and heading up the sidewalk. The Gershwins and their lawnmower followed close behind.

* * *

The rooster's foot hurt, and that made him angry. The little clown had nicked him with the chainsaw. The rooster decided he needed an army.

The rooster began calling his hens to him and circling them. One by one, the hens looked up, fully self-aware. They began to really *think*. And the hens were angry, too.

Chapter 12

"WHEN I WAS A KID, I used to imagine there was a world on the other side of my bedroom wall," Meridian began to explain. "I pretended it was where all the missing things went: the toys I couldn't find, my *Alice in Wonderland* book, all the socks, and that sort of thing. And when Misty, my kitten, disappeared, I made up a story about how she went there and was adopted into a kingdom of cats, ruled by a Cat Lord. The story grew from there."

"That's probably where my class ring went," Belinda realized.

"And my reticulating saw," Carl added.

"The world Meridian invented is, indeed, just on the other side of the wall," Mr. Gray, the Cat Lord, confirmed. "All the walls, actually. And now, it's pushing through into your world."

"And so . . . you're actually from a world that came outta my daughter's imagination?"

"Yes, Carl. I am the Cat Lord."

Carl looked at the Cat Lord's feathered cloak, opened his mouth to ask a question, then closed it.

"So, Meridian's kitten really did end up in a kingdom of cats?" Belinda asked.

"Yes, absolutely. Misty is alive and well in Detritus, where cats never die. Of course, in *your* world, she was eaten by a coyote many years ago."

"Okay, so how do we stuff all this imagination back into Meridian's head?" Carl asked.

"I have a plan for that," the Cat Lord said. "I think we can use Meridian's imagination to close the door . . . once I'm safely on the other side, of course. I have no intention of staying here."

"And first, we have to bring Artie home," Meridian reminded him.

"Get me home, and I'll shove your Artie back through the door."

"What about the shadow wights that have already slipped through?"

"What the heck's a 'shadow white'?" Carl asked.

"That's what possessed my clown lamp and Mrs. O'Dell's dog," Meridian explained. "The shadow wights are servants of the Shadow King."

"Nope. Don't like any of that," Carl said. "When this is over, we're getting you some therapy."

"She doesn't need therapy," Belinda said. "She needs to write a book!"

"No, no, no, no, no," the Cat Lord said. "Don't write any of this down! That's the worst, most permanent damage you could do. That will make it all very . . . *solid*."

* * *

Making Rose Marie, Zelda, and especially the lawnmower wait outside, Sheriff Amory walked all through the Gershwin home, looking for anything out of place. In the kitchen, he found evidence that someone had been making a sandwich. The rest of the house was the kind of neat and tidy that made him wish he had taken off his shoes at the door.

The sheriff was about to give up his search when he stepped on something hard in the hallway. Bending down, he saw something white and about the size of a half-dollar. It was a tooth—a really big one. The sheriff pulled a nitrile glove from his pocket and used it to pick up the tooth, which he slipped inside a crumpled evidence bag he pulled out of his other pocket.

After Amory finished his tour of the house, he rejoined the trio out on the lawn. "Well, if you've got poltergeists, they didn't show themselves," he told them. "I did find a tooth, however." He pulled the bag out of his pocket so they could see. "Any of you recognize this?"

"It's not mine," Mowey said. "I still have all my teeth."

"That's a big tooth," Rose Marie observed. "My lamp tried to bite me, but that looks a little big for a bedside lamp, don't you think?"

"It looks like a Bandersnatch tooth," Mowey said.

Zelda burst out laughing. The others looked at her. "Beware the Jubjub bird and shun the frumious Bandersnatch!" she said. "It's from the poem 'Jabberwocky.' Lewis Carroll, anyone? *Alice in Wonderland*? Although I believe Jabberwocky is actually from *Through the Looking Glass*."

"Oh. Book stuff," the sheriff said. "Gotcha."

"I paid good money for her to know all that," Rose Marie said.

Amory pocketed the tooth. "I'm going to send this to the lab to see if we can find out what kind of animal it came from. In the meantime, if you'd feel safer, why don't you all stay with a friend or relative? Is that doable?"

"We can stay with my sister," Rose Marie said.

"There's no way Aunt Edna is going to let Mowey stay in her house," Zelda pointed out. "We should stay with Mike." Mike was Zelda's younger brother.

"Yes, that's a good idea," Rose Marie agreed.

"Will you hang around a few minutes while we pack?" Zelda asked the sheriff. "The house behaves itself around you."

"Yes, ma'am. If any poltergeists show their faces, I'll shoot them dead."

* * *

The Cat Lord's cottage in Detritus was nestled among the trees. It was constructed of rock and what appeared to be sea glass, with glints of green and blue among the brown, white, and gray. The main structure had a steeply pitched roof. Additions had been stuck on at some point in time, one on each side, hanging on like shy children.

A black kitten, who looked a lot like Belinda's new kitten, Pineapple, was curled up on the cottage's top step. She looked up as they approached.

"So, how is this Cat Lord guy going to help us?" Artie asked. "Because it doesn't look like he has an army hiding anywhere."

"The Cat Lord doesn't need an army," Lanora informed him. "He can weave magic."

"Okay. That's cool, I guess."

"I don't trust him," Calvin said. "The Cat Lord is the Cat Lord's friend and no one else's."

"Meow," the kitten said. "The Cat Lord's not home."

Although Artie had been arrested by giant crabs and was currently traveling with an animated skeleton, he was a bit surprised to hear words coming from the kitten's mouth. "You look like my mother's cat," he told her.

"I *am* your mother's cat," Pineapple said.

"Where is the Cat Lord?" Lanora asked.

"He's not here. He's off fighting shadow wights and teaching science class."

"Do you know when he'll be back?"

"He can't come back. He's stuck in the *other* world."

"Oh, well, so much for that plan," Calvin said, turning to leave.

Lanora grabbed Calvin by the humerus. "How do we get him *un*stuck?" she asked the kitten. The kitten shrugged, then started grooming.

The front door opened, and the world's oldest woman looked out at them. "Hey wot's all this here, eh?" she asked.

"Mayzell!" cried Lanora, and the two women embraced.

"Prepare to be hugged," Calvin whispered to Artie. But there was no way to prepare for the sheer magnitude of the hug he received from this old woman whom he had never met. She was a plump old grandmotherly sort of person, soft and squooshy. Her hug was all gingerbread and cocoa.

"Come in! Come in! We got the cookies and tin cans all afloat fer ya!"

Artie leaned toward where Calvin's ears should be and whispered, "I heard 'cookies,' but nothing else made sense."

"Mayzell's soul is pure light, but her brain's a bit addled," Calvin explained. "Too much age and sun."

They went inside the cottage. Inside, the cottage was bigger than it looked from the outside. Artie wondered whether that was a trick of architecture and decor or whether it was magic. The main part of the cottage was divided into a sitting area full of soft chairs, two sofas, and more blankets and pillows than were strictly necessary, all gathered around a stone fireplace. A skylight in the ceiling left a soft patch of sun on the floor.

Three cats lazed in the warmth of the sunny spot, while another two cats perched on the furniture. Artie could see a kitchen and dining area at the back of the house and a door that he hoped was a bathroom. Did they have indoor plumbing in this world? He peered toward the kitchen and spotted a normal-looking sink.

"Mayzell, is there a bathroom I can use?" Artie asked. He hoped this wasn't about to turn into one of those dreams where you have to pee but can't find a suitable bathroom.

"Of course, sweet pup! Follow me!" Mayzell waddled through a doorway and took two more turns that made no sense to Artie. The house was definitely bigger inside than out. "Here's the loo. You can find yer way back to the kitchen all right? Follow the smell of warm cookies!" And with that, Mayzell left Artie to his business.

It was a more or less ordinary-looking bathroom. After Artie peed and washed his hands, he couldn't resist a brief snoop through the medicine cabinet. It contained five amber glass bottles, each with a handwritten label. Artie picked each up and read them: "For worms,"

"For heartbreak," "For UTI," "For fighting," and "For fleas." There was also a tube of something that had no label. A small wooden box had the words *Robert's Tincture—Stay Out!* written in black sharpie.

Artie opened the box and peeked in. A short, squat glass bottle sat on a bed of tissue paper. It looked leaky around the lid. Artie picked it up carefully. It smelled like camphor. He tucked it back inside the box and returned the box to the medicine cabinet. Realizing his fingers were a little wet, he wiped them on his jeans.

Artie followed the smell of cookies back to the kitchen, unaware of the tincture that was soaking into his body, weaving magic everywhere it went.

* * *

Galactic Books and Other Stuff was locked up for the night. One by one, the books fell asleep, dreaming science fiction dreams of adventure and cunning, technology and lore. The fantasy section fought dragons and wove spells, went on quests, and solved riddles.

The *Star Wars* chess set stirred. A lone Ewok stepped forward one square. A stormtrooper two paces away stepped forward, blaster ready. Han Solo was still missing, so the heroes were at a disadvantage. The Empire was feeling confident.

A ripple of magic coursed through the shelves. In the gaming section, polyhedral dice began to roll. The whole building vibrated with a rhythmic purr deep in its throat. The building opened an eye, saw that it was night, then settled back down and slept.

Chapter 13

WEDNESDAY BROUGHT GRAY DRIZZLE to Biddleborn, which most everyone agreed was fitting for the day of Jazz Miller's funeral. School had been canceled for the day, as it was assumed the entire student population would have used Jazz Miller's funeral as an excuse not to attend anyway.

Meridian and Carl had spent the night at Belinda's house, but they had to brave their own house to get ready for the funeral. Since Meridian's car was still at home and Carl's truck had been destroyed, Belinda gave them a ride. "Be careful," she said. "I'm going to go to the police and report Artie missing."

"You sure about that?" Carl asked. "They ain't gonna find him if what that Robert the Cat Lord fella says is true."

"Yes, I'm sure. For one, it will look suspicious if I don't. And then, there's the 'what if' factor. What if we're wrong about . . . everything? What if he's been kidnapped . . . by humans?"

"Yeah. That all makes sense," Carl agreed. "Well, let us know if you need anything. And I ain't just saying that."

Belinda hugged them goodbye, promised to keep them in the loop, and left to go report her son as a missing person. As for Carl and Meridian, they crossed their scorched yard and went into the house. After a brief room-by-room check to make sure there were no demon clowns, giant killer dogs, or armies of spiders just waiting to get them, Meridian went up to her room to get dressed for the funeral.

Carl went outside to check on the chickens and goats. The chickens, normal-sized, were gathered together in one corner of the yard. When Carl approached, they got quiet and all turned to watch him. He stopped and looked at them. "Did I interrupt a secret meeting?" he asked.

The rooster crowed. Carl sighed. "Isn't that just lovely?" He threw them some chicken feed and went to take care of the goats. The goats were behaving exactly like ordinary goats—that is to say, they bellowed for their breakfast and then fought for the best spot at the hay feeder. And the chickens ate quietly, each with one eye trained on the woods.

* * *

Artie, Calvin, and Lanora had spent the night at the Cat Lord's cottage, where the guest rooms were cozy, coming equipped with one cat each. Pineapple had slept draped across Artie's chest. It was the normal sleeping-dreaming-waking cycle that convinced Artie he wasn't in a coma. He was really in some other world, possibly a parallel universe in which the laws of reality were different and in which Jazz Miller was a skeleton-thief and Meridian some kind of gorgeous princess. And that meant he needed to get home.

Artie lay on his back and stared at the ceiling, which was made of rough wooden beams. He remembered he had been doing his homework when, suddenly, his house was being eaten by an inky, buzzing blackness. He had grabbed the kitten and ran, and at some point, he fell and landed here.

Artie wondered if his house still existed. He wondered if his mother was okay. He had no idea how to get home.

Pineapple stirred and stretched. Artie stroked her fur and gave her scritches on her tiny kitten head. She wrapped around his hand and began to chew. "Ow! Stop that," Artie reprimanded her.

"Sorry," Pineapple said. "I thought you wanted to play."

"Nope. Sure didn't."

"Oh, but . . . *I* want to play." She sat up and looked at him with sad kitten eyes.

Artie sighed and gave the kitten his hand. She wrapped back around it and began to chew. Artie took it as long as he could, then pulled his hand away and hid it under the blanket.

"Oh! I love this game!" Pineapple said, pouncing on the lump made by Artie's hand as he moved it under the blanket.

"We need to get home," Artie said.

"Yes!" Pineapple pounced, then darted away so she could pounce again.

"Don't suppose you have any ideas?"

"All you need is a map." The kitten pounced, then she abruptly stopped to groom.

"A *map*." Artie thought about the map Gorgeous Meridian had drawn on the wall. Of course, all he needed was a map! Artie threw the blanket off, accidentally covering the kitten, and scurried out of bed. All he needed was a map.

* * *

When Elijah opened Galactic Books and Other Stuff on Wednesday morning, everything seemed to be in place, except it looked as if someone had started a game of chess. He frowned at the handcrafted pewter figurines that were no longer set up in neat rows. He couldn't remember whether he had looked at the chess set before closing up the night before. He was pretty sure he would have noticed if they had been out of place.

Elijah made a mental note to ask Meridian about the chess set. Setting the chess pieces back on their assigned squares, he once again mentally cursed the dark forces that stole his Han Solo. Next to the mental note about the apparent game of chess, he added a note about finding a new Han Solo on eBay.

Elijah switched on the Open sign, then settled in behind the counter. He was completely unaware of how on edge all the books were that day.

* * *

Jazz Miller's funeral was held at the First Baptist Church, where the Miller family attended services each Sunday going back three generations. The sanctuary was packed full, with most of Biddleborn having turned out for the occasion, along with Jazz's friends and family from out of town.

Cheese Fry was nervous. Writing the eulogy had been a struggle. Every time he got about halfway through, his hand would start writing gibberish of its own accord. After many failed attempts, he had finally gotten enough written to feel he could probably just wing the rest of it. He had never spoken in front of so large a crowd.

The Strangler sat next to Cheese Fry, looking uncomfortable in a suit and tie. "Norma Bellows sighting," he whispered. Cheese Fry followed his gaze. Norma Bellows was standing at the back of the room, wearing a short black dress and a pair of enormous glasses. Her hair was teased like it was 1986.

Cheese Fry frowned and turned his attention back to the pastor, who was telling about the time Jazz Miller figured out how to fill the baptistry and accidentally flooded the sanctuary. It had been a hot summer day, and the heat caused the water to evaporate, forming a cloud that one of the deacons thought was the Shekinah glory of God, like in the Old Testament.

The attendees sang "Be Thou My Vision," and then the pastor introduced the next speaker, Chad Davenport. Cheese Fry gripped his notebook and made his way up to the pulpit. He cleared his throat and looked out at the crowd.

"Jazz Miller was my best friend," Cheese Fry began. "Maybe he was everybody's best friend. We met in first grade, when I was a shy, goofy kid in glasses who got picked on by the other kids. Jazz Miller pretended I was cool, and then others started believing it. He did that for other people, as well. He genuinely liked us all and wanted us to like each other. He was really cool, and his coolness was contagious."

That was the point where Cheese Fry's notebook scribbles became nonsense about the return of Jazz Miller. So, Cheese Fry closed his notebook, cleared his throat again, took a deep breath, and improvised, which is exactly what he imagined Jazz Miller would have advised.

"I think everybody has a favorite Jazz Miller story," Cheese Fry continued. "Mine was when we were fourteen, and Jazz found a lock-picking set at a yard sale. He spent the whole summer teaching himself how to pick locks, not because he wanted to steal anything but because he imagined the great practical jokes he could pull.

"On the night before school started, Jazz roped several of us in to helping him. He broke into the school, and we spent the next few hours moving classrooms around. We took everything from Ms. Gershwin's room, all the posters and books and everything, and set it up in Mr. Connolly's room. We put Connolly's stuff in Mrs. Dawson's room. We took the skeleton from Kirchner's science class and set it up in Mr. Mayfield's office. And, of course, we got caught because it was a signature Jazz Miller move."

The audience chuckled, and some attendees wiped their eyes. Cheese Fry looked around as he gathered his thoughts. His eyes landed on Norma Bellows, who stood with arms crossed, leaning against the back wall. She flashed her middle finger at him.

Cheese Fry's scalp began to feel tight. The back of his neck tingled, and he was suddenly hot. "I think Jazz Miller will be missed, but I hope we'll continue with what he taught us." The edges of his vision blurred, and words began to bypass his brain as they came out of his mouth. "Before we know it, he'll be back. He'll save us all from the shadows. Jazz Miller will save us all."

Something tickled in Cheese Fry's throat. He opened his mouth to cough, and a thousand moths flew out. He heard his mother scream just before consciousness left him, and he hit the floor.

* * *

The heavy knock on Robert Gray's door was not wholly unexpected. Across worlds, that knock means one thing: the law has arrived. He opened the door to find Sheriff Amory standing there. "Good afternoon, Sheriff. What can I do for you?" Mr. Gray smiled.

The sheriff didn't return the smile. "What brought you to Biddleborn, Mr. Gray?"

"Ah, I see. Stranger in town, must be the killer."

"It often works that way."

"Yes, I suppose it does." Mr. Gray sighed. He was reasonably sure that the lawman wouldn't believe the truth. "I'm just passing through, really. But I got a bit stranded, so I found a job and a place to stay."

"Stranded, huh? Something wrong with your car?"

"I don't have a car."

"Then how did you get here?"

"I was either pulled here through a rift in reality, or someone else brought me in their car and kicked me out. You can believe either story you like."

The sheriff studied Mr. Gray. And the Cat Lord studied him back. "Where were you when Dale Kirchner was killed?" Amory asked.

"You think someone mauled him to death with fetal pigs?"

"I think someone has a sick sense of humor."

"I was teaching English when the science teacher was killed. I have about thirty witnesses who can testify to that."

"So, you were at the high school when he died. I thought so. And where were you Monday night around seven?"

"After work, I stopped by that bookstore downtown, then ate dinner at Miss Lindy's. I was probably back here by seven."

"Can anyone corroborate that?"

"The bookstore and diner, yes. Well, not to the part about me being back here at seven, they can't . . . unless there's a busybody around, paying attention to my comings and goings."

"And yesterday, did you have a class the last hour of the day?"

"Can't you get my schedule from Mr. Mayfield?"

"I absolutely will, but I thought I'd ask you first—give you a chance to cooperate."

"I was teaching freshmen that hour. Believe me, if I were going to murder anyone, it would have been some of the students in that class, not the other boy."

"Will you be staying around Biddleborn for a while?"

"I plan to."

"Then I plan to be a busybody, paying very close attention to your comings and goings. You understand?"

"Yes, sir."

"Good." The sheriff gave Mr. Gray a long, hard look before turning away and heading back to his car.

Robert Gray, the Cat Lord, watched the sheriff for a moment, then closed the door. He had a feeling the sheriff was going to be a nuisance.

* * *

Norma Bellows and the thing that lived inside her stood at the end of Blackbird Lane, contemplating the way the darkness shimmered with crimson light. As it was the middle of the afternoon, the darkness at the end of Blackbird Lane would have been unusual in its own right, but the red that seeped through added to the nightmare. Norma was afraid, but the thing that lived inside her found the darkness and its blood-red light to be quite beautiful.

The darkness began spinning, and an enormous shadow oozed through the light. It puddled on the ground in front of Norma and her guest. Norma's eyes rolled up, her body went limp, and she fell into the shadow at her feet, disappearing from this world.

Chapter 14

SHERIFF AMORY CALLED for volunteers to help look for Artie McClintock. They searched Biddleborn—all of it and the surrounding woods and fields.

Belinda made flyers and passed them out. Meridian and Carl helped. It wasn't necessary, of course; everyone knew who Artie was and what he looked like. And after what happened to Jazz Miller and Dane Peterson, no one expected to find Artie alive.

* * *

Meridian helped search the woods for Artie, but, of course, she knew—or hoped she knew—that they wouldn't find him. Afterward, Carl was reluctant to let Meridian go home, so she went to Galactic Books instead.

"You're early!" Elijah said.

"Yes. Good observation. Very astute."

"Did you see anyone playing chess last night with the *Star Wars* chess set?"

"Nope."

"Did *you* start a game?"

"I don't play chess."

Elijah frowned in thought. "Okay. Well, the set was all messed up this morning. Looked like the Empire was winning."

"Good to know."

"Are you clocking in early?"

"Is that all right?"

"Fine by me."

Meridian clocked in. Elijah let her take the counter while he set up a new display. A fellow from Biddleborn, Barry Brockmeier, had written a dystopian novel about the zombie apocalypse. He was to come in on Saturday for a signing. In the meantime, Meridian perched behind the counter, stared into the middle distance, and attempted to make everything right.

Lanora and Calvin were in the Cat Lord's cottage. Their new friend, Artie, who was very safe and healthy and having a good time, sat petting a kitten. A knock sounded at the door. It was . . .

Meridian blanked on the name. She needed something . . . wizardly sounding.

"Hey, Meridian! Do we have any zombies?" Elijah was at the action figure display.

"Um . . . there might be one." Meridian hopped off her stool and went to the back of the store. Next to the break room was a storage area of mostly forgotten things along with seasonal displays and a crap ton of spiders. Meridian dug through the box, looking for zombies and trying out various wizard names: Old Ron, Merlinson, Jensen Ackles . . .

Meridian found a zombie action figure that also happened to be a wrestler—a combination she decided would be truly terrifying in real life. She took it out to Elijah. "Ah! Zombie Undertaker! Very good," he said.

A knock sounded at the door. It was Old Randolph the Wise but Ungrateful. He peered out from under his hat at everyone.

"Come in, child! Hey, wot!" Mayzell said, ushering Old Randolph into the kitchen so she could properly fetch him some tea. "Have yerself a seat while I spin the old kettle, eh?"

Old Randolph looked at the very happy, very healthy Artie and said, "We must get you home. You are needed there, and the Cat Lord is needed here. I know a spell that will cause you to switch places."

"Was this the only zombie we had?" Elijah asked.

Meridian blinked at him. "It was the only one I saw."

"The display looks weird with only one zombie. We need more."

"Okay."

"You hold down the store. I'm going on a zombie hunt."

"Okay."

Old Randolph pulled a vial out of the pocket of his robe. "Here, drink this." He handed the vial to Artie, who happily and healthily drank it down.

* * *

Although she knew it was a terrible idea, Zelda unlocked the front door of the house from which she and Rose Marie had so recently escaped, and she slipped inside. She had brought Rose Marie's cane in case she needed a weapon. Zelda couldn't resist the idea of a Bandersnatch, if Mowey's theory were correct. She was an English teacher, after all.

If the Bandersnatch was real, what else might really exist? Hobbits? Zelda was really hoping for hobbits. She stood in the foyer. It was hard to believe how normal and quiet the house was after the chaotic terror of the night before. It was almost *too* quiet, like students when they're plotting mischief. Had Zelda been wise, she would have turned around and left. But, alas, wisdom did not prevail.

Outside, the grass was humming. Zelda could feel its unrest. She moved through the house, peeking around doorways and occasionally standing still to listen. She made it all the way to the den before disaster slithered out of the shadows. The darkness oozed up from the floor. It had teeth, and Zelda briefly wondered if it was a Bandersnatch.

The creature wrapped itself around Zelda, and she hit it with the cane. It snarled, and its mouth was definitely the source of the tooth the sheriff had found. Zelda screamed. The Bandersnatch opened its mouth, and Mowey rolled into the room, his blades already spinning.

Zelda swung the cane and threw herself to the floor. The Bandersnatch let go. But it lunged at Mowey, and he lunged back. Darkness flew from his blades, and the Bandersnatch disappeared where it splattered. Its teeth hit the floor and scattered.

Zelda picked one of the teeth up and put it in her pocket. She looked at Mowey, triumphant. "We killed a Bandersnatch!"

Mowey turned off his motor. "We should go, in case there are more."

"Okay. You're right. This was probably a bad idea anyway." Zelda turned to leave just as the room was swallowed in darkness.

"Oh no," Mowey whimpered.

* * *

The Cat Lord was back home, in his lovely little cottage, surrounded by Warrior Princess Lanora of the Sands, Calvin of the Thieves' Guild, Mayzell, and Old Randolph the Wise but Ungrateful. He could have hugged them all.

"It didn't work," Lanora said.

"Give it a minute," Old Randolph replied.

"What didn't work?" the Cat Lord asked. His voice sounded odd.

"Maybe he needs more, eh? A tipsy wipsy vial more?" Mayzell suggested.

The Cat Lord noticed his hands. They looked peculiar. "Oh, God." He pushed himself up from the kitchen table and ran to the bathroom mirror. He *really* ran, full of energy. And his ability and desire to do so strengthened his conviction that Old Randolph had screwed up big time.

The Cat Lord looked in the mirror, and Artie McClintock's face looked back at him. He frowned, and Artie frowned. The Cat Lord roared in anger, but the sound was more comical than frightening. The Cat Lord, in the body of seventeen-year-old Artie, stomped into the kitchen. "You! You . . . bungling old fool! Look what you've done to me!"

Old Randolph the Wise but Ungrateful stood up. "Well, I suppose

I'd best be going. It's getting . . . late. Er . . . I have errands to run." He backed toward the door.

"Fine. Get out! I'll fix this myself!" the Cat Lord shouted.

Old Randolph turned and ran.

"Goodbye, Old Randolph! Come again for tea and seahorses, eh?" Mayzell set about gathering the empty teacups.

The Cat Lord sat down. A horrible thought had just occurred to him. If he was stuck inside Artie McClintock, then Artie McClintock was likely walking around looking like him. He put his head down on the table and moaned.

* * *

Even though everything seemed quiet, Carl didn't trust that his home wouldn't become the scene of some new terror once again. Unfortunately, he had no idea how to prevent shadow widgets or whatever they were called from messing with his stuff. He needed to call in an expert.

Carl drove Meridian's car to the Paradise Motel and knocked on the door to room six. Robert Gray opened the door. "Carl!" He threw his arms around him. Stunned, Carl wiggled free of the embrace. "It's me! Artie!"

Carl looked at him. "*Artie?*"

"Yes!" Artie, trapped inside the middle-aged body of an imaginary person, pulled Carl into room six and closed the door. "So, do I look like Mr. Gray to you?" he asked.

"You're sure you're Artie?"

"I'm not sure of anything anymore."

"Yeah, I hear ya." They looked at each other for a moment. Then, Carl poked Robert Gray/Artie in the chest. "You feel solid."

"Yeah."

"Okay. Tell me what happened. Hang on, let me sit down." Carl walked over to the room's ancient-looking upholstered chair and sat.

"Um . . ." Artie sat on the bed. "I don't know where to start. I don't even know what day it is or anything. I was doing my homework when the house started buzzing, and stuff came out of the walls. Then, suddenly, I was in some other world, with a girl who looked like Meridian and a . . . skeleton who sounded like Jazz Miller."

"Right. Robert Gray said you were in a place that is basically Meridian's imagination."

"Huh. I guess that makes sense. Kind of."

"Okay. So, you was there. Were you you, or were you Robert?"

"I was me. I think. And then, we went to the Cat Lord's Cottage."

"Gotcha."

"And this old wizard came in and gave me a potion to drink. It was supposed to send me home. I think. But then I was here, and now I'm Mr. Gray, the substitute teacher who's teaching Mr. Kirchner's classes."

"Yeah, you missed the part where we all learned that Mr. Gray is the Cat Lord."

"Oh. Uh-oh. The wizard said we'd switch places, the Cat Lord and me. I thought he meant I'd go to my world and he to his, but . . . in our own bodies. Not . . . this." He held up the Cat Lord's hands.

"It's my understanding that this is somehow Meridian's doing. So, let's go see if she can help," Carl suggested. "In the meantime, I don't suppose you know how to banish shadow widgets from my home?"

"Shadow *wights*. And yes, I can kill them with my lightsaber," Artie offered.

"Actually, I think you have a real sword hiding in that weird, feathered cape thing you're wearing."

"Oh yeah? That's cool." Artie started digging through the Cat Lord's pockets, which he discovered were frighteningly infinite. He pulled out a lead pipe, a vial of black liquid, a box of cigars, two cats, and a can of tuna. Finally, he found the sword and pulled it out. "Is it a magic sword, you think?"

Carl flicked the can. "Seems like regular metal. But what do I know?"

"Maybe Meridian can pretend it's magic for me."

"Yeah. Just don't get yourself in trouble with it."

Artie smiled . . . with the Cat Lord's face.

* * *

After a long, discouraging day of searching for Artie McClintock, Sheriff Amory drove all the way to Springfield to show the tooth he had found in the Gershwin house to Dr. Frieda Lowenstein-Smith, a professor of zoology. He was hoping whatever it belonged to was responsible for what happened to Dale Kirchner. Possibly Dane Peterson, too, although it was a human who stuffed him inside the lockers. But maybe an animal was involved.

The sheriff parked outside the professor's house. The tooth was inside a plastic evidence bag in his pocket. He pulled it out to look at it one more time. Something black was growing around the tooth. The root was embedded in what appeared to be a chunk of black meat. Sheriff Amory held it up to the light. It was growing, whatever it was.

Amory was starting to suspect the professor might not be able to help. *Maybe I should have scheduled an appointment with a priest instead*, he thought. He got out of his car and walked up to the professor's door. Since he was there, he figured he might as well see what she thought.

Inside the evidence bag, black flesh grew around the tooth, and a second tooth was beginning to form.

Chapter 15

ZELDA AWOKE AT THE END of Blackbird Lane, a lawnmower digging into the small of her back. She sat up and rolled off Mowey. She tried to stand, and the world spun a bit. Her stomach felt heavy.

Mowey pulled himself upright and moaned. "What happened?" Zelda asked him.

"No idea. There was a shadow . . ."

"But how did we get *here*?"

Mowey shrugged.

Something niggled at the corner of Zelda's memory. There had been something dark, with sunburnt eyes. All around her, the trees whispered their concern. She shook her head and pulled out her cell phone. Rose Marie was going to be upset with them for going off and having an adventure without her.

* * *

When Carl picked up Meridian at the end of her shift, Robert Gray was with him. Mr. Gray smiled at Meridian. She did not return the smile but crawled into the back seat of her own car. "When are you going to get a new truck?" she asked Carl.

"I dunno."

"I hope the two of you aren't becoming best friends."

Mr. Gray looked at Meridian over the headrest. "No, *you're* my best friend," he said.

"Nope."

"Believe it or not, yeah, you are," Carl said. "Tell her something only you would know."

"That might not work," Artie replied from Mr. Gray's body. "If the Cat Lord came from inside her head, he might know stuff even I don't know."

Meridian frowned at them. "Just tell me what's going on. Because something obviously is." She sighed. "Oh. Dadgummit. You're Artie, aren't you?"

Artie used Mr. Gray's body to smile at her. "I am! How did you know?"

"I should have given the wizard a more majestic name. I just blanked."

"So . . . you can help? Because I really don't know how to teach science. Also, what happens when I have to pee? I don't want to pee with . . . well, ya know. And he's me right now, so . . ."

Meridian leaned back and stared out the window.

"So, can you help me?" Artie asked again.

"Not until you shut up."

"Oh."

The Cat Lord, looking out from Artie's eyes, decided to take matters into his own hands. He closed his eyes and began to weave magic, this time not to shape reality but to send his own consciousness back into his body and to draw the consciousness of Artie back into his. Later, he would send each body to its proper home.

"Ow!" Artie put a hand to Robert Gray's head. "Ow! Ow! Ow!"

"Meridian, I think you're hurting him," Carl said.

A string of light joined the two men. Their souls sped along its path, each to its own rightful body.

"Oh, this is much better," the Cat Lord said.

"You're not Artie anymore?" Carl asked.

Robert Gray flipped the sun visor down and looked in the mirror. "No, I'm the Cat Lord again! Thank God," he said.

"I'm still here, though," Artie said, using Mr. Gray's mouth to speak.

"Yeah, we know, Mr. Cat Lord," Carl said. "Now, Meridian's gotta figure out how to send you home and bring Artie here."

"No, it's me, Artie. I'm still here."

"Stop talking through me, you little—" the Cat Lord warned him.

"Why am I still here?" Artie, still trapped inside the Cat Lord, was starting to panic.

The Cat Lord looked over the headrest at Meridian. "We're going to have to work on your ability to do magic." The Cat Lord closed his eyes and used his thoughts to speak to the extra soul residing in his body. "*See the bright string, Artie? Follow it. It leads to your body.*"

"*I did. I'm in my body. I'm just also . . . here. I'm in both places,*" Artie thought-spoke back.

"*That's not possible. You're a mere mortal. Your soul doesn't divide.*"

Artie shrugged one metaphysical shoulder. "*I don't know what to tell you.*"

"*Well, if YOU can do it, I can do it.*" The Cat Lord divided his soul, sending one part along the string and into Artie's body. He looked through Artie's eyes at Lanora, Calvin, and Mayzell, who were drinking tea and trying to solve the problem of Artie and the Cat Lord's switch. "*Maybe we can make this work,*" he said to Artie. "*But you're going to have to learn some magic if you're going to be my hands in Detritus.*"

"*Real magic? Do I get a sword?*"

"*We'll see.*"

"*Cool.*" Artie smiled with both of their faces.

* * *

By the time the sheriff pulled the tooth out of his pocket to show the professor, it had grown quite a chunk of flesh, which was hanging off like a tumor. Another tooth was just beginning to poke through the skin. "I have no idea what this is," Dr. Lowenstein-Smith said. "It's about the right size for a grizzly bear, but look at the shape. It's too broad. And see how it curves?" she asked.

"What about some kind of cat?" the sheriff asked.

"Again, it's too broad, and the shape is . . . unusual. Not to mention whatever *this* is." The professor poked at the blob of flesh with a pencil. It squirmed, and she dropped it.

The sheriff picked the tooth up with a tissue from the professor's desk. "Sorry about that. It seems to be . . . growing something."

"You might want to take it to a priest," the professor suggested.

* * *

Norma Bellows kneeled before the Shadow King. She was only herself now. The old woman with the enormous glasses—the Shadow King's emissary—stood behind her. Norma trembled, certain she was about to die. Or worse.

The Shadow King looked just as Norma had imagined him, back when she and Meridian Page had first told stories about him, trying to scare each other at a sleepover when they were eight years old. The house Meridian lived in with her mother had a finished basement. When Norma would come over, she and Meridian would sleep on the sofa bed in the basement, laughing and telling ghost stories until they finally fell asleep.

Meridian's basement had been full of shadows. To make them less scary, the girls invented tales about them. It was Norma who christened the darkness under the stairs the Shadow King.

Now, the Shadow King hovered over Norma, all inky blackness except for the red hatred in his eyes. She knew he had sharp teeth and claws without needing to see them. She knew he was strong enough to crush her bones. She knew he could drive her mad with his magic. She had given him those powers.

“Tell me, child, where does the magic of Biddleborn reside?” the Shadow King asked, his long fingers stroking Norma’s hair.

“I guess it’s in Meridian’s basement. But not the house where she lives now. Her *old* house.”

“No. Try again.”

“Maybe it’s . . . wherever children tell each other stories.”

“You will take me there.”

Norma continued to tremble as the Shadow King poured himself inside of her. Once she was fully possessed, her fear left her. She smiled, but with her eyes full of hatred.

Chapter 16

"THIS IS THE WORST IDEA you've ever had," The Strangler said to Cheese Fry as they stood over Jazz Miller's grave in the darkness, each holding a shovel.

"We don't have a choice. You heard the prophecy."

"Dude. You ain't a prophet."

"Then explain the moths."

"I don't know. All I know is I don't want to dig up Jazz's grave. We're gonna get caught, for one thing. And also, it's gonna be gross."

"It'll be fine," Cheese Fry assured him. "They *just* buried him—he's not gross yet. And the grave is still fresh, so no one will even know it's been disturbed."

"Worst idea ever." The Strangler stuck his shovel in the fresh dirt and started digging. Cheese Fry joined him. "So, you think . . . what? He's gonna hop up out of his coffin? Like some kind of Jesus?"

"Yeah, I think so," Cheese Fry confirmed.

"That's messed up. You know that, right?"

Cheese Fry shrugged, then resumed digging. Even with the dirt still loose, they dug for a long time. Finally, The Strangler's shovel hit Jazz's coffin.

"About time," Cheese Fry said. "Have you noticed that no one on TV gets this dirty when they dig up a grave?" They uncovered the coffin, then grabbed the crowbars they had brought with them.

"If he's really alive in there, couldn't we just knock?" The Strangler asked. “Like, wouldn’t he make some noise for us?”

Cheese Fry wiped his forehead, leaving a streak of dirt that was all but invisible in the darkness. “That’s a good point.” He tapped on the coffin with the crowbar—three light taps.

Silence.

And then three taps came from inside the coffin. “I’m gonna puke,” The Strangler said.

Cheese Fry pried the coffin open. The thing that sat up in the coffin had been dead much longer than Jazz Miller. It was a skeleton dressed in medieval-looking clothing. A feathered hat sat on its head. “This isn’t the Cat Lord’s cottage,” it said. “Where am I? How did I get here? Good heavens! Am I in a casket?”

The skeleton sounded like Jazz, but it was far too decomposed to be him. The Strangler dropped his crowbar, scrambled out of the grave, and ran.

* * *

“Pay attention,” the Cat Lord said to the teenager lurking in his head and the teenager sitting across the table from him. He, Carl, and Meridian were sitting in Belinda’s kitchen. Belinda poured everyone coffee, then sat next to Mr. Gray. She stared at him, trying to catch a glimpse of her son in his eyes.

“Weaving magic is like telling a story, which means you can’t be afraid to take risks,” the Cat Lord continued. “Also, it’s the details that make it work.” As he spoke, Mr. Gray wove a string of light through his fingers. As the pattern grew in complexity, the light changed colors. He let it go, and a butterfly flew around Belinda’s kitchen.

“But how did you pull the magic out of the air to start with?” Meridian asked.

“Pretend hard enough, and it’ll happen. Of course, it helps if you have magic inside of you.”

“I don’t think I do.”

"You must, or I wouldn't be here."

"I know *I* don't," Artie said.

"The fact that you said that from inside my head suggests otherwise," the Cat Lord pointed out.

"Oh."

"How do I know what pattern to weave?" Meridian asked. "Are you going to teach me?"

"No. Your hands already know. You hold the picture in your mind, paying attention to the details. Your hands will automatically weave what you're picturing."

"Okay." Meridian pretended to pull a string from the air. She wove it through her fingers.

"You might want to practice with a real string first, to get the feel of it," the Cat Lord suggested. "If you had actually pulled magic just now, I think you would have created a cyclone. What were you picturing?"

"Um . . . a string of light."

The Cat Lord frowned at her.

"Can I try it?" Artie asked. Artie used the Cat Lord's fingers to pull a string of magic from the air. He wove it in a complicated net that turned green, then blue. A plate of spaghetti appeared on the table. Belinda and Carl clapped.

"He had an advantage," Meridian said. "He used *your* fingers."

The Cat Lord shrugged. "If you're in battle, you don't get to whine that your enemy has an advantage."

"I don't get why I can't just make a potion like Old Randolph did."

"You saw how well *that* worked, right?"

"But I wouldn't bungle it. I have a better wizard name than Old Randolph does, so I'm sure my potion would be better. 'Meridian' sounds like an evil sea witch."

"The other problem with you making a potion is that you're *here*. Your plants don't have the same magical qualities as the plants in Detritus. Have you tried to have a conversation with one of your plants?

They're idiots."

"So," Carl said, "Is anyone going to eat that spaghetti?"

* * *

Reality blurred at the end of Blackbird Lane. Norma Bellows stepped through the darkness. The Shadow King poured out of her. Then, he went in search of children telling stories.

* * *

Sheriff John Amory put the teeth inside a ten-gallon aquarium that once held a fish named Freddie. Freddie had long since departed, and the sheriff kept meaning to acquire a new fish. He and fish made the perfect roommates. Fish were quiet, which he liked.

The thing growing around the teeth wasn't exactly quiet. It made a small mewling sound. And it had grown an eye, just above the first tooth. The eye looked at the sheriff and blinked.

The part of Sheriff John Amory that made practical decisions, such as wearing comfortable shoes, was fairly certain he needed to kill whatever was growing in the tank. But the curious part of Sheriff John Amory, the part that investigated sounds in the night, wanted to see what it was going to do next. And the practical part wanted to beat it with a hammer, then throw it in a wood chipper.

Instead, the sheriff went to his refrigerator and pulled out a container of red wigglers left over from his last fishing trip. He popped open the lid and dug out a worm. He tossed the worm into the aquarium.

The creature turned its eye toward the worm. It slithered toward the worm, then pounced on it. It made slurping sounds as it ate.

Amory's practical side suggested that was the sound the creature was going to make when it ate the sheriff in his sleep. He tossed the thing another worm, then secured the aquarium lid with duct tape. The practical part of him insisted on bungee cords as well, which he wrapped around the bottom of the tank and fastened on top. He'd need a better setup, but it was late at night, and this was the best he could do for now.

* * *

Zelda said good night to her brother Mike, then retired to the guestroom. Mike had given up his room so Rose Marie could have a proper bed and a nearby bathroom. He and Mowey were camped out in the living room.

After the initial shock, Mike seemed to have accepted the talking lawnmower as just one more of life's little oddities. Zelda suspected that by the time they were able to return home—if that ever happened—Mike and Mowey would be the best of friends.

It had been a long week, and it was only Wednesday. Zelda turned down her bed, then put on her pajamas and brushed her teeth. She could still feel the adrenaline from her fight with the Bandersnatch. How on earth was she going to sleep?

Zelda opened her laptop and found the Microsoft Word document she had named *Spark of Night*. Her main character, Holmes Peabody, had just narrowly escaped a car bombing. Now, he was talking to the woman who would later betray him. Zelda, like many English teachers, was an aspiring novelist. She had self-published one book, *Destiny Takes a Bow*. She was hoping to find an agent when *Spark of Night* was finished.

Zelda wrote about Holmes for an hour, unknowingly spinning magic that drifted from Mike's house like smoke from a chimney. In room seven of Biddleborn's Paradise Motel, a man named Holmes Peabody was now brewing coffee in a coffee maker that probably contained as many germs as the bathroom floor of that same establishment. The tap water smelled of chlorine, and the coffee itself came in pre-measured packs. Holmes had low expectations for the taste, but caffeine is caffeine, and he was going to need it if he hoped to stay awake long enough to thwart a killer.

Someone knocked at the door of Holmes's room. He peeked through the spyhole. A woman with dark hair and darker eyes stood on the other side. She wore a red dress. To the people of Biddleborn, she looked like Zelda Gershwin but with better hair.

Holmes opened the door. "Looks like you found me," he said.

Zelda flashed her signature wicked smile. "Looks like I did." She stepped into room seven and closed the door.

Chapter 17

ARTIE SAT IN the Cat Lord's kitchen, a piece of parchment open in front of him. The pen Mayzell had given him was really just a feather and a bottle of ink. Artie dipped the quill and practiced writing. He wrote his name at the top of the parchment, along with the words *Biology Notes*.

Artie would be listed absent from biology class that day, but he could at least attend the class by listening in through Mr. Gray's ears. He watched through Mr. Gray's eyes as his classmates took their seats. Meridian was sitting in her usual spot, next to Artie's empty chair. He noticed that Cheese Fry was also absent. But Norma Bellows was present and watching their teacher with more interest than she had ever shown anyone else at Biddleborn High School.

"*Is Norma Bellows even in this class?*" Artie asked.

"*Who*?" Mr. Gray asked back.

"*The girl in black, by the door. She's sitting in Cheese Fry's usual seat.*"

"*I have a student named 'Cheese Fry'?*"

"*He's on your roster as Chad Davenport. But that's not my point. My point is that Norma Bellows never comes to school. And I don't think she's even in this class.*"

Mr. Gray flipped open the grade book and scrolled down the names. There was no Norma Bellows. He looked at the girl. She looked back defiantly. "*She's been playing with Shadows*," Mr. Gray realized.

Artie looked closely at Norma through the Cat Lord's eyes. He hadn't spoken to her in years, and he hadn't really even thought about her. He knew she and Meridian had been friends when they were young, before Meridian's mom died. Now, Norma ran wild—as wild as one can be in Biddleborn, anyway.

A shadow crawled across Norma's face. Far away, in another world, Artie's body jumped. "*So, what does it mean?*" he asked. "*Is she . . . possessed?*"

"*No. Just . . . accompanied. She has some very unsavory friends. I think we need to keep an eye on her.*"

"*Does she know I'm here?*"

"*The beauty of our current situation, Artie, is that you are NOT here, remember? Now, shut up and let me teach.*"

* * *

Elijah was alone at Galactic Books. The store wouldn't be open for another half hour. He had already put the *Star Wars* chess set back in order. If he found out who kept playing with it, he was going to frown at them *so* hard. He couldn't imagine that it was Meridian. She was more responsible than most of the adults he knew.

Maybe Galactic Books has a ghost, Artie wondered. *Wouldn't that be exciting?* he thought. He figured he could probably use it to draw in more customers. People love a good haunting, especially if it's happening on someone else's property.

As if in answer to Elijah's thoughts, the bell over the door jingled. But the door remained closed and locked. "Um . . . hello?" Elijah called out.

A copy of *The Silmarillion* fell to the floor. And on the chess board, an Ewok stepped forward. Although his instinct was to run, Elijah forced himself to remain very still, with his eyes fixed on the chess set.

A stormtrooper stepped forward. The Ewok gripped his spear in both hands. Leia shifted positions on her speeder bike.

Slowly, Elijah reached into his pocket and pulled out his cell phone. He opened the camera app, setting it to video. This was going to go viral.

* * *

After the incident with the moths at Jazz's funeral, Cheese Fry had no trouble convincing his mom that he was sick and needed to stay home from school. After his mom left for work, Cheese Fry opened his closet door. "You can come out now," he said to Calvin of the Thieves' Guild.

The skeleton was definitely not Jazz Miller, Cheese Fry had decided, unless people turned into fantasy characters when they died. This was his first time digging up a grave, so he couldn't be sure that it didn't always happen this way. Would Dane Peterson be a talking skeleton, too? He hadn't been buried yet—but when he was, perhaps Cheese Fry could dig him up and see if he, too, had taken on a new persona in death.

Calvin crawled out of the closet and stood. He looked around with interest at Cheese Fry's room. He walked over to Cheese Fry's dresser and examined his lightsaber. "Artie has one of these," he said. "He used it to fight the scarecrows."

"Artie McClintock? You know Artie?"

Putting the lightsaber back, Calvin turned to Cheese Fry. "Yes. We met in a dungeon. Come to think of it, I don't know what his crime was. Anyway, he seems a decent chap. He's from your world—*this* world—I take it. He's been our traveling companion for a couple of days. Seems to have ended up in Detritus by mistake."

"Ended up where?"

"Detritus. It's where I'm from. Quite frankly, I have no idea how I ended up in that coffin, but I can tell you it was a horrible place to wake up. Last I knew, I was tucked in safe and sound at the Cat Lord's cottage."

"I don't suppose you know what happened to the body that was supposed to be in that coffin?'

"No idea. I assume it's in Detritus. It'll be quite a shock when the others find it. They'll think I somehow died and recomposed."

"So, how do we get you back home?"

"Well, it's my understanding that the Cat Lord is trapped somewhere in your world. He's quite powerful, especially when it comes to weaving magic. I think we should find him and see if the two of us together have enough magic to open a door."

"Cool. How do we find him?"

"We'll draw a map. But first, I don't suppose you have something to eat? I'm so hungry that I'm about to waste away to mere bones."

* * *

Meridian sat outside at lunch, eating her yogurt. The bench beside her was empty, and she wondered what Artie was doing. Was he sitting in the teacher's lounge, talking inside the Cat Lord's head? Or was he having an adventure in Detritus?

Meridian was a little jealous at the thought of Artie on an adventure. If one of them were going to somehow end up in Detritus, it should have been her. Maybe she could figure out how he did it. The door to Detritus had to be inside her head.

Glancing around, Meridian determined that no one was looking at her. The whole campus had a somber feel to it. She closed her eyes and thought about magic-weaving. She had created Detritus with her mind, so she saw no reason to get her hands involved. She pictured a thread of magic, with light changing colors, from blue to red. In the teacher's lounge, the Cat Lord looked up, hopeful.

"May I sit here?" a voice interrupted Meridian's magic. Strings of light flickered out. In the teacher's lounge, the Cat Lord felt the magic disappear and resumed his conversation with Zelda Gershwin.

Meridian opened her eyes. A girl sat on the bench next to her. The girl was vaguely familiar, sporting dark hair and too much makeup.

"English class?" Meridian asked.

"Right. I think I accidentally took your seat the first day."

"Yes."

"Sorry."

Meridian shrugged. She wanted the girl to go away.

"I'm Dezi, but people call me Bird."

"Ah, with a name like that, you'll fit right in. Welcome to Biddleborn, where we give people strange nicknames. I don't have one, but I think that's because Meridian lends itself to manipulation: Mer, Mermaid, Prime Meridian, Meridian Prime, . . . I never needed an official nickname."

"What about your friend? Artie?"

"His real name is David." This wasn't true, but Meridian heard the lie come out of her mouth and couldn't pull it back in. That happened sometimes.

"Oh. I see. I was really rude to him the other day."

"He'll get over it."

"You think? I mean, you think he's okay? Do you know where he is?"

Meridian sighed. Now, she really wanted this girl to go away. "I have no idea, but I'm sure he's okay. He's really smart." She hoped that was true.

They sat in silence for a moment. Meridian got her hopes up that the awkwardness would drive Bird away. But the girl continued asking questions. "Is he your boyfriend? He's not, is he? I mean, because if he is, you know, I'll respect that."

Meridian toyed with another lie, but she didn't know how to make it convincing. Unless . . . "No, he's not my boyfriend. We're just friends. But he *is* dating my cousin, Lanora."

"Oh. I guess I thought . . . never mind."

"You thought he was flirting with you?"

"Yes."

"He wasn't. He was just being friendly. He's a goof who doesn't know any better." Meridian forced her face to smile. "Sorry about that. I'll yell at him for you if you want."

"No. Please don't. In fact, please don't mention any of this . . . when they find him."

"Okay, sure. I won't say a thing," Meridian assured Bird.

* * *

In the teacher's lounge, Robert Gray poured coffee for Zelda Gershwin. His smile was suave as he handed it to her. Inside his head, Artie groaned. "*Oh, God. You're flirting with Ms. Gershwin? Please just kill me now.*"

"*Shut up, boy.*"

Zelda smiled back at Mr. Gray as she accepted the coffee. "Thank you, Robert." Their hands touched briefly as the cup was exchanged. Zelda blushed.

"*Someone, please, just kill me now.*" Artie groaned again.

"*Shut up, boy. Seriously. Go play in Detritus.*"

* * *

Mowey could feel the fabric of the world. It was thin, like a favorite T-shirt. He poked at it, feeling for an opening. It wasn't that he wanted to go home. He just wanted to know where the door was, in case he needed it. And in case Rose Marie and Zelda needed it. He felt certain they would be safer in Detritus.

Mowey knew there was a door at the end of Blackbird Lane, but that door led to darkness and shadow. He wouldn't dare take Rose Marie and Zelda through that opening. For now, he followed the thin line of reality to Mike's backyard. It was a tidy spot without any extra ornamentation. The grass was short, which Mowey found disappointing. He really wanted to mow.

A yellow butterfly flitted past. "Hi!" Mowey called out to it. Drawn to the magic of a talking lawnmower, the butterfly landed on his handle. "Do you happen to know if there's a way to get elsewhere from here?" Mowey asked it. The butterfly fluttered and moved its feet in a pointing motion. "Oh. No, that's the wrong world. But I guess it would do in a pinch. Thank you."

The butterfly kissed Mowey and flew away. Mowey squinted at the door the butterfly had indicated, wondering about the world behind it.

Chapter 18

"I CAN'T FIND CALVIN," Lanora announced to Artie and Mayzell.

"Maybe he went all sour-belly up," Mayzell suggested. "Wouldn't be the first time, eh?"

"I'm sure he didn't just leave," Artie said. "Maybe he has a brilliant idea for defeating your uncle, but he had to make arrangements or try something first. Gather supplies?"

"No. Something feels wrong." Lanora looked at Artie, her pretty eyes brimming with tears. "Calvin is a thief, not a hero. Perhaps he was too ashamed to say goodbye."

"Oh." Artie felt a sucker-punch of guilt. He fully intended to leave Lanora and Detritus as soon as he could. "Well . . . that sucks."

Lanora put a pretty hand on Artie's arm. "You'll help me, won't you? You'll be my hero?" Her eyes were enormous, and Artie couldn't look away.

"Er . . . sure. I mean . . . yes. Yes, I'll help you."

The tears that had been threatening spilled prettily down Lanora's cheeks. "Thank you, Artie."

"*You really are a fool, aren't you?*" the Cat Lord cut in.

"*Yeah, I think so. I need your help, Mr. Gray, er . . . Cat Lord, sir.*"

"*Sorry, kid. You're on your own. Except for my prying voice every now and then, that is.*"

Lanora hugged Artie. He was so busy blushing that he almost forgot to hug her back. She pulled away, but her hand stayed on his arm for longer than was strictly necessary. Inside his head, the Cat Lord laughed.

"*Shut up, Cat Lord. Er . . . please, sir.*" Artie was blushing even more now.

"So, I guess we need a plan," Lanora noted. "And probably a map. Blueprints! Mayzell! I need more of that parchment. Oh! And does anybody have a dragon?"

Artie had a plan, but first, he needed magic. And he knew exactly where to find it.

* * *

Cheese Fry didn't own a trench coat, so Calvin's disguise consisted of a Jedi robe. "Keep your hood up," Cheese Fry instructed him. "People will assume you're just wearing a mask."

"Why would they assume that?"

Calvin had drawn a map that supposedly led to the Cat Lord. Cheese Fry was a little skeptical, as the map looked nothing like Biddleborn. He was fairly certain the skeleton was confused about how maps work, but he wasn't going to argue. He was, after all, riding around town with a talking skeleton he had pulled out of Jazz Miller's coffin. So, he was pretty sure the regular rules of physics or whatever no longer applied.

By nature, Cheese Fry was a good kid—a rule follower. Except when he was with Jazz Miller, that is. And being with this skeleton felt a little like being with Jazz. The voice was the same. And the insistence that his plan would work was the same.

They drove past The Strangler's house. Cheese Fry wondered if he was at school or was still recovering from the shock of the night before. Then, they passed an old woman talking to a lawnmower. Calvin waved at them.

The map led them to the high school. "Oh no. We can't come here.

I'm supposed to be sick," Cheese Fry remembered. "My mom called in for me."

"But this is where the Cat Lord is. We need his magic to get me home."

"There's no Cat Lord at the high school. Just a bunch of teachers who are going to wonder why I'm here when I'm supposed to be home. And a bunch of students who are going to notice that you're a skeleton."

"Then let's be careful not to get caught. And I resent being called a skeleton."

"Then what do you want to be called?"

"I'm a *thief*."

"Is that what the kids are calling it these days?"

They blinked at each other, which was quite a feat for the one of them who had no eyelids. Cheese Fry led Calvin around to the gym, to the side door that Jazz Miller had always preferred for his nighttime pranks. They ducked inside.

Class was going on, which meant only a few students were aimlessly roaming the halls. Cheese Fry and Calvin walked purposely past a freshman boy who merely glanced at them. Cheese Fry avoided eye contact as they passed and led Calvin toward the science rooms.

"Stop. I just had a brilliant idea," Cheese Fry announced. "But you're probably going to hate it."

Calvin looked at him. "Brilliance is always appreciated. Speak."

Cheese Fry smiled and told him his plan. Calvin did, indeed, really hate it.

* * *

A woman stood on the sidewalk outside of Miss Lindy's Diner, the establishment where Holmes Peabody was hoping to find not only a greasy burger but also some information. She handed Holmes a flyer as he walked by. "Have you seen this boy?" she asked him.

Holmes glanced at the picture. It was of a teenage boy with a shy smile. Poor kid. “He been missing long?” Holmes asked.

“Since Tuesday night.”

“I see. Any idea where he might be?”

“No. His mom owns Miss Lindy’s Diner.” The woman nodded at the restaurant. “She said she thought he was in his room doing homework, but when she called him for supper, he wasn’t there.”

Holmes looked at the flyer again. “I’ll keep my eyes open. Sure hope you find him.”

“Thank you,” the woman said.

Holmes pushed open the door of Miss Lindy’s and took a seat at a booth in the far back where he could keep an eye on the street. He stuck the missing person flyer in his pocket. It was a dangerous world, and nobody knew that better than Holmes Peabody.

* * *

Sheriff Amory was not home. He was off supervising a team of divers as they searched Gilbert Lake for the body of Artie McClintock.

In a corner of the sheriff’s darkened living room, something black stirred inside a ten-gallon aquarium. It had three jagged teeth, above which one open eye looked around the room. A second eye, still closed, was half the size of its mate.

And now, the thing had feet. The feet were overlarge for the rest of it, so walking was difficult. The thing could shuffle for a while, but then it would fall over and roll for a bit.

The sheriff had been experimenting with different foods. So far, chicken nuggets were the clear favorite. The thing looked up at the screen that the man had to move aside to give it food. The man wasn’t home, and it was hungry. The food was up there, somewhere above the screen.

The thing jumped, but without real legs, it couldn’t jump very high. It jumped again, then fell over. It had to find a way to get to that screen. The chicken nuggets were up there somewhere.

* * *

After lunch, Norma Bellows went to the art room. Norma Bellows wasn't taking art. Nevertheless, she stood in the doorway, scanning for the right seat.

There.

She walked to the table at the back of the room, where the new girl was sitting, drawing in her notebook and ignoring the students shuffling in around her. Norma slid into the seat next to her. "Hi," she said. "I'm Norma."

The girl looked up. "Hi. You can call me Bird."

"It's nice to meet you."

"Same."

Norma looked over at Bird's drawing. It was of a sad-looking cat about to be eaten by a Bandersnatch. "Nice."

"Thank you."

The teacher, Mrs. Clark, hit a service bell that sat on her desk. "Okay, people, let's get those sketchbooks out. You know what to do." She looked around the room, her eyes snagging on Norma for a moment.

Look away, Norma thought hard at Mrs. Clark. And the teacher did.

"Impressive," Bird said. "Looks like you've been practicing."

Norma smiled. "So, what happens next?" she asked.

Bird was shading in the Bandersnatch's shadow. "That depends on your level of daring."

"My level of daring is pretty high."

"Cool. Then I vote we open some doors and maybe close a few others. Mix things up a bit. These people are far too comfortable."

"Do we get to kill anybody?" Norma asked in a whisper.

Bird smiled. "You bet."

"We should start with the new biology teacher," Norma said.

Chapter 19

CHEESE FRY PUSHED OPEN the biology room door in time to hear his new science teacher say, "And that, dear children, is the wonderful way baby earthworms are made." He dragged a naked Calvin into the room. Mr. Gray looked at them both, his eyebrow raised in a question.

"I found this skeleton by the gym," Cheese Fry announced. "I thought maybe it belonged in here."

The corner of Mr. Gray's mouth twitched a little. He nodded toward the skeleton model that hung in the far corner of the room. "Put him over there for now."

Calvin was certain everyone could see him blush. Cheese Fry arranged him next to the other skeleton, then took his usual seat. He could feel Calvin staring at him through the rest of the lecture.

Finally, the bell rang. Cheese Fry's classmates gathered their belongings and pushed toward the door. After the last student left, Calvin let out a sigh. "I hate both of you," he stated. "Give me my clothes."

Cheese Fry opened his backpack, pulled out Calvin's clothing, and handed it to him, a little alarmed at Mr. Gray's *lack* of alarm that his new skeleton model was alive and cranky. But as Mr. Gray spoke, Cheese Fry began to understand. "So. Calvin. Last I knew, you were in my cottage, eating my food. How did you end up here?"

Calvin straightened his clothes and tightened his belt. "I'm not sure. Cheese Fry here dug me out of his friend's grave."

Cheese Fry smiled weakly. "I have a really good explanation for that, Mr. Gray."

"I'm sure you do, but you should probably save it for someone else. If you want to dig up all the graves in Biddleborn, be my guest. It's no concern of mine."

"Oh, well . . . So, you've already met Calvin. Oh, wait." Cheese Fry turned to Calvin. "*Him? He's* the Cat Lord?"

Calvin nodded. "In the flesh."

"A condition in which most of us find ourselves," the Cat Lord teased. He walked to the classroom door and peered out into the hall. Satisfied, he flipped the latch, locking them in. "The last thing we need is for some student who wasn't paying attention when I gave their homework assignment to suddenly realize they need to come ask me about it as a ruse to leave some other dreadful class."

"I've used that trick a time or two," admitted Cheese Fry.

"We need to get back to Detritus," Calvin said. "As it turns out, I can't walk around in this world without arousing suspicion."

"That is unfortunate because you're probably going to be here for a while," the Cat Lord informed him.

"But you're the Cat Lord. You have all that magic. And with my cunning, surely we can open one little door."

"We could, indeed. Except someone seems to have barred the doors from the other side."

"But how did I get here, then? And how did Artie get *there*?"

"Those are excellent questions. As best as I can tell, someone is playing a game of chess."

"I will not be used as a pawn!"

"Oh, I imagine you're at least a rook."

"So . . . who or what is playing chess? And is that a metaphor?" Cheese Fry asked.

"It's mostly a metaphor," the Cat Lord confirmed. "But something brought us here. And something took Artie to Detritus. Pieces are being arranged. Or maybe I'm wrong. Maybe it's all just happenstance. But I don't tend to believe in happenstance, especially not when the door gets locked behind me."

"Do you think this is the Shadow King's doing?" Calvin asked.

"I think that's giving him far too much credit. In fact, I rather suspect he, too, is a chess piece."

"So, we're being manipulated by something or someone strong enough to play with the Shadow King as if he were a game piece? I sure don't like the idea of that."

"Nor do I."

"I'm pretty good at chess," Cheese Fry announced.

They both looked at him.

"I mean . . . never mind. While I'm here, could you tell me what our homework assignment is, Mr. Gray?"

"Earthworms."

* * *

Artie stood in the Cat Lord's bathroom, holding the box that said *Robert's Tincture—Stay Out!* He opened the bottle and sniffed. It smelled like fresh-cut grass and alcohol, with just a hint of something rotten, like an orchard in late September.

"I hope I don't regret this." Artie drank the tincture. It burned all the way down, then sloshed around like lava in his stomach.

"*You're going to regret that*," the Cat Lord chimed in, a bit too late. "*I sincerely hope you ate something first.*"

Artie's whole body felt like it was on fire. Whimpering, he reached into the shower and turned on the cold water. Still fully clothed, he stepped under the spray.

The water didn't stop the burning; it just made Artie soggy and shivery on top of the pain. He turned off the shower and sat in the tub. His skin looked normal, but it felt red and bubbly. The fire was inside of him. Magic—consuming him from the inside out.

"*Aren't you going to help me, Cat Lord!*" Artie pleaded. "*How do I make it stop burning?*"

The Cat Lord sighed in Artie's head. "*This incredibly poor decision is on you. But while the magic is fresh, you might want to use it.*"

"*How?*"

"*Tell a story. Better yet, write it down. Weave with ink.*"

The burning began to ease, replaced with a jittery tingle, as though Artie had just consumed a pot of coffee chased by a six-pack of energy drinks. His mind vibrated with the same intensity, and he stripped off his wet clothing. He needed to use this magic before it diminished.

"I'm a wizard," Artie said. "No, a Jedi-Wizard. Wizard-Jedi." He giggled. Naked, Artie ran through the Cat Lord's cottage screaming, "I'm the greatest Jedi-Wizard to ever live!"

* * *

Although she knew it was a waste of time, Meridian took off work to go with Belinda and a handful of other BHS parents to Darmstadt, the next town over, to hand out Artie flyers. Once they hit Darmstadt, they split up. Meridian went with Belinda and Mrs. Davenport.

"What about doing a prayer vigil for Artie?" Cheese Fry's mother asked them. "I'm sure Mr. Mayfield would let us have it at the high school. I know Chad and Josh would be willing to help put it together."

Belinda nodded. "Yes. That would be really appreciated."

Mrs. Davenport looked at Meridian. "Oh, yeah. That would be great," Meridian said. She was trying to picture Cheese Fry and The Strangler putting a prayer vigil together. Mrs. Davenport was delusional.

Darmstadt was only slightly bigger than Biddleborn. They walked up and down Main Street, stopping in businesses and asking people if they had seen Artie. They tacked flyers up in supermarkets and on power poles.

After the flyers were gone, they walked back to Mrs. Davenport's car. Darmstadt, like Biddleborn, was a fairly quiet place. It had a different feel to it than Biddleborn, however. Meridian looked around, suddenly aware of the difference.

Darmstadt felt so . . . *normal.* Safe. It felt like real life. Biddleborn almost felt like it had a buildup of static electricity these days, as though a pent-up energy was just waiting to shock someone. Biddleborn was a daydream.

Back in the car, Meridian leaned her head on the window and closed her eyes.

Lanora wove magic, her hands filled with light. She turned to Calvin—

Meridian opened her eyes. Somehow, she *knew*. Calvin wasn't there!

* * *

No one saw Galactic Books and Other Stuff move two doors down, even though it happened just before supper time, right as kids were getting home from whatever they practiced after school and parents were bustling home from work. The bookstore traded places with Wishy-Washy, Biddleborn's only laundromat. Everyone noticed afterward, of course, although the more practical members of Biddleborn society convinced themselves the two buildings had always been in their new locations. Because buildings don't just trade places, obviously.

Elijah was flummoxed, standing on the sidewalk in front of the laundromat, worrying that this would somehow affect his lease. His ghost theory seemed a little flimsy now. It had to be something bigger. A parallel universe?

Elijah looked around. *Where am I?* he wondered.

* * *

Zelda had given a short story writing assignment to her freshmen. She did it to herself every year. She felt it was good for them, but oh, the horror of grading those stories.

They were freshmen. They couldn't help it. It was more than bad prose, though—they simply didn't know enough about the world and how it worked, so even the good stories tended to be childish. And the bad stories, Lord help. Occasionally, Zelda would find a few stories that weren't too bad. But most of them were the kind of dreadful that drove her to a mini existential crisis.

Zelda gathered the papers into two stacks on Mike's kitchen table. She had pulled out all the papers from students who were fairly good writers. This was the shorter stack. The other stack was the soul-killing stack. She'd grade a few soul-killers, then reward herself with a good story.

Digging through the stack, Zelda pulled out Nate Jacoby's paper, certain it would be the worst. She flipped through, happy to see it was mercifully short—shorter than she had asked for, but she wasn't going to complain. Poor Nate. He wrote English like it was his third language, although he was born and raised in Biddleborn.

> *The zombies were mad of poop. They ate people. One day a man ran from a zombie but he triped on a log. The zombie cot him and was about eat his head of when the man pulled out a nif and killed the zombie. then poop feel from the sky.*

Zelda skimmed the rest of it—nearly a full page—then wrote 90/B at the top. It was the longest paper Nate had ever written for her.

Outside, something began to fall from the sky, plopping in fat drops against the windows and roof. Zelda assumed it was rain. She pulled another paper from the soul-killers. Rags Davis. She had gone to school with his father, Franklin, which she tried not to hold against the boy.

> *One time, when it was really dark out and there were ghosts, a little boy and girl were in a graveyard. I think I see a ghost, said the little girl. but she didn't know the boy was a ghost. and then he stabbed her in the eye with a nazi bayonet that he had hid in his*

pocket next to his grenade launcher and flame thrower. he had real big pockets.

Zelda laughed out loud. She wrote 100/A at the top. Oh, that Rags Davis. He managed to work grenade launchers and flame throwers into every assignment.

And so, Zelda sat, grading papers at Mike's table, while outside in the darkness, a heavily-armed child ghost haunted the smelly streets of Biddleborn.

* * *

The tooth waited patiently, squatting down on its feet. It had grown claws from its feet, and it had a plan for using them.

Sheriff John Amory had had a long day. His investigations were going nowhere. Although he felt like the deaths had to be connected, he couldn't find anything that tied them together. The only thing the victims had in common was their connection to Biddleborn High. The crimes seemed almost random and opportunistic. And weird.

The sheriff had stopped on his way home to get a cheeseburger for the tooth monster, speaking of weird. The creature shrank back from him as he approached the aquarium, looking up at him with one big eye and one little eye. It now had four jagged teeth—the fourth just barely pushing up from the gums.

The thing was the ugliest creature Amory had ever seen, and the practical part of his brain was certain he needed to kill it. But how do you kill something that can grow from a single tooth? He would need to pulverize it. Maybe burn it. Possibly both.

The sheriff had built a wooden frame for the aquarium and rigged up a series of clamps to hold the lid in place. He undid the clamps and opened the lid far enough to chuck a cheeseburger inside. The creature jumped, digging claws into John's hand. It ran up his arm as he flailed. He heard it hit the floor and scamper away. It took the cheeseburger with it.

“Dadgummit,” the sheriff said. The practical part of his brain replied, *I told you so*.

Chapter 20

"DO YOU WANT TO TALK to Chad about the vigil before I take you home, Meridian?" Mrs. Davenport asked.

"Sure." Meridian arranged her face into her most concerned expression and climbed the Davenports' stairs.

Meridian had only been in the Davenports' house once, but she knew Cheese Fry's door was the one covered in Pokémon posters. She knocked and heard a kerfuffle inside the room. The door opened a couple of inches, and Cheese Fry peeked out. "Meridian? What are you doing here?"

"Ah, good. Let her in," said a voice behind Cheese Fry.

Cheese Fry pulled Meridian into the room and shut the door. He seemed to be the only person in the room. A very large black and white cat sat on his bed, watching Meridian. The room was a mess, with clothes strewn everywhere. The closet door was open, and a skeleton was visible, sitting cross-legged on the closet floor.

"Your mom thinks we need to hold a prayer vigil for Artie," Meridian said to Cheese Fry, although her attention was on the skeleton. "You have a skeleton in your closet."

"Uh, yeah. That's, um . . . from school."

"You stole one of the school's skeletons?"

"Yeah . . . I mean, no. It was Jazz's final prank."

"Actually, although they haven't met in the . . . flesh, as it were, I believe Meridian knows Calvin." This came from the cat, and now

Meridian recognized the voice she had heard welcoming her into the room.

"Always with the flesh jokes," Calvin said.

"Oh! Calvin! Hi." Meridian sat on the bedroom floor. Her legs no longer seemed to be working. She had accepted the Cat Lord's presence in Biddleborn, but seeing Calvin made her feel as if the edges of her sanity were starting to blur. Whatever tether she had to reality was definitely coming loose.

"My lady," Calvin greeted Meridian. "I don't believe we've met. Though, you look familiar. Are you perhaps kin to Lady Lanora of the Sands?"

"Uh . . . kind of. Wow. You're really here. I don't know why I made you a skeleton. Sorry."

"I believe it was hundreds of years in a dungeon that made me a skeleton."

"Oh. Yeah."

"Since you're here, why don't you help us?" the cat said. "Calvin seems to be in the same predicament in which I find myself, and he seems to believe that the two of us together, you and me, could weave enough magic to unbar the door to Detritus."

"So, Meridian knows about this?" Cheese Fry asked the cat. He turned to Meridian. "You know about this?"

"I think this is partially my fault, actually," Meridian admitted.

"No," said the cat, which suddenly morphed into his Mr. Gray, the Cat Lord, form. "I've revised my theory. I mean, yes, our existence is your fault, and we thank you for it. But I think someone else is playing havoc with reality."

"I was in Darmstadt earlier, and it felt so . . . calm," Meridian informed them. "I think whatever's happening is only happening in Biddleborn."

"Let's hope it stays that way. If it's contagious, all our worlds are doomed," the Cat Lord pointed out.

They heard footsteps coming up the stairs. The Cat Lord returned to his cat form, curled up, and feigned sleep. Calvin slumped against the closet wall. Mrs. Davenport knocked and opened the door in one swift motion. "Do you kids need anything? Want me to order a pizza?"

Cheese Fry smiled at his mom, a little too brightly. "That would be great!" His face was a little pinker than normal.

Mrs. Davenport smiled back and winked at him from behind Meridian's back. "I'll let you know when the pizza's here." She started to close the door, then stopped and pushed it back open. "Where did *he* come from?" She was looking at the cat.

"Uh . . . I found him, Mom. And he looked hungry."

"That cat doesn't look like it's *ever* been hungry."

"He was all alone." Cheese Fry gave his mom his saddest eyes.

"He looks like he belongs to someone. You'll have to try to find the owner. Someone probably misses him."

"Yes, ma'am," Cheese Fry agreed.

Mrs. Davenport closed the door. They waited for her footsteps to recede down the stairs before anyone spoke. "She meant you're fat, in case you missed it," Calvin eventually said to the cat.

"So, what do we do?" Meridian asked the Cat Lord.

"I think we need to gather as much magic as we can. Let me work on that. It shouldn't be too hard; there are puddles of magic popping up everywhere. And I think we need a place to use as our fortress, as it were. I recommend your bookstore. It seems to have some latent power of its own."

"So, what do you need us to do?"

"For now, plan your prayer vigil. That boy, Artie, needs all the divine help he can get. Pray he grows a brain. Meet us at midnight. Bring your imagination with you."

* * *

Sheriff Amory wished he had a shovel, but he didn't want to go all the way out to his shed to get one. Instead, he grabbed the fireplace poker.

The truth was that Amory didn't want to kill the monster. He didn't know why, except that he felt it was important. It seemed like some kind of scientific discovery—an alien life form. Heck, he shouldn't have kept it, he decided. He should have turned it in to some shady government agency.

Poker in his right hand, the sheriff peeked behind the sofa. Something scurried behind him. He whirled around. His cell phone rang, but he ignored it.

"I'm doing this wrong," Amory told himself. He went to the kitchen and dug through the freezer. Finding pizza rolls, he scattered them on a plate and popped them in the microwave. He kept an eye on the kitchen doorway as they heated.

The sheriff's cell phone rang again. He pulled it from his pocket and looked at it. Geraldine. "Yeah?" he answered.

"Got another body for you. This time, it's that schoolteacher. The one who tried to kill herself."

"Where?"

"Alley behind Miss Lindy's."

"Okay. I'm on my way." As the sheriff spoke, the tooth creature peeked into the kitchen. "You want some pizza rolls?" he asked it, pulling the plate out of the microwave and putting it on the floor.

The creature crept to the plate, keeping one cautious eye on the sheriff. It sniffed the pizza rolls, then started eating.

Amory kneeled down beside the creature, though aware that he was needed at a crime scene. The thought of finding Zelda Gershwin's body in an alley made him sick. He hoped it wasn't suicide.

"If I pick you up, are you going to bite me?" The sheriff held his hand out to the creature as if it were a dog or cat. It backed away, then turned and scurried from the room. "Wonderful." Sheriff Amory put the plate on the counter, grabbed his gun, and left the house, locking the door behind him.

* * *

Artie McClintock, the world's greatest Jedi-Wizard, now fully clothed, and Princess Warrior Lanora of the Sands gathered an army of ghosts. They marched through the night, arriving at her uncle's castle just before dawn. "I don't like this. Ghosts aren't often trustworthy." Lanora kept her voice low as they set up camp along the beach.

"You trusted Calvin, and he's a thief," Artie pointed out. "And he's also dead, just not . . . ghostly."

"That's different. I *know* Calvin. I don't know these ghosts, and neither do you."

"I don't need to know them. They're under my power. And they're not just ghosts; they're Jedi-ghosts."

"You keep saying that, but I have no idea what it means."

Artie unrolled the parchment on which he had drawn a blueprint of the castle. "Look. There should be a trap door right over there." He pointed to a group of palm trees. "There's a tunnel that leads straight under the castle."

"So, we broke out of the dungeon; now, we're breaking back in?"

"And then there's a secret passageway to the throne room. While the ghosts keep the guards busy, we'll slip inside and deal with your uncle."

"You make it sound so easy."

"Sure. Easy peasy lemon squeezy."

"I don't know what that means either. You're a mysterious man, Artie McClintock." Lanora kissed his cheek.

Artie called the ghost general—a spirit he was calling Benny—to him. He didn't know Benny's real name. The ghosts made him uncomfortable, if he were being honest. But since the guards couldn't very well kill them, they seemed the ideal soldiers.

"Hey, Benny. You guys ready to rock and roll?" Benny looked at

Artie gravely. "Okay. So, you guys keep the guards busy. Chase them and, you know, fight them with your lightsabers. Er . . . but don't go dark side, okay?" Benny nodded. "Cool." Artie turned to Lanora. "You ready?"

"Lead the way."

They found the trap door among the palm trees. Artie and Lanora brushed the dirt and rocks off it, then pulled it open. The tunnel yawned away into darkness. It smelled of time.

Artie held up his Jedi-Wizard staff and said, "Fire!" in what he thought of as a wizardly voice. A flame burst from the top of the staff, turning it into a torch. Gripping the staff, Artie climbed down into the tunnel, followed closely by Lanora.

* * *

Norma Bellows hadn't had this much fun in years. Bird had a map of all the doors. The ones to be closed were marked with a red X. Those doors mostly led to Detritus. The doors to be opened were circled in green. Behind the green doors was all kinds of chaos. Norma could feel it, so many stories swirling around.

But first, they needed power—lots of it. They ran through the streets of Biddleborn, laughing. Near Miss Lindy's Diner, a group of police and curious onlookers were gathered. Lights were set up in the alley, and someone was taking pictures. It looked like a crime scene.

"Looks like the night is primed for chaos," Bird observed.

There were lots of places in the real world that were brimming with power. In Biddleborn, there was Galactic Books, but its location right on Main Street made it a risky choice. It was too likely to get the young ladies caught, especially with so many police already out and about.

The high school library was another powerful place and an easier option. Biddleborn High School was notoriously easy to break into. Norma and Bird entered through a ground-floor window near the science labs. The halls echoed with their laughter as they ran to the library.

The library door set off an alarm. "Guess we'd better hurry," Bird said.

"What do we do?"

Bird smiled. "Do you know where your power comes from, Norma? It comes from the stories they tell about you—their 'Norma Bellows sightings.' We need to make it a better story."

Bird stretched her arms, and a set of wings unfurled from her back. Her skin turned to black leather, and a set of horns pushed through her forehead. Smiling, she plunged a talon through Norma's heart.

Norma's body dropped to the library floor. Her ghost stood still. Had breathing been an option, the surprise would have stolen all her air.

"Well, now that that's over with, let's go open some doors," Bird said. She gathered Norma's ghost, who opened her mouth to scream. But Bird gripped her in fiery hands. Norma burned, her soul hardening into a small metal object that blazed in Bird's leathery hand. The object was . . .

A key.

Chapter 21

THE BODY IN THE ALLEY behind Miss Lindy's Diner was Zelda Gershwin's, dressed to the nines. "Must have had a hot date," Jerry Benson said. "I've never seen her dressed this nice."

"Lot of good it did her," Sheriff Amory replied. "So, what we got, Jerry?"

"Looks like a gunshot wound to the head. Close range. There's a gun over by the dumpster." Jerry nodded toward where Sonny Rogers was photographing the scene.

"Keep your thumb outta the picture this time," the sheriff reminded Sonny. "I didn't think Jerry was gonna let you take pictures anymore."

"I've been practicing at home." Sonny was not a crime scene technician, but Biddleborn was small, so sometimes, the officers were called upon to develop new skills. He was probably the worst photographer in the whole department, but he was enthusiastic, and enthusiasm is a hard trait to find sometimes.

"Why would her killer leave the weapon, Jerry?" the sheriff continued. "You think he panicked?"

"Or *she*. But maybe. Or it's not a murder weapon at all. She was wearing a holster."

"Zelda Gershwin was armed? Really?"

"Yeah. I don't suppose she has an identical twin?"

"Wouldn't that be something." The sheriff looked around. This murder—if it was a murder—didn't seem at all connected to the other deaths. But any murder in Biddleborn was unusual, and the way Zelda was dressed—and possibly armed—was also unusual.

Maybe the world was going mad. Briefly, Amory thought about the strange toothy creature running free in his house. What if it was all connected? He found the tooth in Zelda's house, after all, so a connection was likely. "Anybody talk to the patrons and staff of Miss Lindy's yet?" he asked.

"Barbara's doing that now," Jerry informed him.

The sheriff rubbed his face. "Okay. Guess I'll go see Rose Marie."

* * *

The Cat Lord, no longer in the form of a cat, and Calvin, still in the form of a skeleton, stood at the end of Blackbird Lane. Calvin threw a rock at the opening between worlds. It bounced back and hit the Cat Lord on the shoulder. "Ow!"

"Sorry."

"Okay. Mark this place on the map," the Cat Lord instructed Calvin. "There's definite magic here, but of the shadow kind. My guess is that this opening leads to the Shadow King's fortress."

"Can we close it?"

"Not from this side. Something's holding it open."

"So, we'd need to be on the other side?"

"We'd need to be on *both* sides. Which isn't possible. Wait!" Robert Gray looked at the opening and thought deeply. He wove a strand of magic as an experiment. It burned white, then faded. "The boy. Artie. He's already on the other side for us."

"I don't think that's a good idea. You can't expect Artie to sneak into the Shadow King's fortress. He'll get killed!"

"Maybe."

"No. There's no 'maybe.'"

"Let's go visit the English teacher."

"Okay. But there's still no 'maybe.'"

"Right," the Cat Lord assured him.

"What we need is a dragon," Calvin posited.

"There are no dragons here. We'll have to make do with frogs. They seem to be conducting some sort of magic. The ones I've seen, anyway."

"We also need stories," Calvin added. "Ones people believe."

"Ghost stories are the most powerful. But first, we must find Zelda. She seems to be a maelstrom of magic in her own right."

* * *

Zelda was unknowingly weaving a maelstrom of magic as the Cat Lord was speaking and the sheriff thought her dead. She had her laptop open. Heidi Starr's past had caught up with her. Holmes Peabody's lover had been shot dead in an alley.

The doorbell rang. Zelda looked at the clock. It was a bit late for visitors, but Mike was a night owl, so she figured she shouldn't be surprised.

Zelda closed her laptop, wrapped a scarf around her hair to hide the bald patches left from the hairdryer incident, and went to the door. "Sheriff Amory! Is everything okay?" she asked, finding him on the other side.

The Sheriff looked at Zelda as if he had never seen her before. He wrapped his big arms around her and lifted her off the ground. She was pretty sure he was crying. This couldn't be good news, but Zelda was certain the people she cared about most—the ones whose deaths would bring a crying sheriff to her door—were tucked safely in the house with her.

The sheriff let Zelda go and wiped his eyes. "Wow! You're okay! You're really . . . okay."

"Yes, I'm okay. What's going on?"

"We found a woman's body, and . . . you don't happen to have a twin sister, do you?"

"No. Just Mike." Mike wouldn't be happy with a lawman at his door.

"Wow," the sheriff said again. He took a deep breath.

"Do you want to come in?"

"No. I'd better . . . you know what, yes. Yes, I would. I think maybe I should talk to Rose Marie. She might know whether you have . . . um, *had* . . . a twin sister separated at birth. Or maybe some kind of cousin. Do you have cousins? Like, one who looks just like you?"

"Come on in. I take it you found someone who looks just like me. That's . . . unusual. But this week hasn't been normal, so why should any of us be surprised?" Zelda led the sheriff into the house and deposited him on the sofa. "Do you want coffee?"

"Yes, please," Amory said. The lawnmower was in the living room. "How ya doin?" he asked it.

"Okay. How about you?"

"It's been a long week."

"Sorry about that."

"I don't suppose you're from outer space?"

"No, sir. That sounds terrifying."

The sheriff nodded. It *did* sound terrifying.

Rose Marie came in, followed by Zelda. Rose Marie was carrying two cups of coffee. She sat one in front of the sheriff. "Good evening, Sheriff," she greeted him. "Zelda said you found a dead body."

"Yes, ma'am. We were certain it was Zelda. Looked just like her. Well, kind of. She was dressed different."

"Different? How so?" Zelda asked.

"Uh . . . you know . . . a little black dress kind of thing and . . . spike heels. Lots of makeup."

"So, she dressed *sexy*," Rose Marie said. "I'm always trying to get Zelda to dress sexier. She's never gonna catch a man in them long skirts."

"So, where'd you find her?" Zelda asked, steering the subject away from her inability to marry.

"Behind Miss Lindy's. Look, I probably shouldn't tell you too much. It's an ongoing investigation, and now, I don't even know who my victim is. Rose Marie, do you have any idea? Is there someone in your family who looks an awful lot like Zelda?"

"Not that I can think of. She got most of her looks from her mother, God rest her crazy soul."

"Grandma!"

"Sorry, Zelda. It's the truth anyhow. But I can't think of anyone else who looks like my Zelda."

The sheriff turned to Mowey. "What about you? You have any ideas?"

"It could have been a doppelganger or bakeneko, or possibly a shadow wight, but they don't stay bodies when they die."

"What was that second thing you said?" Rose Marie asked.

"Bakeneko. It's a cat that can change its shape."

"Well, there you go," Rose Marie said to the sheriff.

Amory was picturing how the tooth he found was growing and changing. What if . . .? "Tell me about that tooth we found."

"Oh, the Bandersnatch tooth?" Mowey asked.

"Yeah. Do Bandersnatches turn into people?"

"I don't think so."

"Well, let me know if you think of anything, Rose Marie. In the meantime, we'll run her prints. And it might not be a bad idea to do a DNA analysis to see if she could be a relative of yours. Maybe one that you never heard about. It happens."

"Okay," Rose Marie agreed. "What do you need from us?"

"I'm guessing just a cheek swab, but what do I know? I'll have Jerry Benson give you a call. He'll probably want all of you, including Mike, to come in, if that's okay. Tell Mike I promise not to arrest him."

"He won't like it, but we'll do our best," Rose Marie agreed.

"Jerry Benson's probably going to hug you, too, Zelda," the sheriff warned.

"Thanks for the warning," Zelda replied.

Sheriff Amory finished his coffee, and Zelda walked him to the door. "I'm really glad you're alive," he told her.

"Thanks. Me too."

* * *

After much deliberation, Elijah decided that the right thing to do would be to tell his family the truth. He called a family meeting.

Elijah's wife, Carolyn, and kids looked at him expectantly. It was almost the kids' bedtime, and they were excited by the prospect of staying up late. There were three of them, stair-stepped in age. Isaac was seven, Orson was five, and Madeleine was three.

"I thought you should probably know that I'm not *your* Elijah. I'm from another universe." Elijah looked at the kids. "You remember when we talked about the multiverse?" Isaac and Orson nodded, and Madeleine stuck her fist in her mouth. "Well, I'm me from a different part of the multiverse. And your daddy is probably where I used to be. It's a nice place, a lot like this one. Except just a little different."

"Are we there too? But other us?" Isaac asked.

"Yup. They look just like you."

"Don't you think it's a little late to start this?" Carolyn asked. "It's not exactly the kind of bedtime story that's going to help them sleep."

"I'm being serious. I walked out of Galactic Books today, and it had *moved*."

Carolyn sighed. "Oh, Elijah. Well, there's nothing we can do about it. If you'll have us, we can be your family. And you can stay here and be our Elijah. Isn't that right, kids?"

"But what about real Daddy?" Isaac asked. "Is he scared?"

"No," said Elijah. "Because he has the other you, and you're all the best family ever."

"Okay. That's all right then."

Elijah and Carolyn put the kids to bed. Afterward, she patted his face. "Am I as pretty as the other Carolyn?"

"Every bit as much."

"Good answer. Now stop scaring the kids with all this multiverse talk."

"I thought they deserved to know."

"You really believe it?"

"Yes. And I need you to at least consider the possibility. I can't prove it to you. I don't think."

"Okay. I'll consider it. But it seems like the whole thing with the multiverse is . . . a glitch. And I don't believe the universe is flawed, not fundamentally, anyway. Certainly, *you're* not a flaw."

"Then why is my bookstore where the laundromat used to be?"

"I don't know. But have you considered maybe seeing a doctor? What if it's your memory that's wrong? What if there's something wrong with your brain?"

Elijah blinked at her. He hadn't thought of that—the parallel universe theory seemed so obvious. "Wow. Okay. Maybe," he agreed.

Carolyn kissed him. "I'll make you an appointment. Promise me you'll go?"

Elijah nodded. "I don't want to, but I will."

* * *

Lanora's Uncle Hoss looked an awful lot like Mr. Mayfield, the principal of Biddleborn High School, except he was wearing a kingly robe and crown. He had a sword strapped to his side, which Artie found a bit intimidating.

Artie *liked* Mr. Mayfield. He didn't want to kill him. Actually, he didn't want to kill *anyone*. He wasn't even sure if he could, even with his mad Jedi-Wizard skills. But these people weren't real. They were inside Meridian's head, sort of. They existed because she imagined them, so it wouldn't be like killing a real person. And this Mr. Mayfield look-a-like was evil, wasn't he?

"This castle is mine!" Lanora announced. "You've oppressed my people long enough, Uncle."

Uncle Hoss laughed. "You should have stayed away, Lanora. You and this peasant boy cannot defeat me."

"What does Meridian have against Mr. Mayfield?" Artie asked.

Lanora looked at him with something like worry in her eyes. Then, she turned back to her uncle. "We have brought an army that, even now, is driving back your guards."

"Those ghosts, you mean? Not likely, child. You'll need more than ghosts."

"Blah blah blah," Artie said. "I just want to go home and finish my biology homework. This isn't fun anymore. And *why* do you look like Mr. Mayfield?" He pulled a string of light out of the air and began weaving. He didn't want to kill Mr. Mayfield, but Lanora wanted her castle back, and that probably felt a lot like wanting to go home to finish your biology homework.

Artie had the Cat Lord's power, but he didn't really know what that meant. *What the heck's a Cat Lord anyway?* he wondered. *Is that just the male version of a Crazy Cat Lady?*

Uncle Hoss drew his sword and started across the throne room toward Artie. Artie frowned, closed his eyes, and imagined him differently. That's all he was, anyway—just imagination. *Something nice, that's what I need. The nicest person I know.*

"Artie?!" someone called out.

Artie opened his eyes. His mom stood in front of him, wearing her Miss Lindy's shirt, with *Belinda* stitched above the pocket.

"Hi, Mom!"

Belinda hugged him fiercely.

Chapter 22

"CARL! CARL DAVIS! Where are you?!" boomed a voice. It was his mother's voice, which worried him because she had been dead for years. Carl got out of bed, grabbed his nine-millimeter and a knife, and slipped into the hallway.

The first thing Carl noticed were the cats. Dionysius had about ten friends over. They were perched at intervals in the hallway, mostly around Meridian's door. She was being guarded.

"Carl! Where are you?!" his mother's voice called out again. "Come help me!"

Meridian's bedroom door opened. Her face peeked out, still rumpled from sleep. "Were you yelling?"

"No. That's my mom yelling."

Meridian blinked. "She's, um . . . dead, though."

"Yup."

"Are we having a cat party?"

"I assume they've been sent as your bodyguards."

Meridian opened her bedroom door wider. "Here, kitties. You want to come in?" Indecisively, they went in, except for a giant orange tabby who stayed right outside her bedroom door. "You okay?" Meridian asked Carl. "You need me to help you with Grandma's ghost?"

"Nah. You stay in your room. I'll call if I need you. You still armed?"

"Yessir."

"Cool." Carl started down the stairs.

"Hey, Carl? Be careful. You could just come hang out with the cats and me."

"After I see what Mom wants. And I think I should probably fix up a litter box in your room."

Carl went downstairs. The house was dark, but a soft, flickering glow came from the living room. Carl followed the muffled sounds of a television turned down low until he entered the living room.

Carl's mother sat on the couch, looking as she had in the last year of her life, pale and worn. She wore a housecoat and slippers and had a blanket wrapped around her shoulders. "You need something, Mom?" Carl asked her.

"I could use a Pepsi," she said. Her eyes were empty and cold in a way they had never been in life.

"Yes, ma'am."

Carl went into the kitchen. The world's oldest woman was sitting at his kitchen table. "Bit of ruddy chaos we've struggled into, eh, lad?"

"Um, yes, ma'am." Carl got a Pepsi from the refrigerator. "Are you a . . . ghost, too? Because I don't recognize you."

"Not a ghost yet, dear. I'm Mayzell, and I seem to have slipped through the walls and landed in some weird someplace or other. This sure isn't the Cat Lord's cottage."

Carl brightened. "The Cat Lord? You know him?"

"Aye. I'm his housekeeper and cat sitter."

"Did you bring all them cats?"

Mayzell looked around. "I don't see any cats."

"They're upstairs, with my daughter."

They heard a crash outside, followed by a screeching, grinding, ripping sound. Carl flinched, then moved to the kitchen window. He peeked out into the night.

"I don't see—" he started. But then, he *did* see.

The broken lawnmower had picked up the broken air conditioner and was pulling it apart. The lawnmower was throwing pieces at the chickens, who had it surrounded. The rooster crowed, and the chickens retreated. Near the toolshed, a bearded old man was building an ark. A line of spiders ran across the kitchen window. Carl jumped back, but they were on the outside of the glass.

"Carl! Where's my Pepsi?!"

"Coming, Mom!"

"Don't you take that to her, child. She'll eat your soul," Mayzell warned.

"I don't suppose you know how to do magic?"

"Just enough for scrubbing and herding."

"That's more than I know. Please come with me."

Carl led the old woman up the stairs. She moved much faster than he thought possible. Carl was a little bit afraid of her. He knocked on Meridian's bedroom door.

The orange tabby was still in the hallway, and it rubbed against Mayzell's legs. "There you are, Larry," she greeted it. "And being a good boy, for once, eh?"

Meridian opened her door. Her eyes widened at the sight of the world's oldest woman. "Mayzell?"

"Aye. And you look a bit like Lanora. You must be the puppet master's mistress, eh?"

"I'm Meridian."

"I forgot the litter box," Carl said. He and Mayzell stepped into the room. Larry followed Mayzell in by walking in front of her.

"What's happening?" Meridian asked. "I heard noises in the yard. And I'm pretty sure the house is covered in spiders."

"I suspect it's about to rain, too," Carl said. "Mayzell here is one of your . . . people? From your story?"

"A character. Yes."

"Good. How about the two of you do some kind of magic?"

"Carl Eugene Davis! Where's my Pepsi?!" boomed from below.

"We should hurry," Meridian said. No one disagreed.

* * *

Zelda's brother, Mike, went to the kitchen for a beer. "You want one?" he asked Mowey.

"I probably shouldn't have another one," the lawnmower said. Mike handed him one anyway.

Mike sat on the floor next to Mowey. "So, were you always a lawnmower? Or are you like those clocks and things in *Beauty and the Beast*?"

"I've always been a lawnmower, ever since I was made."

"And that's like, normal, where you come from?"

"I guess."

"Cool. I think I'd like to go there someday. Just to visit."

"Oh, you'd like Detritus! Except for the shadow wights. But you'd be safe enough in Roanoke."

"Ain't that in Virginia?"

"I don't know. What's Virginia?"

"Are there people there? Humans, I mean?"

"Oh, lots. And animals. Ghosts. Monsters. I saw a train one time. He was really nice."

"Do the animals talk?"

"Some of them."

"Cool. I could get me a talking dog. We'd hang out, ride the train—Wait," Mike interrupted himself, "can you ride the train, or is that offensive?"

"I don't know what that means. Of course, you can ride the train."

"Awesome." There was a thud above them. Something heavy landed on the roof. "Dude. What was that?"

"It was too big to be a sock or a Tupperware lid," Mowey noted.

"Definitely. Is that what falls from the sky in your world?"

"Mostly. The lost things of your world. The forgotten things. The

Detritus."

"Oh, I gotcha. *That's* why it's called Detritus."

"I found a really nice class ring once. I traded it at the market—"

"Shhh. Listen."

There were footsteps across the roof. Then, there was another wump, followed by a slide.

"I think it fell off," Mowey said.

"Let's go see what it is." Mike grabbed a knife from the block and led the way to the door.

"I think I should go first," Mowey suggested. "I'm harder to eat."

"Good point."

Mowey rolled outside, Mike following close behind. They could hear someone moving around in the yard. Then, a voice: "I demand to be returned to my castle at once!" A man dressed in a king's costume came stomping toward them. He had a very pointy sword.

"Uh-oh," Mowey whispered to Mike. "It's a king. They're the worst."

"Crap." Mike started to leave, but it was too late. The king had seen him.

"You there! I demand help."

Mike looked down at his knife, then looked at the man's sword. "Okay, okay. How can I help you . . . your highness?"

"First, you can kneel to your king. Second, you can take me back to my castle."

"Yeah. Sure thing. I gotta get something first. Hang on." Mike turned and ran.

Mowey looked awkwardly at the king.

"Where did he go?" the king asked. "That coward! I'll have him thrown in a dungeon! No, hanged! I'll have him hanged!"

The king ignored Mowey—lawnmowers were basically just servants, after all. He stepped up to Mike's door and tried the knob. It was unlocked, so he pushed his way inside. Mowey followed.

The king stomped through the house, ready to yell at someone. "What is all that racket?" Rose Marie asked. "Mike, is that you?" She had come out of her bedroom, wearing a nightgown and housecoat. Her slippers looked like pandas. She was carrying a baseball bat.

"You!" shouted the king. "Kneel to your king!"

"Zelda! We've got a lunatic in the house! Mike!"

"I'm not a lunatic! I'm your king!" He raised his sword.

Rose Marie swung the bat with her frail, ninety-year-old arms. The king swung his sword, which connected with the bat. Rose Marie said, "Oof," dropped the bat, and staggered backward.

Mowey started his motor. He was about to attack when the king slumped to the floor. Mike stood over him with a shovel.

Zelda came out of her bedroom. "What's going on? Good heavens! Is that Mr. Mayfield? What have you done to my boss?"

"He tried to attack me," Rose Marie said.

"He tried to violate my civil rights," Mike said.

"He's starting to wake up," Mowey pointed out.

"Quick! Let's tie him to a chair," Rose Marie suggested. "Zelda, get the duct tape."

"This is a bad idea," Zelda said. But she fetched the duct tape anyway. And they hoisted the king into a kitchen chair.

"Is this treason?" Mowey asked. "Because I've never committed treason before."

"It can't be treason," Rose Marie assured him. "He's just a high school principal pretending to be a king. Besides, we're Americans. We don't even like kings. And you saw him try to attack me, didn't you?"

The king opened his eyes and frowned, realizing his predicament. "Let me go at once!" he demanded. "I'll have your heads for this!"

"Mr. Mayfield? What on earth has gotten into you?" Zelda asked.

"Oh! I know!" Mowey shouted. "He's a doppelganger!"

The others looked at the king, squinting at his face. "Well, I suppose . . ." Zelda said.

"We should call the sheriff," Rose Marie urged.

"Nope. Let's not do that," Mike said.

"Yes! Call for the law! That's exactly what you need to do!" the king said. "Send it by your fastest pigeon!"

"Okay. I agree," Zelda said. "Not about the pigeon; let's call the sheriff. Either he's a doppelganger, or he's gone completely mad. Either way, we need help."

"Don't tell the sheriff I hit him with a shovel, okay, Zelda?" Mike pleaded. "Tell him *you* hit him. The sheriff likes you; he won't care if you hit him. He'll assume the guy deserved it."

"I don't know that he *likes* me."

"Sure he does. I've seen how he looks at you."

Zelda blushed. And Rose Marie smiled with glee. "Well, in that case, let's get the sheriff over here," she said.

"This is TREASON!" the king screamed. Mowey shuddered at the suggestion.

Mike tore off a strip of duct tape and stuck it over the king's mouth.

* * *

The past twenty-four hours had changed Cheese Fry's life; he was certain of it. The clock on his cell phone told him it was time to leave if he was going to meet Calvin, Mr. Gray, and Meridian at Galactic Books. Whatever exciting, dangerous thing they were about to do, he wanted to be part of it.

Cheese Fry stuffed his body pillow under the blanket on his bed. It was an old trick, to be sure, but still effective—so long as no one heard him leave. Jazz Miller had taught him the art of sneaking out.

Cheese Fry wasn't sure what kind of gear would be needed, but he decided on a flashlight, a notebook and pen, a cigarette lighter, and a box of granola bars. He stuffed it all in his backpack, then threw in a pair of scissors, just in case. He was pretty sure scissors didn't get the respect they deserved.

Cheese Fry opened his window and climbed out onto the roof. A tree was strategically placed for his escape, and he had often wondered if his parents were responsible for the positioning of the tree. Did they plant it intentionally so their son could have adventures?

To get downtown, Cheese Fry would cut through Clyde J. Anderson Park. He liked cutting through the park at night because of the danger. If he timed it right, there might even be a drug dealer in the park. It would just be Ross Jacoby, whom he had known since preschool, but still.

The streets of Biddleborn were unusually dark, so Cheese Fry stopped and dug out his flashlight. He glanced up at the streetlights. They were on, but the light seemed dim. And brown. The light seemed brown.

Cheese Fry headed toward the park. Shadows slithered along the periphery, and a faint whispering seemed to follow him. He stopped and listened.

The whispering seemed to be coming from the trees. That was okay—trees whisper. But the sidewalk may also have been whispering, and that worried Cheese Fry. Then, there was another sound: the rustle-plop of frogs hopping across lawns and sidewalks. He swept his flashlight's beam across the ground in front of him.

Frogs! A dozen or so. Cheese Fry had spent enough time in Sunday school to know that a plague of frogs is a bad sign. He ran to the park. And that's where he found Ross Jacoby, Biddleborn's very own drug dealer, swinging his fists at what appeared to be a shadow.

"Get away! No!" Ross screamed. "Help! Somebody help me!"

Cheese Fry, an army of frogs at his feet, paused a moment. The shadow grabbed Ross by the throat. *How do you fight a shadow?* Cheese Fry wondered. *With light. Of course!*

Cheese Fry screamed what he imagined was a very fierce war cry. He ran toward the shadow and Ross Jacoby, his flashlight ready. The frogs followed. Plop plop plop plop plop.

"Ross!" Cheese Fry called out while aiming his flashlight's beam at the shadow. The shadow flinched and dropped Ross Jacoby. "Turn on your cell phone's flashlight!"

Ross moaned and whimpered but started fumbling with his phone. The shadow grabbed his ankle. He screamed and dropped the phone.

Cheese Fry wished he had a bigger light. Something like . . . *a fire*! He ran to the nearest trash can and dragged it over toward the struggle. He dumped the contents of his backpack on the ground and snatched up the notebook and cigarette lighter. While Ross Jacoby screamed that the shadow was *eating* him, Cheese Fry lit a sheet of notebook paper on fire, then dropped it into the trash can.

The garbage took a few seconds to ignite, during which Ross screamed at Cheese Fry to hurry. The fire grew. Cheese Fry pulled his cell phone out and turned on the flashlight feature. He shined both of his flashlights at the shadow.

The shadow let go of Ross. It snarled at Cheese Fry, backing away from the light. Cheese Fry stepped toward it, lights held high. And the frogs plopped all around.

The shadow lunged at Cheese Fry, grabbing him by the throat. Cheese Fry kicked. He tried to pry the shadow's hands away, but it was like trying to move a brick wall. The frogs circled around them. Plop plop plop plop plop plop plop squish.

The shadow screamed in rage and dropped Cheese Fry. As Cheese Fry fell, he noted that his scissors were sticking out of the shadow's back. The shadow disappeared, taking the scissors with him.

There were fifty or so frogs gathered around Cheese Fry as he sat up and rubbed his throat. "You okay?" he asked Ross Jacoby.

"It bit me! I hope it didn't have rabies."

"You should go to the ER. Tell 'em a dog bit you. Or a hobo."

"Nah. I'll be fine." Ross Jacoby limped over and sat next to Cheese Fry. The frogs moved out of his way. "What's with the frogs?"

"No idea. They seem to be following me."

"You're the Frog King. Cool. So, what was that thing?"

"I'm not sure, but we probably shouldn't stay here in case it comes back." Cheese Fry stood, then helped Ross up. "Seriously, you should go to the ER."

"Nope. I'm coming with you. You look like a guy who's running away. You saved my life, so I'm honor-bound to protect you."

Cheese Fry blinked at Ross. "That's, um . . . nice? Or possibly weird. But you should go to the ER. And I'm not running away. I'm meeting people for, um . . . some Dungeons and Dragons."

"Cool. Let's go, Cheese Fry!"

"Remember that time you threw dirt at Meridian Page? I don't think she's forgiven you."

"So?"

"She's part of the D&D group."

"It's probably time for me to apologize to her anyway, don't cha think?"

"I guess," Cheese Fry agreed reluctantly, not really wanting Ross to join them.

"Look. I don't believe you're playing Dungeons and Dragons. You're a nerd, but not quite that much of a nerd. Whatever you're doing, you need backup. So, here I am. Besides, the ER asks too many questions."

"Well . . . okay then." Cheese Fry put everything back in his backpack, except the scissors, which seemed to have been carried to another world.

And that is the story of how Biddleborn's only drug dealer ended up joining Cheese Fry as he made his way to Galactic Books, followed by an army of frogs. Plop plop plop . . .

* * *

Orson clung to Mr. Fred, his stuffed llama, as Isaac thought up fresh details to embellish the tale of The Thing That Lived under Orson

Schmidt's Bed. It was a saga he had been working on for the past three weeks. As an older brother, he felt it was his solemn duty to keep Orson entertained, and possibly terrified.

"And then, one night, the Thing got tired of being crowded. He got tired of keeping all of his arms and legs squooshed up against his body under the bed. And he decided he was hungry." Isaac paused for emphasis. "You know what he was hungry for?"

"Don't say it," Orson begged.

"He was hungry for . . . STUFFED LLAMA! Muahahaha!"

Orson hugged Mr. Fred tighter. Suddenly, there was a scraping sound from under Orson's bed. Both boys paused, listening.

"Isaac!"

"I heard it, too!" The last thing Isaac wanted to do was put his feet on the floor. But if there was a monster, *someone* had to turn on the light. And, as the older brother, that someone had to be him.

Isaac put his feet on the floor. He took two quick steps before a tentacle reached out and wrapped around his ankle. Isaac screamed. Orson screamed. Mr. Fred screamed. And Orson screamed harder.

As the Thing pulled, Isaac grabbed hold of Orson's bedpost. Another tentacle had just wrapped around his other ankle when Elijah opened the bedroom door and flipped on the light. "No!" Elijah yelled, throwing himself at his oldest son.

Isaac lost his grip on the bed post. He hit the floor. A third tentacle wrapped around his body. Orson sobbed while telling his llama, "Be strong, Mr. Fred. You gotta kill that thing."

Elijah was trying to stomp on tentacles while holding on to Isaac. "Carolyn!" he called out.

Orson took a deep breath, kissed his llama, and threw it at the Thing.

Carolyn appeared in the doorway. "What is— Oh!"

"Get a knife! Then, call 911!" Elijah directed her. Now, a tentacle wrapped itself around Elijah's body. Carolyn ran.

Mr. Fred kicked the Thing. He bit it. He kicked and bit at the same time. A tentacle wrapped around his throat. Mr. Fred spit. And his saliva sizzled where it landed. The Thing screamed. All of its tentacles let go and retreated under the bed.

Elijah scooped up Isaac. "Come on!" he said as he also reached for Orson, who scooped up Mr. Fred. They all ran from the room, nearly colliding with a knife-wielding Carolyn in the hallway. Three-year-old Madeleine was right behind her.

"Run! Run! Run!" Elijah yelled, steering his family down the stairs.

"What happened?" Carolyn asked.

"Mr. Fred spit lava at it," Orson explained.

The family ran through the kitchen. Elijah plucked his car keys from the hook by the door.

"What about Sasha?" Isaac asked.

"I'll get her," Carolyn replied.

"No. I'll get her," Elijah said. "Give me that knife. Here, take the keys." Elijah stuffed Isaac in their SUV. "I'll get the dog and meet you out front."

"Daddy!" yelled Orson. "Here! Take Mr. Fred with you." Elijah took the stuffed llama from his son. Apparently, in this universe, stuffed animals really could protect you from the boogie man.

Sasha's crate was in the living room. The puppy, a mix of lab and golden retriever, was quivering with excitement when Elijah kneeled down to free her from her nighttime prison. He pulled her out and held her and the llama in a bear hug as he ran back toward the kitchen. He still gripped the knife, but he would have to put the puppy down to use it.

The puppy growled as Elijah approached the kitchen doorway. Then, Elijah paused. He backed away and ran for the front door instead.

Elijah could hear something following him. It was knocking knick-knacks and pictures to the floor as its tentacled body moved through the house. As Elijah reached the front door, something wrapped around his ankle. "Not again!" he shouted. He dropped the puppy and the llama and turned, knife ready.

The Thing was uglier than Elijah had imagined. It was lumpy and brownish-green, like a giant booger with tentacles. Its eyes were bloodshot—all seven of them. And it had a hungry, sharp-looking mouth that reeked of vomit.

Elijah stabbed the Thing. The Thing's body oozed around the knife. Then, Mr. Fred attacked, spitting lava.

The Thing backed up and loosened its grip on Elijah. Elijah scooped up the puppy and jerked open the front door. As he ran, he could hear the battle between the stuffed llama and the tentacled monster.

The SUV was on the street, door open and ready. Elijah threw himself and Sasha into the passenger seat, shoving her toward Isaac so he could close the door. "What about Mr. Fred?" Orson asked.

"Mr. Fred is killing the monster for us. He'll be all right," Elijah reassured his son. "He's very strong and resourceful. Spits lava, you know."

"That's right!" Isaac said. "Mr. Fred will defeat him. For sure!"

Carolyn pressed down hard on the gas, and the family SUV rocketed forward through the streets of Biddleborn.

"Where are we going?" Elijah asked. He thought maybe there was a protocol for dealing with monsters in this part of the multiverse.

"To the police station," Carolyn answered. "You got a better idea?"

"No. That's as good a place as any."

* * *

Downtown Biddleborn was full of ghosts. They arrived from every era since the town's establishment. And there were even a few rugged ghosts from the area's wilderness days. A handful of Native American ghosts rounded out the assemblage. The sidewalks were alive with the dead.

The Cat Lord and Calvin, pockets full of magic, followed their map to Galactic Books. "With all these ghosts around, I guess you can take that mask off," the Cat Lord said. "No one's going to be surprised that you're a skeleton."

"Thank goodness. This thing is hot." Calvin pulled off the ski mask Cheese Fry had given him. It was standard black and had been used in many a nighttime adventure for Cheese Fry and Jazz Miller. Calvin wiped a skeletal hand across his face. "I think I'm even sweating."

The bookstore appeared to be having a party. Ghosts were everywhere, dancing and drinking while a ghost band played jazz in the children's section. Galactic Books had once been a saloon, then had aged into a speakeasy, and finally had settled into its role as a drugstore through the forties all the way to the mid-sixties.

Then, after a mysterious death, the Galactic Books building had sat vacant until 1980, when it became Biddleborn Public Library. It was a function the building served until the library moved to a newer, squatter building. The building then became Schmidt Books & Things when Elijah's father bought it in the early nineties. After Elijah took over the family business, the name changed to Galactic Books and Other Stuff, and the focus shifted to sci-fi and fantasy.

The ghosts came from every season of the building's life. A soldier who came home from World War II minus a leg was telling his story to Clyde J. Anderson, a Biddleborn citizen whose mysterious death had left the building desolate for over a decade. Girls in poodle skirts drank root beer floats next to frontier women in long layers and flappers in short dresses. A ghost librarian with stern eyes behind cat eye glasses walked around, shushing the crowd. But no one listened to her.

"How come you're not a ghost?" the Cat Lord asked Calvin.

"I don't know. Guess I'm stuck to my bones."

"This chaos is giving me a headache. We need some ghost spray."

"I'll see what I can find." Calvin headed to the break room.

The Cat Lord went to the Dungeons and Dragons section. He needed something to hold the magic, and he remembered seeing some dice on his last trip to the store. And . . . there they were.

The Cat Lord chose a set of jade dice, seven in all, and lined them up on the counter. Taking the magic from his pockets, he let the strands of light fall onto the dice, soaking in like water on sand. The dice began to glow faintly.

Calvin came back with a can of Raid. "I found this."

"That'll do." The Cat Lord rummaged for paper. He couldn't find any regular paper, but Galactic Books used paper bags for customers who only bought a small number of items. So, he tore a bag apart and taped part of it like a label on the can of Raid. He found a sharpie and wrote *Ghost Spray* on the makeshift label.

"I'll do the honors," Calvin said. He turned to a ghost cowboy and sprayed him with the Raid. The cowboy faded. Next, Calvin sprayed soldiers and debutantes, the whole jazz band, and library patrons. He sprayed teenagers and old people. The librarian followed Calvin around as he sprayed. She seemed to approve.

After the ghosts were gone, Calvin returned to the counter, setting the spray next to the magic dice. "What about her?" the Cat Lord asked him, nodding toward the librarian. She was straightening the books in the Manga section.

"I kind of like her."

The Cat Lord shrugged. "I guess we might need a ghost before the night is over."

The walls buzzed around them. Magic bled from the air. The dice began to shiver.

"Well, at least we seem to have a surplus of magic to work with," Calvin noted. "I hope the young lady is able to get here without too much trouble."

"I suspect getting here will be a bit of a quest," the Cat Lord said. "Which is good. It'll prepare her for what comes next. Now, if you'll excuse me, I believe we need an English teacher."

"The librarian won't do?"

“The librarian will definitely help, but what we chiefly need is an aspiring novelist.”

Chapter 23

FOR THE SECOND TIME that night, Sheriff John Amory pulled up outside Mike Gershwin's house. The door opened before he even knocked. Zelda motioned him inside, already explaining.

"So, you know that woman who looked like me? Well, we found a man who looks like Mr. Mayfield. Only he thinks he's a king. He tried to attack my grandmother." Zelda led the sheriff to the kitchen, where Mr. Mayfield, dressed in robes and a broken crown, was duct-taped to a chair.

"What happened to his crown?" Amory asked.

"Oh. Um . . . I hit him," Zelda lied for Mike. "With a shovel. In self-defense. Well, not *self*-defense. In Grandmother defense. But that counts the same, right?"

"Absolutely. Defending your grandmother is always the right thing to do." The sheriff looked down at the high school principal. He reached out and tore the duct tape from the principal-king's mouth.

"This is treason!" the king immediately shouted. "Arrest them at once! They deserve to be hanged!"

The sheriff considered putting the duct tape back. But he needed information. "Hey, there . . . your highness. What's your name?"

"King Hoss, Ruler of the Sands and Keeper of the Rocks."

"That's quite a name. So, you're telling me you're not Arthur Mayfield, Principal of Biddleborn High School?"

"Of course not! I'm the king! That treacherous niece of mine sent me here. No, it was that *boy* who was with her. I need you to arrest them, too!"

"And did you attack this woman?" the sheriff pointed at Rose Marie.

"She was insolent, and she called me a lunatic. She tried to hit me with a cord of wood."

The sheriff looked at Rose Marie. "It was a baseball bat," she said. "I keep it by my bed in case a lunatic breaks into the house."

"And that's when you hit him with a shovel?" Amory asked Zelda.

"Yes. He knocked away Grandmother's bat with his sword. I thought he was going to kill her."

"Of course I was going to kill her! She refused to kneel to her king!"

"Okay," said the sheriff. "This seems like a mental health crisis, which is outside of my wheelhouse. Let me make a phone call." He pulled his cell phone out of his pocket and stepped out of the kitchen to call a crisis worker.

"Where is he going?" the king asked. "Isn't he going to arrest all of you?"

"He's calling the loony bin to come take you away," Rose Marie replied.

"So, are we sure this really is Mr. Mayfield?" Mike asked.

"He sounds like a real king to me," Mowey said.

The king looked at Mowey for the first time. "You! Untie me, and I'll give you lawns to mow!"

"Pretty sure you said you were king of the sand and rocks," Mowey corrected him. "You don't have any lawns."

"I can get lawns! Lots of lawns!"

"Don't listen to him," Mike said. "A king is nothing more than a politician. He has no intention of getting you lawns. Besides, *we* have a lawn. Two lawns, actually. And you're welcome to mow them any time."

The sheriff stepped back into the kitchen. "Sonny's on his way to help me get his highness to the hospital. The crisis worker is going to meet us there."

When Sonny arrived, the sheriff untaped the king, who promptly bit him. "Ow. Bull Hockey!" the sheriff exclaimed. Sonny, who was younger and in better shape, stepped in to help wrestle the man to the floor, where the sheriff slapped on a set of handcuffs.

"Don't forget to read him his rights," Rose Marie reminded them.

"Oh, I won't." The sheriff informed the king of his rights as Sonny collected the sword.

"Do you always keep your lawnmower in the house?" Sonny asked.

"He gets scared outside in the dark," Rose Marie explained.

Sheriff Amory and Sonny ushered the king to Sonny's squad car. A very large black and white cat watched from Mike's yard as they drove away, the sheriff following Sonny and the king.

* * *

"Ice cream!" shouted Mayzell. "I'll bet they'll all be wanting some, eh?"

Carl and Meridian looked at her, then looked at each other. Carl's eyebrows silently said something to Meridian like: "*This one isn't going to be much help, is she?*"

Meridian's look answered silently: "*Sorry, no. She's a little senile. But she does know a little magic.*"

Spiders started pouring under Meridian's bedroom door. The cats pounced. "Ah!" Carl shouted, dancing a bit where he stood. He looked at his hand and realized he was still holding a can of Pepsi.

Mayzell slipped off her shoes and sat on Meridian's bed. "Ice cream, ice cream, ice cream," she sang. "And plenty of lollipops!"

The crunching, screeching sounds from the yard stopped as Meridian and Carl were stepping on spiders. "Carl! Oh, Caaaaarrrl!" His mother's voice seemed to have moved to the yard. Daylight streamed in from the window, dragging birdsong along with it. The surviving spiders turned and fled under the door.

"We've got chocolate and daisies," Mayzell whispered. Her eyes were unfocused, and she had a smile across her lips.

Carl and Meridian looked out the window. Night had been replaced by an aggressively beautiful day. The trees were heavy with bluebirds and cardinals. Flowers had sprung through the ground. Indeed, there were a lot of daisies.

And ice cream. There was an ice cream social in the yard, with cloth-covered tables here and there for the partygoers to gather around as they ate. A long table held tubs of ice cream, various toppings, and all kinds of candy. There were plenty of lollipops.

"She did magic all right," Carl said as he watched his broken lawnmower and broken air conditioner sit down at a table together to eat their ice cream.

"We'd better leave before they run out of ice cream," Meridian suggested.

"All right," Carl said. He watched as the ghost of his mother danced with the old, bearded man who had abandoned his ark-building for now.

Meridian touched Mayzell's arm. "Let's go. We need to get downtown to the bookstore. We're supposed to meet the Cat Lord at midnight . . . assuming it's still nighttime."

Mayzell slipped her shoes back on. "It's always every time," she said cheerfully. "We'll grab some lollipops on our way. Come on, kitties!"

* * *

"This is Detritus?" Belinda asked, looking around the castle.

"Yeah," Artie confirmed. "Oh! Introductions! My bad." Artie cleared his throat. "Lady Lanora of the Sands, I'd like to introduce you to my mom, Belinda of Miss Lindy's Diner."

"I'm very pleased to meet you," Lanora said.

"Yes. It's good to meet you, too."

"Your son has done my kingdom a great service. You should be very proud of him. He's the greatest Jedi-Wizard I've ever met."

"A Jedi-Wizard, huh?" Belinda looked at Artie. "You couldn't just pick one? You had to be both?"

Artie shrugged. "I couldn't decide."

Belinda laughed and hugged him. "What happens next?"

"The Cat Lord has a plan," Artie informed her. "Let's get back to his cottage. But first, we gotta go see a guy about a dragon."

* * *

Downtown Biddleborn was still full of ghosts. Cheese Fry and Ross Jacoby, accompanied by an army of frogs, moved through the ghosts, trying to avoid eye contact with any of the spirits. They had learned the hard way that the ghosts took eye contact to mean you wanted to hear their story or see how terrifying they could be.

The ghosts were like carnies, but instead of trying to get you to throw darts at balloons, they were looking for volunteers to be haunted. Cheese Fry didn't have time to be haunted, though. Ross Jacoby's rescue had cost him too much time.

"Dude," Ross said eloquently. "Do you think this is the apocalypse?"

"Something like that."

"I'm glad it ain't zombies."

The night was ripe with magic, and Ross Jacoby had just accidentally set a small apocalypse in motion with his words. A zombie stumbled out of the Biddleborn Post Office, about twenty feet ahead of the boys. "Dagnabbit," Cheese Fry and Ross both said.

The zombie was wearing the long, blue shorts of a US postal worker. But his shirt was missing, as was his left arm.

Cheese Fry grabbed Ross's sleeve. "This way, hurry." He pulled the drug dealer across the street, through a crowd of ghost children playing marbles in the middle of Main Street. Cheese Fry and Ross ducked into the alley that ran between Miss Lindy's and Hobby House, where crime scene tape still cordoned off the area where a Zelda Gershwin doppelganger was found murdered earlier in the evening.

Cheese Fry grabbed the bottom of the fire escape ladder that clung to the side of the hobby shop and pulled himself up. "Come on, Ross!"

"Hurry! That zombie can move! Like a turtle that don't want to take a bath."

Cheese Fry hurried, contemplating turtles, baths, and the mysterious life of Ross Jacoby. Below him, an army of frogs plopped against the building, frustrated at their inability to follow. But a few bright green tree frogs stuck to the bricks and began to climb.

Cheese Fry reached the roof and looked around. Galactic Books was four buildings away. The buildings on Main Street were connected—chunks of brick businesses, divided by side streets and alleys strewn here and there.

Ross fell onto the roof. "I think maybe I should have gone to the Emergency Room."

"Told you."

"Good thing that zombie's missing an arm." They ran across the Hobby House roof and jumped down to the roof of Wishy-Washy, the town's laundromat. "It stinks up here," Ross noticed. "The whole town kinda stinks tonight. You noticed?"

"Yeah. Like a sewer overflowed somewhere."

"Exactly."

The roof of the Thirsty Hippo, a dive bar famous for its occasional fight, was a bit higher than the laundromat, slowing them down as they had to scramble up a brick barrier. Cheese Fry could tell Ross was slowing down and encouraged him. "Just one more roof, and we'll be there. Mr. Gray might know what to do about your leg."

"That weird sub?"

"Yeah. He's actually some kind of wizard or something."

"I guess nothing will ever surprise me again."

They reached the roof of Galactic Books. The access door was locked, of course. Jazz Miller would have known how to open it, but Cheese Fry was at a loss. Fortunately, his compatriot was not bound by the rules of polite society. Ross Jacoby pulled a set of lock picks and a butter knife from his pocket. "You're gonna have to get yourself a set of these if you're going to sneak around at night, saving the world from apocalypses," he told Cheese Fry.

"I guess so. But what's the butter knife for?"

"It's the world's most versatile tool."

It took longer than Cheese Fry thought it would, but eventually, Ross opened the roof access door of Galactic Books and Other Stuff. Using Cheese Fry's flashlight to guide the way, they climbed down a set of stairs and found themselves in a cluttered office area. An old dryer, like the kind you find in laundromats, was pushed up against one wall. A dirty coffee maker sat on top of it.

They found a door leading to another set of stairs and climbed down into the store. Only, it wasn't Galactic Books. They were inside Wishy-Washy!

"That's weird," Cheese Fry said. "We went across four rooftops. We should be in Galactic Books."

Ross Jacoby shrugged. "I'm just following you, Frog King."

A headless ghost was folding clothes in one corner. A tired mother ghost was stuffing ghost coins in a vending machine. A trio of restless dead children were running amok around her.

A thud against the front glass drew both boys' attention. A horde of zombies was scratching and clawing at the windows and doors.

"Crap. Let's get outta here," Cheese Fry said. But Ross was already halfway to the stairs. A crack of thunder sounded nearby.

* * *

Elijah drove, but the universe kept changing. It was like a bad dream, where you're late for your piano lesson because you can't find the right house.

"The police department should be right here," Carolyn said. "I'm certain of it." But the lot was empty. In fact, Biddleborn looked like a ghost town.

"I don't like the looks of this," Elijah said. He checked the gas gauge. There was a quarter of a tank left. He kept driving.

With a suddenness that caused the car's occupants to squint, day replaced night. They drove down a country road. Elijah recognized it as Paulson Mine Road, and he marveled at the scenery. The day was aggressively cheerful. Even with the windows rolled up, the family could hear birdsong.

"I think Meridian lives out this way," Elijah noted. But he realized that it wouldn't be the real Meridian, would it? And what could the teenager do to help, anyway?

And then it was night again, and the road was slick with rain that pelted the windshield. Elijah turned on the wipers. The car turned onto the highway, headed toward Darmstadt. Elijah glanced at the gas gauge again. He hoped they were in a universe with gas stations—and that his debit card would work.

They passed an old church, and suddenly, they were in downtown Biddleborn. "I don't like this at all," Carolyn said.

"Okay. Don't panic," Elijah reassured her. But there were zombies, and therefore, panic was the most rational choice.

Chapter 24

AFTER HE WAS SURE the lawmen were gone from Mike Gershwin's house, the Cat Lord transformed back into his human form. He had no real plan for convincing the English teacher to come with him. Instead, he was hoping to use what he believed to be his considerable charm and rugged good looks.

The Cat Lord, in the form of Robert Gray, knocked on Mike's door. A voice from the other side said, "If you're a king, go away. We don't like your kind."

"I'm not a king." *Just a lord.*

Zelda's brother opened the door. "What do you want?"

Mr. Gray, completely accustomed to unprovoked hostility—and even more accustomed to provoked hostility—put on his most trustworthy face. "I need to speak with Zelda."

"Absolutely not. I don't know you, but you look untrustworthy." Mike slammed the door. But, undeterred, Mr. Gray knocked again. "Don't open that," he heard Mike say from behind the door.

The door opened anyway. Zelda's face looked out, wary at first. But when she realized it was Robert Gray, she smiled. He smiled back, self-assured as a cat.

"It's late," Zelda said.

"I noticed you had some excitement here. The sheriff was leaving as I arrived."

"Oh, um. Yes. Why don't you come in?"

"Don't let him in," Mike said from behind Zelda.

"Mike, where are your manners?" an elderly voice asked.

Zelda led Mr. Gray into her brother's kitchen, where everyone was still gathered. Too late, she realized the chair still had duct tape on it. But Mr. Gray didn't notice.

"Robert, this is my brother, Mike, and my grandmother, Rose Marie." She hesitated. "And that's Mowey. He's our lawnmower."

"Hello. Nice to meet all of you."

"It's very nice to meet *you,*" Rose Marie said, her eyes smiling with all sorts of meaning in Zelda's general direction.

"I'm going to bed," announced Mike. "If this guy turns out to be a psychotic king or some kind of monster, just know I was against letting him in the house. You're all on your own." Mike left the kitchen.

"Sorry about him," Zelda said. "We had an incident. It seems Mr. Mayfield has gone mad and thinks he's a king of some sort. He was rather . . . testy."

"Oh, *that* king. That's not Mayfield. That's King Hoss, who isn't truly a king at all. He's the king's brother, always trying to wheedle his way onto the throne. You know the type."

"I suppose it's a common enough stock character."

"Exactly."

With a deep intake of breath, Mowey exclaimed, "You're the Cat Lord!"

"Indeed, I am," Mr. Gray confirmed. "I assume you are yet another displaced resident of Detritus?"

"He's the Cat Lord," Mowey said to Rose Marie and Zelda.

Mike's voice drifted in from the living room, "I told you so."

"Is that the male version of a crazy cat lady?" Rose Marie asked.

"Absolutely not," Mr. Gray said, straightening his blazer even as it revealed its true nature as a feathered cloak.

"Oh!" Zelda exclaimed when she saw the cloak.

"Well, ain't that something?" Rose Marie said. "You're not here for

Mowey, are you? Because we aren't ready for him to go home. Unless he really wants to. But we'd at least want to throw him a party or something."

"No. I'm not here for your lawnmower, although he could probably be of service if he so desired. I'm actually here to ask for Zelda's assistance."

"My assistance?"

"Yes. I'm not sure you realize it, but you have quite a lot of magic coursing through you. There are . . . *forces* afoot in Biddleborn. Will you help us vanquish them?"

Zelda blinked at him for a few moments before speaking. "You're sure?" she finally asked.

"I'm always sure."

"Is it a Bandersnatch?"

It was Mr. Gray's turn to blink for a moment. "I wouldn't rule out the possibility of a Bandersnatch or two."

"We defeated one, Mowey and I," Zelda informed him. "Mowey and . . . me, is it?" She frowned for a moment, mentally working out the grammar.

"Zelda has one of its teeth," Mowey said. "The sheriff has one, too."

"Oh, now that's a bad idea."

"Is it?" Zelda asked.

"Sure. Unless you *want* to raise a baby Bandersnatch. They'll eat you out of house and home if you're not careful. Might take a few of your fingers in the process."

"Maybe I'd better get rid of that tooth. Excuse me for a moment." Zelda left the kitchen. Mowey, Rose Marie, and Robert Gray stood in silence until Zelda returned with a small creature growing out of a large tooth. "Is this a baby Bandersnatch?" she asked.

"Yes," Mr. Gray confirmed. They go through quite an awkward stage at first."

"It sure is ugly," Rose Marie said.

"It gets even uglier," Mr. Gray informed her.

"Will you take it?" Zelda asked Mr. Gray. "It doesn't belong here."

"No. It truly doesn't. How about this? I'll take the Bandersnatch off your hands if you'll come with me."

"Where are we going?"

"The bookstore. Galactic Books."

"Oh." Zelda looked disappointed.

"There's magic there—lots of it. We'll use it as our fortress while we weave a spell to open the door to Detritus wide enough for those of us who wish to return."

Zelda looked at Mowey. "You should come with us, then."

"I'm coming, too," Rose Marie announced.

Mike stomped back into the kitchen. He was holding Rose Marie's baseball bat. "No one's going anywhere without me."

"Then, it's settled," Mr. Gray said. "Zelda, we're going to need you to do some writing. If you have a favorite quill and a bit of parchment, you'll want to fetch them."

"I'll grab my laptop. Be right back."

* * *

Carl was in the driver's seat of Meridian's car. Meridian sat beside him in the passenger seat. Mayzell was in the back with a dozen cats begging for her ice cream.

They were driving through chaos. Assorted items flew through the air as if an invisible tornado were stirring Biddleborn like cake batter. A doghouse flew by, narrowly missing the car. "There are shadows," Meridian said.

"Of course there are shadows," Carl replied.

"No, I mean, there are shadow *wights*. I think they're following us."

"Dagnabbit bull corn."

"Such language!" Mayzell said.

Carl glanced in the rearview mirror. "Sorry, ma'am."

"Mayzell, can you get rid of the shadow wights?" Meridian asked.

"Not without my knitting needles and so many feathers, I'm afraid. Looks like the Salt Boy is at it again."

"I'd forgotten about the Salt Boy," Meridian said.

"An assault boy? What the heck is that?" Carl asked.

"No. Salt. Not assault," Meridian corrected him.

"Y'all are crazy; you know that? I'm the only sane person in this dadgum car."

"Language!" Mayzell squeaked.

"Sorry, ma'am."

A teenage boy in a top hat stood in the middle of the highway. He wore a long, purple coat with lace at the wrists. Carl slammed on the brakes.

"Oh, crap on a cracker! It's him," Meridian said.

"Language," Mayzell whispered.

The Salt Boy carried a bucket of salt. He threw some at the car. Meridian opened her door.

"What are you doing, Meridian? Shut that!" Carl demanded. But Meridian ignored her stepfather and got out.

"Salt Boy! We need your help!" Meridian pleaded. The Salt Boy laughed.

Meridian stared at her creation. The Salt Boy. She had invented him years ago, based on a neighborhood brat who liked to vandalize. Meridian had once watched him throw salt at birds. Meridian, only a child at the time, thought of him as a hardened criminal. This image was strengthened when he was finally sent to juvie, where Meridian imagined him wearing a striped prison uniform and breaking rocks with a sledgehammer all day.

The Salt Boy had terrorized Detritus for a while in Meridian's imagination, throwing salt at his enemies, burning their eyes. That was before Meridian thought up some better, more frightening villains: the shadow wights.

"Why should I help you?" the Salt Boy asked, pulling a handful of salt from his bucket and throwing it at Meridian. She saw it coming and closed her eyes. It hit her face and stuck in her hair.

"Because you want to go home."

"No, I don't."

"Because you want the Cat Lord to be in your debt."

"I don't like the Cat Lord."

"You don't have to like him."

"I don't like you either."

"You don't even know who I am, Salt Boy." The Salt Boy stared at Meridian, and she remembered his eyes were full of holes. She looked away before she got trapped inside of one. "Please help us, and I'll give you a gift," she continued to plead.

"What could you possibly give me?"

"I'll make you the true king of Detritus."

The Salt Boy took a step closer to Meridian and squinted at her. "You have this power?" Shadows swirled around them. The Salt Boy flinched, grabbing a handful of salt.

"Here come them shadow whites!" Carl yelled from the car.

The Salt Boy laughed. The shadows swirling around them grew milky. "Shadow whites," whispered Meridian. "Good one, Carl."

The Salt Boy threw salt at the albino shadow wight that had surrounded them. It screeched and disappeared in a puff of white smoke. "Did you kill it?" Meridian asked.

"No, it'll be back."

"Will you help us now?"

"Yes. But you'd better keep your promise."

"I will."

A garden gnome flew out of the air and smashed into Meridian's car, leaving a dent she couldn't afford to fix. She winced. "Let's go, Salt Boy," she said.

"Okay, but I'm not riding in the back with that old loon."

* * *

Inside Artie's head, Robert Gray outlined what he needed the boy to do. Artie held a map he had drawn on the back of a proclamation King Hoss had been carefully writing just before the confrontation that sent him to another world's psych ward. Artie used the map to lead his mother and Princess Lanora to the home of Sir Walter the Esteemed Owner of Many Books. The Cat Lord had assured Artie that Sir Walter was the man to see if you wanted a dragon.

"You don't have to come with us," Artie said to Lanora. "Not that we're not glad to have your help. But I'm guessing you have a lot of work to do now that your uncle is gone."

"You have helped my family tremendously. I owe you my help."

"Nah. We're friends. Friends don't owe each other unless one of them borrows money."

"And even then," said Belinda, "there isn't always an expectation of being repaid."

"I know that you are a powerful wizard and Jedi, but you still may need a little extra magic to accomplish the Cat Lord's task," Lanora insisted.

"Yeah, that's true," Artie said. He smiled at the princess. "Thanks."

Lanora smiled back, then blushed.

Sir Walter's house sat high on a hill. It was tall and blue. The bricks were the pale blue of a summer sky—on earth, anyway. In Detritus, the sky was always a swirl of pinks and browns. The house's trim was the dark blue of the Detritus sea.

Artie had never seen so many flowers. They hung in pots and grew in wagons and buckets and even out of the ground. "Oh, how pretty!" Belinda exclaimed. "I like Sir Walter already."

Artie knocked on the door. Shuffling and a set of very heavy footsteps from inside told him his knock was about to be answered.

The door opened. A dragon filled the doorway. He wore a vest that looked as if it were made of copper, and a pair of pince-nez sat on his nose. He held a book, with one massive claw stuck in to hold his place.

"May I help you?" the dragon asked. His voice was deep and husky.

Artie gaped until his mother nudged him. "We're looking for Sir Walter," he said.

"You have found him."

"Oh. I see." Inside Artie's head, the Cat Lord laughed.

"The Cat Lord sent us," Lanora jumped in. "We have need of your help."

The dragon sighed, long and deep. "Let me find a proper bookmark." He turned and walked into his house, leaving the door open. "Well, come inside!" he called to his guests. They did.

The house was bigger inside than it had seemed outside. It was built for a dragon. Bookshelves lined every wall, stuffed with books. It was the only real furniture. Giant, soft-looking rugs covered the floors. Although it was warm outside, a fire burned in the hearth.

The dragon picked up a black feather that was lying on a rug near the fire. He slipped it inside the book he was holding. He slid the book onto a shelf, sat himself on the rug, and pulled his glasses off his nose. He used a corner of the rug to clean his glasses, then returned them to his face. They were very large glasses, and Artie found himself staring at them.

"So, what does the Cat Lord need from me?" the dragon asked.

"He said we need a dragon to help us get home," Artie explained. "And to help him get back. He's trapped in our world, and we're trapped here in his. Except for Princess Lanora. She lives here."

The dragon smiled toothily at the princess. "Hello, Lanora. I know your father well. I hope he will soon return to us, abandoning this folly of looking for the Lost Well of Remembering."

"I hope so too, although I'm not so sure it's folly."

Artie made a mental note to ask Meridian about the Lost Well of Remembering.

"This is a beautiful home," Belinda said. "I've never met a dragon before, and I confess you're not what I expected."

"No? What did you expect?" the dragon asked.

"In all the stories I've heard in my world, dragons live in caves, sleeping on piles of gold."

"Ah. Yes. I've met those fellows. I prefer soft rugs and books."

"Isn't it dangerous for you to live in a wooden house?" Artie asked. "I mean, do you breathe fire?"

"Quite right. That's why I coated the wood in a thick layer of magic, to protect against the occasional sneeze."

"And the books? They're pretty flammable, too."

"I had a chat with them. They've promised not to burn."

"Oh. That's all right then. So, will you help us?"

"That depends on what you need me to do."

"Come with us to the Cat Lord's cottage. Help us . . ." Artie paused and tilted his head while listening to Mr. Gray's voice. "Help us forge a key."

The dragon sighed, looking with longing at the book he had just slid onto the shelf. "I suppose I can do so," the dragon agreed. "The Cat Lord is my friend. And he owes me money. I'd hate for him to be banished forever in a world without *me* in it."

Chapter 25

CHEESE FRY AND ROSS were on the roof of Galactic Books. They had peered over the sides of the buildings this time to find the correct one. "I swear this building used to be over there," Cheese Fry said, gesturing toward the laundromat.

The roof access door was, of course, locked. Little sticky frogs plopped around Cheese Fry and Ross as Ross set to work. "Those frogs would be more useful if they had piranha teeth or something," Ross Jacoby said just before being bitten by a frog. "Ow! Consorn dadgum fiddlesticks!"

"Oh, wow. He really got you," Cheese Fry noted.

Ross Jacoby's other leg was now bleeding. "Tell your frog army to stay away from me."

"I'm not sure they listen to me, but . . . hey, frogs, leave Ross alone. He's on our side."

Plop plop plop plop plop. The frogs plopped away.

"Did that work?" Ross asked.

"I guess so."

Ross continued to poke at the lock. The butter knife was now in use, for no reason Cheese Fry understood. "Hey, Ross. Tell me again how the butter knife works."

"This little tool is almost magic, I think. You'll notice the tip of this one is broken off, which makes it better than a screwdriver. You can wedge it in most any place. It's a mini crowbar, screwdriver, and chisel rolled into one."

"And tell me it's a great lock pick that opens any door."

"Well—"

"No. I literally want you to say those words, Ross. I'm testing out a theory."

Ross held up his broken butter knife and inspected it. He shrugged. "Sure. This thing'll open any door."

"Cool."

Ross turned his attention back to the lock. As soon as the butter knife got near, the lock clicked open. "Whoa! That was—"

"Magic," Cheese Fry finished.

"How?"

"It's like when you mentioned zombies, and suddenly, there they were. Then, you said the frogs needed teeth, and bam! You're some kind of wizard, I think."

Ross giggled. "A wizard." He liked the sound of that. He pulled the door open, and the two boys slipped inside the bookstore.

Downstairs, a skeleton sat watching a *Star Wars* chess set play itself. "Hi, Calvin!" Cheese Fry said.

"He's a skeleton," Ross pointed out.

"I'm *not* a skeleton," Calvin said. "I'm a member of the Thieves' Guild."

Ross opened his mouth to argue, then decided against it. "Sure. That's cool. Have you got a first aid kit?"

"What would I need with a first aid kit? I'm a skeleton."

Cheese Fry, followed by frogs again, went in search of a first aid kit.

* * *

With the Salt Boy riding shotgun, Carl drove down a ghost- and zombie-clogged Main Street. "Wish I had brought a rocket launcher," Carl said. He pulled out his cell phone and called his brother Franklin. "Hey, there's a zombie apocalypse or something happening on Main Street. Might want to gear up and come down here. Bring the tank."

There was a whoop of excitement from Franklin, and then Carl hung up. Zombies rocked the car. "I don't think we can wait for Uncle Franklin," Meridian said from the back seat. Mayzell sat next to her, knitting a cat sweater.

The Salt Boy sighed. "I hate zombies. They stink."

Carl put the car in reverse and floored it. "Wish I had my truck," he said. "Hey, anyone got a magic spell to turn this car into some kind of vehicle of destruction?"

"No! Not my car!" Meridian yelled. "Do. Not. Turn my car. Into. *Anything.*" She glared at everyone in turn.

Carl backed down Main and backed onto Park Street, which seemed to be zombie-free. "At least it seems to be a localized apocalypse," he said.

"I think we would be better off on foot," the Salt Boy suggested. "Maybe we could pretend to be zombies."

"Wouldn't they smell us or something?" Carl asked.

The Salt Boy shrugged.

Mayzell set her knitting aside. Leaning forward, she said, "You might want to send the cats to clear the mice away before you go a rovin' in the moonlight, eh?"

Carl blinked at her, then glanced at Meridian, who shrugged. "It's not a bad idea," Meridian said. "They're the Cat Lord's cats."

"So . . . *magic* kitties?"

"Yes. Magic kitties."

Carl stuck his finger out to the nearest cat, a small orange tabby. It stretched and touched its nose to his fingertip. "Nose touch," he said. The cat rubbed its face on his hand. "You be careful out there fighting zombies, okay?"

"And don't spoil your whole dinner, eh?" Mayzell chimed in.

They opened the doors and put the cats out. "Go kill zombies," Meridian told them. The cats wandered off, except for one that hopped up on the hood of the car and began to groom.

"I don't know that they understood their orders," Carl said, watching as one cat started investigating a dumpster.

"I say we make a run for it," Meridian suggested.

Carl looked at Mayzell. "Can you run?"

"Aye, I can scrub and herd with the best of 'em."

"Okay. Let's think this through. How does magic work?" Carl asked.

"We weave stories, I guess," Meridian answered. "But there's more to it, I think."

"Mayzell, show us how you scrub."

Mayzell brightened. She pulled three strands of light from the air and began to weave them together. Meridian's dashboard dust disappeared, replaced by a shine and the smell of lemons.

"I don't think we can scrub the zombies to death," Meridian said.

"She can also herd, though," the Salt Boy reminded her.

"Can she herd zombies?" Carl asked. He turned to Mayzell. "Can you herd zombies?"

"Oh, probably. If I can herd cats, I can probably herd just about anything."

"Well. There you go. That's our plan."

"Where would you like them, dear?"

"Anyplace away from where we're going."

They got out of the car and crept to the corner of Park and Main. The zombies were gathered around the laundromat, which, strangely, was located where Carl would have sworn Galactic Books should be. But the bookstore was two doors down.

"Someone must be trapped inside Wishy-Washy," Carl said. "Mayzell, see if you can herd them away from there. Maybe lock 'em inside the post office? It's night. No one will be there for hours."

"Okey-dokey-pokey-lokey," Mayzell sang. She pulled several

strands of colored lights from the air—blue and green and gold. The lights began to flash as she wove them, as if she held a tiny discotheque.

The others watched while Mayzell wandered out into the street with flashing colors and cheerful song. The Salt Boy took off his hat and pulled out a handful of salt. He passed the hat to Meridian. "Take some, just in case." She put her hand in and came out with a fist full of salt. Carl did the same, but with more skepticism.

The zombies shuffled toward Mayzell, one by one, and then in hordes. Then, the Cat Lord's cats joined the fray. One of them, a sleek Siamese, pounced on a zombie's shuffling foot. A tabby joined, then a lanky black cat. The three of them took the zombie down like lions pouncing on a gazelle. The other zombies failed to notice, too entranced by the lights. Now, the ghosts were following as well, but more out of curiosity than any sort of mesmerism.

"Okay, let's go. Quietly," Carl said. He stayed between the teenagers and zombies, gun ready, as they ran-crept to Galactic Books. Hundreds of frogs hopped out of their way.

Meridian had her key ready when they reached the door. She had no sooner stuck it in the lock when the door opened. A skeletal arm motioned them inside.

* * *

Elijah and his family watched as a very old woman, holding a pulsating ball of colored lights, wandered onto Main Street at the other end of the block from where they sat motionless and panicky in their SUV. "Is that a witch?" Orson asked.

"I'm not sure," Elijah responded.

The zombies shuffled toward the woman. "Should we save her?" Isaac asked.

"I'm not sure of that either."

But the zombies merely shuffled along after the woman. Most of the ghosts drifted after her, too, but from a greater distance.

A trio of cats attacked a zombie. "Cool!" both boys said. "Do you think Sasha could do that, Dad?"

"I doubt it. She's just a puppy."

"But when she grows up, she'll be a lot bigger than a cat," Isaac pointed out.

"I hope Sasha never, ever, ever meets a zombie in her life," Carolyn said, ending all speculation.

"I think we should make use of this distraction," Elijah suggested. "Everyone ready? I'll take Madeleine. Carolyn, you grab Sasha. Everyone stay close together." They opened their car doors as quietly as possible, slipping out into the zombie-infested night.

"Look!" whispered Carolyn, pointing as best she could with a puppy in her arms. Meridian Page, her stepfather, and a teenage boy in a top hat and theatrical-looking coat were running toward Galactic Books.

"Looks like we have some allies. I hope," Elijah said. "Okay, let's go."

Their run was more of a light jog, given the length of Orson's legs. No one was willing to leave the boy behind. Hundreds of frogs jumped out of their way. Orson stopped, amazed, slowing them down further. He picked one up. "Ow! It bit me!" He began to cry.

"Come on! Cry later!" Isaac said, grabbing his brother's arm and pulling him along.

They reached Galactic Books and fell against the door. Evidently, Meridian had locked it behind her, which was wise in light of the apocalypse going on. Elijah pounded on the door, then pulled out his key. But the door opened, and Meridian's face appeared.

"Hurry inside!" Meridian said. "And don't mind the skeleton. He's on *our* side."

* * *

Mike, Rose Marie, and Zelda sat on the bench seat in the cab of Mike's truck. Mowey and the Cat Lord rode in the truck bed. The Cat Lord tried to maintain his dignity as he was rocked to and fro and forced to cling to the side to keep from toppling off the wheel well. To keep both hands free, he stuffed the baby Bandersnatch in a pocket of his cloak. "Go to sleep," he told it.

"What are you going to do with it?" Mowey asked.

"I have an acquaintance who rehabilitates them. I'll probably—"

The truck stopped abruptly, throwing the Cat Lord from his perch. A teenage girl stood in the road. Robert Gray recognized her as one of his students. The girl, Bird, held a golden key in her hand. "Oh," he said. He reached inside his cloak for his sword.

The girl turned the key, and the sky ripped in two. Darkness poured out—darkness with . . . teeth.

Chapter 26

WHEN THE CALL CAME, no one at the Biddleborn Police Department believed it. Zombies on Main Street? Must be a prank, probably in honor of that kid who died. But the police responded anyway.

When the police arrived, Main Street was quiet. A half-dozen cats were gathered outside the post office, and a lonely child ghost sat on the sidewalk outside Miss Lindy's, looking forlorn. The most unusual thing happening on Main Street seemed to be the number of lights that were on inside Galactic Books and Other Stuff.

Sonny Rogers went to check out Galactic Books while the other officers, Jerry Benson, Chip Harding, and Sheriff Amory, spread out to check the other buildings. Sonny tried the door, but it was locked. He unholstered his weapon with his right hand and knocked with his left hand. "Police!" he called out. "Elijah, you in there?"

Elijah opened the door and peeked out, looking nervous. "Hey, Sonny."

"You working late?"

"Actually, just . . . did you know there are zombies in the post office?"

"In the post office, huh? That why those cats are over there?"

"Yes, I think so."

"You ain't been smoking crack, have you, Elijah?"

"No. You know I wouldn't do that."

“You mind if I come in and have a look around?”

Elijah glanced behind him, looked back at Sonny, then stepped aside to let him in. Carolyn Schmidt and her three children were in the children’s section, reading a book. Carl Davis sat behind the counter with his stepdaughter Meridian, Chad Davenport, and some other teenager whom Sonny had never seen. This new boy was dressed like a magician.

“You guys having a party?” Sonny asked as he looked at his watch. “It’s after midnight. What are you all doing here?”

“Hiding from zombies,” Carl said.

“And ghosts,” Meridian added.

“And shadow wights,” said the teenaged magician.

A very old woman emerged from the back of the store. She held a tray of freshly-baked cookies. “Hi, there, Jolly Copper Lad. You want a chocolate biscuit before you fight them zombies, eh? Sing ’em off to sleep, I always say.” She offered him a cookie.

“Oh, no . . . well, just one won’t hurt, I guess.” Sonny plucked a cookie from the tray and ate it in two bites.

“Are you going to warn the other officers about the zombies in the post office?” Elijah asked. “I think they need to know.”

Sonny sighed. He pulled his radio from his belt. “I’ve got a group of civilians in the bookstore. They say the zombies are in the post office.”

There was a burst of static on the other end, then the sheriff’s voice. “Roger, Rogers.”

Sonny started to return the radio call when Jerry Benson’s voice came on. “Hey, Sonny, any of those civilians look like they’ve been bitten? They’re not salivating over your brain, are they?”

Sonny rolled his eyes. “You’re hilarious,” he said into the radio. He clipped the radio back to his belt. “But I guess Jerry has a point. Are you all okay?” he asked the people gathered in the bookstore.

Everyone looked at each other. “Sure. We’re fine,” Carl answered.

“Oh, for Pete’s sake,” Carolyn Schmidt said, standing up from the children's section. "Actually, Sonny, Ross Jacoby is here. He didn't want you to know it because he's convinced you'll arrest him for . . . existing, I guess. But he has been bitten by something."

"It wasn't a zombie," Cheese Fry said. "It was a shadow wight. I don't think he's going to . . . turn . . . or anything." He looked at Meridian. "Right?"

"Right."

"And," Cheese Fry continued, "there might also be a skeleton who . . . sounds like Jazz Miller. But his name is Calvin of the Thie— Um, Theater Club. Or something."

Sonny nodded. There was the name: Jazz Miller. This was definitely a prank, although he was surprised to find so many adults in the room. The Schmidts were good people, and the old lady seemed nice. Carl Davis was less of a surprise, though.

"I'll go get Ross," Carolyn said. "It'll frighten him less, I think. Is that okay, Sonny?"

"Sure, ma'am."

"I'll help," Cheese Fry said. "He's having a hard time walking," he explained to the officer.

Shots rang out from the general direction of the post office. "Sounds like someone found the zombies," Carl said.

Sonny ran to the door and looked out. Jerry Benson was screaming. And Sheriff Amory was shooting into the post office.

"Lock this door after me!" Sonny instructed. He ran out into the night.

* * *

The Shadow King walked through Clyde J. Anderson Park. The night was full of stories. He could feel them tugging at the darkness, begging it to come to life. Sometimes, when the story was heavy enough, the darkness obeyed.

The one who called herself Bird had opened a lot of doors. The

Shadow King made a mental note to thank her, right after he tore the key away from her. Or possibly after he killed her and absorbed her power.

But first, the Shadow King had another girl to kill. Once Meridian Page was dead, the Shadow King would be free.

* * *

Artie, Belinda, Lanora, and Sir Walter the dragon squeezed inside the Cat Lord's cottage. For its part, the cottage grew to accommodate its large guest. "Wish my house could do that," Belinda said. "Thanksgiving would be far more pleasant."

"So, where is the Cat Lord?" Sir Walter asked. "How do I get to this other world?"

"He goes by the name Robert Gray there. And he had a plan," Artie remembered. "Let me ask him." He flinched. Then, his eyes popped back open. "He's currently busy fighting all the legions of hell. But he says for us to make ourselves at home."

"Any idea where Mayzell is?" Sir Walter asked. "Perhaps off to the Roanoke Market?"

Artie and the women shrugged.

"Wherever she is, she must have taken the cats," Lanora pointed out, gesturing to the empty furniture.

"Curious," said Sir Walter. He looked closely at Artie, adjusting his pince-nez for a better view. "You have a . . . connection . . . to the Cat Lord? Er . . . Robert Gray?"

"Yeah. He's in my head sometimes. And vice versa. It's kinda annoying."

"Very good. I can use that."

"Cool. I think. What do you need me to do?"

"I need you to be in active communication with him. When you spoke with him earlier, the path lit up. It would be most helpful if I could see it."

"Okay. But he's someplace really creepy right now."

"All the more reason to get me there in a hurry."

"Good point." Artie closed his eyes and directed his thoughts toward his science teacher. Suddenly, he was looking through Mr. Gray's eyes at a horde of monsters. Some were shadows with sharp teeth and bleeding eyes. Others were milky white. Mr. Gray was hacking at them with his sword. A lawnmower fought beside him.

"*Not now, kid!*" Mr. Gray said.

"*But Sir Walter's here. He wants to use the path to come to you.*"

"*Oh, well, in that case, make yourself useful.*"

It occurred to Artie that he could, in fact, be useful. He was a great Jedi-wizard, after all. Although he wasn't sure you could use the Force on a shadow. That left wizardry. So, Artie began to weave. And Sir Walter began to weave, too.

Mr. Gray hacked at one shadow as another grabbed him from behind. He threw himself to the ground and rolled. "*I'm too old for this.*"

"*You're doing fine,*" Artie encouraged him.

"*Please tell me that isn't a tornado you're creating.*"

"*Don't worry, Cat Lord; I have it under control.*"

Mike Gershwin ran at the shadows with a baseball bat and a knife. In the truck, Zelda's laptop finally loaded. She clicked on Microsoft Word, opening a new, blank document.

A tornado made of light began to churn around the shadows, dissolving them where it touched. Mr. Gray got to his feet. "Mowey! Mike! To the truck!"

A milky white shadow was gripping the lawnmower by the handle. Mike ran at it with his bat swinging. Meanwhile, Zelda began typing: *The albino shadow let go of the lawnmower and was sucked inside the tornado of light.* With a scream, the shadow white was sucked into the blazing whirlwind.

Light grew all around Mr. Gray—a thick strand of it that led from his head to a spot in the air some thirty feet away. It glowed a brilliant green—the color of dragon flesh—and Sir Walter appeared in his coppery vest. He pulled his glasses off, cleaned them, and looked around at the chaos.

Zelda typed: *A very good dragon appeared out of nowhere. He was very friendly and mostly ate fruit.*

Sir Walter had a sudden craving for peaches. He hoped this world had some. "Cat Lord! Good to see you!" he exclaimed as a shadow wight bit down on Mr. Gray's leg.

"Ow! Good to see you, Sir Walter. A little help?"

Sir Walter waded into the fray, tossing shadows here and there. He breathed on a nearby tree, igniting it.

A group of shadows began circling the truck. "Uh-oh," Rose Marie said. "Zelda!"

Mike and Mowey, back to handle, fought through a horde of shadow wights. Zelda typed: *The truck in which the heroines sheltered began to glow from within. The light was brilliant in its purity, a radiance that destroyed any shadow that dared come near.* The shadow wights screamed and dissolved.

Sir Walter picked up the tornado and began to shape it like clay. He forged it into a sword that spun and pulled like a cyclone made of lightning. "Bet you wish you had one of these," he said to Mr. Gray.

"I am a bit jealous," Mr. Gray confirmed, stabbing a shadow wight through the middle with his ordinary, non-cyclone sword.

Sir Walter swung the cyclone sword and killed a half dozen shadows. He smiled, and the light reflected off his teeth.

In the truck, Zelda typed furiously.

* * *

A tank rolled onto Main Street. Franklin Davis had arrived.

Zombies were spilling out of the post office. Two officers were shooting at them while a third dragged a fallen comrade to safety. Franklin made a mental note that the fallen comrade would have to be dealt with later. For now, he had a town to save.

Frank rolled his tank into the crowd of zombies. "Oh, yeah!" he shouted with glee.

* * *

The lights dimmed inside Galactic Books. "That can't be a good sign," Carl said.

A hissing sound, like a punctured tire, seemed to come from the walls. The group stood. Those with weapons gripped them, ready.

Darkness swirled, and the Shadow King poured out of the ventilation system, materializing in the middle of the room. He was all darkness and teeth, like a shadow wight, but bigger. There was a suggestion of bulk, muscle, hair, and leathery skin. His arms were long, his knuckles brushing the ground. His crown glinted red in the dim light.

Carl shot at the Shadow King. The bullet went straight through and lodged inside a bookshelf.

Teeth gleamed. "Hello, Meridian Page," the Shadow King greeted her menacingly.

"No!" Carl shouted.

Meridian's body pumped epinephrine and norepinephrine into her system, preparing her for fight, flight, or freeze. Freeze had always been her favored response, though. As much as she wished she could fight, she instead froze, her mind slipping away.

At long last, Lady Lanora stood before the Shadow King. The monster thought victory was his—that he would soon be devouring royal flesh. But Lanora smiled. "You've lost," she said. She pulled the key from her pocket—

"That's not going to work this time, child," the Shadow King said, interrupting Meridian's imagination. He knocked Carl out of his way, slamming him into the counter. Then, the Shadow King reached across the counter and grabbed Meridian's throat, pulling her close to his face. "This time, you die."

Chapter 27

WHILE SIR WALTER KEPT the shadows busy with a swinging cyclone sword, the Cat Lord wove magic. The girl, Bird, had the key. The Cat Lord had to find her. The people at Galactic Books were counting on him. But the girl had the key, and that was more important.

The Cat Lord took the magic he had made and spun it. It flew from his hands and rose above the fray, the cyclone, and the dragon. And then, gravity brought it down because physics, too, is a kind of magic.

As the magic dropped, it grew. The web of magic dropped like a net, entangling shadows in its light. Sir Walter used the distraction to turn the cyclone into a club. He beat the remaining shadows with it until they dissolved.

Mike put down his bat. And Mowey stopped his motor. The battle was over. Shadow dust coated the ground. And the Cat Lord had disappeared.

* * *

Jerry Benson had a sudden craving for brains. He stopped screaming and staggered to his feet. The place where the zombie had bitten him no longer burned. But his legs weren't moving quite as smoothly as they used to. They felt heavy.

Jerry's friends—his fellow officers, his brothers—were running and waving their arms at a tank that was rolling over a group of zombies. A small group of the living dead had broken off from the main horde and was staggering after his friends. Jerry stumbled after them, too, but not to help. Those days were finished.

Jerry's life was behind him, and what did he have to show for it? All he had ever done was work, and what does work accomplish? He hadn't built anything tangible. All he was leaving behind was a dirty apartment, and even that would soon be cleaned out and rented to someone else. His stuff was just yard sale fodder. His whole life was meaningless, a chasing after the wind.

Jerry opened his mouth to voice his existential angst, but all that came out was "braaaaaiiins!"

* * *

The Salt Boy saw his chance at the throne in danger. He didn't care one iota about Meridian Page, but, by gosh by golly, he was going to save her. The Shadow King grabbed Meridian by the throat, and the Salt Boy threw himself at him and climbed him like a kitten scaling a human leg. He grabbed the Shadow King's crown and threw it. Then, he dug his thumbs into the Shadow King's eyes.

The Shadow King screamed and dropped Meridian. He flailed at the Salt Boy and grabbed him with one huge hand. Meridian crawled to Carl.

Running up behind the Shadow King, Calvin stabbed his sword into the Shadow King's back. The Shadow King swung around and hit Calvin with the Salt Boy, using the teenager as a club. Calvin and the Salt Boy both flew across the room, hitting shelves and knocking books to the floor.

Cheese Fry clicked on his flashlight and shined it on the Shadow King's face. The Shadow King flinched. He picked up the *Star Wars* chess set and threw it at Cheese Fry. "No!" Elijah yelled.

An apparition appeared. It was faint at first but then resolved into a clear image. The ghost caught the chess board. The pieces fell all around him, running when they hit the floor.

The ghost was Jazz Miller. He gently set the chess board down with a nod at Elijah. Then, Jazz picked up Calvin's sword and launched himself at the Shadow King. The Shadow King roared in frustration and dissolved. Jazz handed the sword back to Calvin, tipped an imaginary hat to Cheese Fry, then turned into a cloud of moths and flew away.

Carl pulled Meridian into his arms. Weeping, she allowed herself to be held.

Calvin of the Thieves' Guild stuffed the Shadow King's crown into his pocket. It would fetch a lovely price at the Roanoke Market, in some of the murkier stalls that bought and sold after hours.

* * *

The tooth monster broke a window and escaped from Sheriff Amory's house. The noise was loud, and the glass was sharp, but it had to be done. The magic and the danger called.

It was dark out—just right for hiding. The creature's feet had grown to their proper size. Its legs were still stubby, but they were strong. Best of all, it had claws and a mouth full of teeth—sharp, sharp teeth.

The thing ran, staying close to the house. Then, it ran in the hedgerow that separated the sheriff's yard from his neighbors'. Then, down an alley. And then, under a fence. A dog barked, with its face close to the creature and full of anger. So, back under the fence the thing went.

The monster ran along the house, then through a flower bed full of sticky stems and soft petals. Its legs were getting tired. It had never run so far. And the night was cold.

Maybe this was a mistake, the tooth monster started to think. But the man with the chicken nuggets was in danger. The creature could feel it. It could feel the danger and so much magic, wild and reckless.

Daddy. The tooth monster had to save Daddy!

* * *

"Could we do what Sir Walter did? Just ride on home like that?" Belinda asked.

"I don't know," Artie responded to his mom. "I don't know if I could keep the path open *and* use it as a doorway at the same time. But *you* could go home that way. In fact, you *should* go home. I think."

"No way. I'm not leaving you."

"I think you're both safer here for—" Lanora said. But the princess disappeared before she could finish her statement.

Artie jumped up from his seat. "Where'd she go?"

"Did she follow Sir Walter?" Belinda asked.

"Couldn't have. The path was closed."

"I don't like this. I don't like being alone in this world. I don't understand its rules, how things work."

Artie agreed, but instead of saying so, he hugged his mom. "I shouldn't have brought you here."

"Oh, baby. Of course you should have. It was absolutely the right thing to do. I was so, so, so worried about you and . . . sad. I was so sad without you."

Lanora reappeared. "Lanora! You're back! Where did you go?" Artie asked.

The princess opened her hand and looked at the golden key she was holding. "I was in the Shadow King's throne room, telling him he had lost. Somehow, I was going to use this key to defeat him."

Artie could feel the key's power. "Dude," he said eloquently.

"You just . . . poofed, and there you were in the throne room? Is that unusual?" Belinda asked.

"I don't know," Lenora answered. "I guess it happens sometimes."

"Where did the key come from?" Artie asked.

Lanora tilted her head and thought about it. "I think . . . *she* created it."

"She? Oh, you mean Meridian?"

"Yes. She was in danger, and—"

"In danger? What kind of danger?"

"I don't know."

"Can you help her?"

Lanora shook her head. She handed the key to Artie. "I think you should keep this safe."

"Actually, I think my mom should probably hold onto it. I tend to lose things." Artie handed the key to Belinda, who slipped it onto the key ring that held her car and house keys. "How do you know Meridian was in danger?" he asked.

"I don't know, precisely. I guess I can . . . feel her sometimes, at the back of my mind. Like when you see something from the corner of your eye."

"You have a connection."

"I suppose so."

"Okay, good. We can use that."

"It's not something I can control, though."

"I can maybe help with that. Or, at least, the Cat Lord can probably help with that."

"Can we use her connection with Meridian to go home?" Belinda asked.

"I think so. Is that okay, Princess Lanora?"

"Yes. I'm willing to help you. Although . . . I will miss you."

Artie blushed.

Chapter 28

"I THOUGHT THIS WAS supposed to be a fortress," Carl said. Meridian sat up, rubbing her eyes. "You okay, Baby Girl?" he asked her.

"Yessir." She rubbed her throat. "I thought I was going to die, though."

Calvin reached out a skeletal hand to each of them and helped them to their feet. "You're right. We need to make this place more secure. It has magic—lots of magic. We can shape it into a shield of sorts."

"Can you wield it against shadows?" Cheese Fry asked.

"And maybe zombies?" Ross Jacoby added.

"Maybe," Calvin replied. "Of course, it would be easier with the Cat Lord's help."

"I don't think we can wait for him," the Salt Boy said.

"We need some stuffed animals," Orson suggested. His mother ruffled his hair.

Calvin looked at him and nodded. "You're right about that, young man."

"How come you're a skeleton?" Orson asked.

"This is what happens if you spend too long waiting for something."

"Oh."

"Another good reason to stop waiting for the Cat Lord," the Salt Boy pointed out.

"Then, let's see what we can do. Does anyone know where we can get some frogs?"

Cheese Fry and Ross Jacoby laughed. "Yeah," Cheese Fry said, "I think we can hook you up." Cheese Fry went to the door and peeked out. He opened it, and a hundred or so frogs hopped into the building. He closed the door.

"Well, that wasn't weird at all," Carl said sarcastically.

"Careful. They bite," Elijah warned.

Calvin picked up a frog and examined it. "This frog has definitely been magicked."

"Like the O'Dell's dog," Meridian mused. "I wonder how many other animals have been affected."

"Wherever stories are told, they've been affected," Calvin said. "Someone, somewhere, believed it, and the story changed reality."

"But if all of this started with me, with my stories, then I don't get it," Meridian said. "I never told a story about that dog. I never even thought about it. But . . . Artie hated it."

"That boy is quite a wizard," Calvin said.

"So maybe it was Artie's hatred that did it?"

"Quite so."

"What about Mr. Kirchner? And Jazz Miller? Did someone make up stories about them?"

"I have no idea."

"So, what do we do now that we have all these frogs?" Elijah asked.

"Herd 'em round and round," Mayzell suggested. "Be sure to put your back into it."

"Let's cut them open," suggested the Salt Boy. "Drain out the magic."

"Nobody's cutting open my frogs," Cheese Fry said. "They're mine. They followed me all the way here, and I'm not going to betray their trust."

"He's the Frog King," Ross announced, helpfully and with just a hint of pride.

"Well, there you go then," Calvin said. "Cheese Fry, you channel the frog magic while some of the others wake the books. Mayzell, Meridian, and I will weave."

"What about me?" the Salt Boy asked. "I know more about magic than Meridian does."

"He has a point," Meridian said.

"You are a veritable wellspring of magic," Calvin told her.

"I don't know what that means. I mean, I guess I do, kinda. But I don't know how to use it."

"And I don't know how to wake no books," Carl said.

"Oh! I do!" Isaac shouted, using his best outdoor voice. "You *read* them!" His mother, unperturbed by his volume, beamed at him.

Calvin pointed at Isaac. "The boy is right." Then, he pointed at Meridian. "And you've been weaving magic for years."

"Well, *I* created the zombie apocalypse," Ross pointed out.

"He did. It's true," Cheese Fry confirmed. "He's also the reason the frogs have teeth."

"Very well. He can join us," Calvin said. "The rest of you, go wake the books."

Carl raised his hand. "Do I have to actually read? Couldn't I just . . . keep a lookout or something."

Calvin shrugged. "Sure. That's not a bad idea."

Elijah and his family grabbed books to read. The others, minus Carl, gathered around the tables in the back, where the Dungeons and Dragons games typically took place.

"Okay," Calvin said, pulling strands of magic from the air, "let's start this story. Meridian, you start. Remember, our goal is to build a fortress."

Meridian closed her eyes and gathered her thoughts. *I can do this.* "Once upon a time, there was a bookstore called Galactic Books and

Other Stuff . . ." she started.

Galactic Books heard its name spoken and opened its eyes—metaphorically speaking, of course.

* * *

Robert Gray disappeared in a flash of magic. "I didn't know he could do that," Rose Marie said.

Zelda closed her laptop and got out of the truck. Sir Walter was cleaning his pince-nez. And Mike was examining Mowey's blades.

"Is he okay?" Zelda asked.

"He's got a broken blade," Mike informed her. Mowey was shaking. Mike patted him. "It's okay, buddy. We'll get you all fixed up. Don't you worry."

Zelda kneeled down next to the lawnmower. "Does it hurt?"

"A little."

"You are so brave."

Rose Marie joined them. "What's wrong with my Mowey?"

"Broken blade," Mike said. "Don't worry. It's an easy fix."

Sir Walter approached the group. "We should probably get going. There's a doorway here that has been unlocked. There's no telling what vile things might be watching us."

"Does it lead to Detritus?" Mowey asked.

"Indeed. Although I suspect it would take you right to the Shadow King's lair."

Mowey shook even harder. "I don't want to go *there*."

Rose Marie put her hand on Mowey's handle. "Do you really want to go home? Because you could just stay here forever if you wanted to."

"Really?"

"Of course, really."

"Sure. We love you," Zelda chimed in.

Mike patted the lawnmower.

"This is touching," Sir Walter said, "but we have been abandoned, it seems, which makes me feel as if I am responsible for your collective safety. Also, it's time for tea."

"We were on our way to a bookstore," Zelda said. "Robert said we'd be safe there while we gathered enough magic to fight the . . . whatever those things were."

"Shadow wights. And a bookstore would be delightful." The dragon smiled. "I'm assuming the Cat Lord, er . . . *Robert* will catch up with us when he's finished with whatever fool quest took him away so suddenly."

"If he can just disappear, how come he doesn't just disappear himself back home?" Rose Marie asked.

"The magic he used created a portal, but it doesn't cross worlds. It crosses time. It was a small portal, so he didn't go far. Just a couple of days back, from the looks of it."

"He went back in time?" Zelda asked.

"Just a little."

"Why?" Mike asked.

"No idea. He's probably either saving the world or taking a nap," Sir Walter suggested. "With Robert, there's usually no in-between."

"*I* could sure use a nap," Rose Marie said.

"Let's get to this bookstore," Sir Walter insisted.

"I don't think you're going to fit in my truck," Mike pointed out.

"I'll follow from above." Sir Walter tucked his glasses safely in a pocket of his vest before spreading his wings.

* * *

The zombie horde had been reduced to a few stragglers, one of which was Jerry Benson. Sheriff Amory, out of ammunition, tased a zombie. It jerked but kept coming toward him.

"Sonny! Chip! Fall back!" the sheriff shouted. What remained of the Biddleborn Police Department ran for cover. "This way!" They ran toward Galactic Books.

Jerry Benson shuffled after them. Then, something flew out of the shadows. It landed on Jerry and tore him apart with enormous, very pointy teeth.

"What in tarnation is *that*?" Sonny asked.

Sheriff Amory didn't answer. Instead, he pulled his officers toward the bookstore as the tooth he found in Zelda's house ate the zombie that used to be his crime scene investigator.

* * *

Lanora sat and tried to find Meridian with her mind—something she had never done before. "I don't think it's working," she said.

"We need that wizard," Artie said. "Old Randolph the Wise but Ungrateful. He's the one who created my link to the Cat Lord."

"But you're a better wizard than he is. Why can't you do it?"

"I'm not sure that I am. I don't know how he did it."

"He was trying to make the two of you switch places."

"And it went wrong. Or maybe it went right. But he gave me something to drink, and I have no idea what was in it."

"That's right. There *was* a potion," Lanora remembered. "I'm not sure we can convince him to come back here. Perhaps we should go to him."

"Okay. All we need is a map, right?"

"Actually, he lives near the Roanoke Market, along the banks of the Green River."

"So . . . no map?"

"No map is necessary, unless it makes you truly happy to draw one."

"Whatever's faster, I suppose."

"When you get home, will you send my friends back here?" Lanora asked.

"Yes. And, you know, if I figure out how to go back and forth, I could come visit you sometimes."

"I would like that," Lanora said as she took Artie's hand, causing him to blush profusely while his mother held in a giggle. "Let's go see Old Randolph."

* * *

The Shadow King was angry and humiliated. He hadn't expected the girl to be guarded by the dead. He stood in the doorway between worlds and called.

He called forth shadows.

He called forth slimy things.

He called forth the hungry, the depraved, and those who, like him, longed for revenge.

He called them forth and told them where to find the girl.

* * *

The Cat Lord didn't need to go back in time very far, just a few hours. He knew where he had seen the girl with the key, but he wasn't sure which class she had been in. More importantly, he knew where he had seen the key—or, at least, the key's aura.

The Cat Lord stood, as Mr. Gray, in his first-hour class, just as he had earlier in the day. He didn't remember what he had been talking about that morning, but he didn't think the students would notice if he switched topics anyway. They never seemed very attentive.

There she was. Norma Bellows. A shadow crawled across her face. Far away, in another world, Artie's body jumped.

"*So, what does it mean?*" Artie asked. "*Is she . . . possessed?*"

"*No. Just . . . accompanied. She has some very unsavory friends. I think we need to keep an eye on her.*"

"*Does she know I'm here?*"

"*The beauty of our current situation, Artie, is that you are* NOT *here, remember? Now, shut up and let me teach. In the meantime, I need you to do something for me.*"

"*What's that?*"

"I need more magic than I have available here. I have a pocketful of light. I need magic from Detritus to forge it into a weapon that can slide through magic. Can you get me what I need?"

"*Sure,*" Artie agreed. "*I can do anything, especially if it means I don't have to listen to you teach.*"

"*I'll remember you said that when I'm grading your next assignment. Here,*" the Cat Lord said while picturing what he needed. "*Got it?*"

"*Yessir,*" Artie confirmed.

Mr. Gray turned his attention back to the class and Norma Bellows. At some point in the next few hours, she was going to cease to be a girl and become a key. Mr. Gray couldn't keep that from happening. But he could put a tracer on her to make her easier to find several hours from now.

"Wildflowers grow wherever they please," Mr. Gray said, walking around the classroom. He needed to walk around Norma three times to create a loop, then cross back through to create a knot. "Up through castles and such. The parts of a wildflower are the piston, the petals, and the cylinder. On a cellular level, they work much the same as—"

Norma Bellows stood up and interrupted. "I need to use the bathroom," she said. She stomped toward the door.

"No. Sit down," Mr. Gray told her.

"You can't make me."

Mr. Gray threw a noose made of magic at her. But Norma Bellows ran from the room, dodging the noose.

"Poop on a pedestal," Mr. Gray muttered. He sighed and continued with the lesson. "The striations on an earthworm. If you look closely enough at an earthworm's medulla oblongata, you'll note the way the muscles flex, like the biceps on a daisy."

Mr. Gray would have to try a sneakier approach to put a tracer on Norma Bellows. One of his cats would have to do it. He glanced at the clock. He still had time.

Chapter 29

FINDING THE DOOR to Galactic Books locked, Sheriff Amory knocked loudly. Carl Davis opened the door and gestured for the officers to come inside. Once they were in, he relocked the door.

The sheriff looked around, assessing the situation. Although the bookstore's front was less exposed than some buildings, such as the laundromat, it still had a very large window. He looked out through the glass, leaning his head against his cupped hands to get a better view of the darkened street. Most of the zombies seemed to be gone.

Franklin Davis had opened the hatch of his tank. Amory squinted to see him better. In the glow of a streetlight, the sheriff watched Franklin fiddle with something in his hands. Amory squinted again. *A grenade.* "Oh no! Not the post office!" the sheriff shouted.

Amory scrambled to unlock Galactic Books. He pushed the door open and stumbled onto the sidewalk in time to feel the heat of the explosion as the Biddleborn Post Office flew apart, throwing mail, debris, and zombie parts all over Main Street. Franklin climbed back inside his tank and drove through the chaos. This was the single greatest night of his life.

The sheriff sighed and went back inside the bookstore. "I think most of the zombies are gone," he announced.

"There are worse things than zombies out there. Far worse," Carl told the sheriff while relocking the door. "If you want to help, how about you grab a book and read? Unless you happen to know how to do magic."

"Is that a skeleton?" the sheriff asked.

Calvin looked at the sheriff and waved. "We're doing magic back here, if you don't mind," he said.

The skeleton, Carl Davis's stepdaughter, Chad Davenport, Ross Jacoby—of all people—and a couple of strangers the sheriff didn't recognize were gathered around a table, playing with colored lights they seemed to be pulling from the air. "Of course you are," the sheriff replied to Calvin.

Amory motioned Sonny and Chip into a huddle. "I have no idea what's going on," he told them, "but we just fought zombies, the street is full of ghosts, and, at this point, I'm willing to believe just about anything, including the fact that there's a skeleton doing magic with a group of teenagers and what looks to be the world's oldest woman. Oh, and if anyone asks what happened to the Post Office, I didn't see anything."

"Me neither," Sonny said. Chip nodded.

"Okay. Good." The sheriff looked around. Elijah and his family were reading. And Carl was watching the street. He waved at someone—probably his crazy, tank-driving brother, the sheriff figured. "Reading a book sounds like a great idea," he told Sonny and Chip in response to Carl's suggestion. "You guys like to read?"

"Sure," Sonny said. Chip shrugged.

"I'm not much of a science fiction fan," the sheriff said, "but I'm sure I can find something. So long as it's not a zombie novel."

The officers spread out, scouting the shelves for something to read. The sheriff grabbed a copy of *Ender's Game* and positioned himself near the window. Something moved on the other side of the glass. He looked closer. One big eye glinted at him in the darkness. The light from the window reflected on a mouth full of oversized teeth. Amory's monster looked up at him.

I should kill it, the sheriff thought. *No, it saved my life. But . . . look at those teeth. It's dangerous!* The thing curled up against the building. *Gosh, golly, darn.*

The sheriff put his book aside, unlocked the door, and stepped onto the sidewalk. The monster perked up and shuffled over to him. It sat at his feet, then leaned its head against his leg. "Well, I guess you'd better come inside," the sheriff told it. "Just don't do anything to make me have to shoot you."

The monster followed the sheriff into Galactic Books. As the sheriff repositioned himself with his book near the window, magic coursed through the bookstore. The walls glowed a faint pink. The whole building sighed. Books fluttered. Action figures stood at attention.

The bookstore was wide awake, its belly full of magic.

* * *

Traveling with a dragon proved to be a bit awkward, especially at night. Mike sat in the back of his truck with Mowey while Zelda drove. He tried to keep an eye on Sir Walter, who was flying behind them, but it was hard to see the dragon in the darkness. All Mike could do was trust that the dragon was keeping up with them.

Biddleborn was quiet until they reached Main Street. There, a ring of ghosts stood watching as the post office burned. "Looks like the mail's going to be late," Zelda pointed out.

"I hope my May issue of *Cosmopolitan* wasn't in there," Rose Marie said.

They pulled up in front of Galactic Books and got out of the truck. Sir Walter landed beside them and helped Mike get Mowey out of the truck's bed.

"Dude. Those are zombies," Mike said, pointing to a pile of bodies. One zombie, still ambulatory, was loitering near Wishy-Washy. It spotted them and started shuffling over.

Sir Walter looked at the zombie. The zombie stopped shuffling and looked at the dragon. Its face twitched. With great jerking motions, it turned itself around and walked back to the laundromat, where it parked itself in front of the window. It stared at its reflection, contemplating life and choices and its place in the universe. “Braaaaiiiins,” it moaned.

Sheriff Amory pushed open the door of Galactic Books. “Is that dragon with *you*?” he asked Zelda.

“Yes. Sheriff Amory, this is Sir Walter. Sir Walter, this is Sheriff John Amory.”

“Ah, a lawman. Very nice to meet you,” Sir Walter said.

“Good to meet you. And I see you brought your lawnmower. Very good.” Sheriff Amory would never be a skeptic again. He sighed. “Why don’t you all come in here? It’s safer.”

Everyone looked at Sir Walter, then glanced at the doorway. “Dude,” Mike said.

“I’ll fit,” the dragon asserted.

With one more glance at the dragon and door, the group shrugged. The humans led the way. And Mike pushed Mowey inside. When it was Sir Walter’s turn, Galactic Books stretched to accommodate him. The sheriff locked the door behind them.

“Sir Walter! You look fresh as a liver toad’s sunglasses!” Mayzell said. She got up from her seat and hugged the dragon.

“You look just as lovely as ever,” Sir Walter replied. It was a true statement.

Calvin shook hands with the dragon. “I’m glad you made it.” Then, Calvin looked at the newcomers. “The Cat Lord isn’t with you?”

“He seems to have run off on a side quest,” Sir Walter explained. “I have no doubt that he’ll eventually show up, probably at the last minute. It’s how he operates.”

“That’s my fault, I guess,” Meridian admitted. She came and stood before Sir Walter, looking up at him. “Hi, Sir Walter. I’m Meridian. It’s nice to see you in real life.”

“Ah. Yes. I know who you are. Someday, when the forces of evil are not crashing at our door, perhaps we’ll share a pot of tea and have a profound conversation about life and the imagination.”

“I’d like that.”

Sir Walter spotted the Salt Boy and frowned. "Why is *he* here?" he whispered to Meridian. Unfortunately, even at a whisper, a dragon's voice tends to boom.

"I'm here because she invited me," the Salt Boy said with a biting tone. "The same reason we're all here."

"That's not why *I'm* here," Ross Jacoby said. Everyone looked at him. He shifted uncomfortably. "Well, it's the truth anyhow," he muttered.

"This is a magical place," Sir Walter said, gesturing to the room around him. "And so many books."

"My daddy owns this bookstore," Isaac informed him proudly.

Elijah beamed, agape at the dragon as if Sir Walter were a rockstar. "Hello, Sir Walter. I'm Elijah Schmidt. Welcome to Galactic Books and Other Stuff. Please make yourself at home."

"Hello, Sir Elijah. Always good to meet another book enthusiast."

"So, what happens now?" Carl asked.

Sirens outside announced the Biddleborn Fire Department's arrival on Main Street. "Dadgummit," the sheriff said. "Sonny, you stay here. Chip, come with me. We gotta keep these guys safe while they work. You got any ammunition left, Chip?"

"No, sir."

"Franklin can probably hook you up with some," Carl suggested. "Nine-mil, right? I'll text him."

The sheriff sighed. "That would be swell."

"I can help, too," Mowey said. "Not with ammunition. But I'm real handy in a fight."

The sheriff looked at the lawnmower. "Oh, why not? Sure, come along."

"I'm coming with Mowey," Mike Gershwin said.

The sheriff's monster jumped up and down. "Oh, look!" Zelda cried. "A baby Bandersnatch!"

"Yeah. Apparently, they grow from teeth," Amory replied.

"I know! I found a tooth and accidentally grew a Bandersnatch. Robert Gray has it."

"Turns out, they're very loyal." With that, the sheriff went out into the night, followed by Chip, Mowey, Mike, and the baby Bandersnatch.

* * *

Robert Gray stepped outside the Biddleborn High School gymnasium. A group of smokers looked at him in alarm, certain they were about to be reprimanded. But Mr. Gray had more important matters to attend to.

"Pspspspsps," Mr. Gray said. Then, he waited. The smokers shifted, uneasy. One of them coughed because cancer always starts years before it's diagnosable. "Smoking is stupid, kids," Mr. Gray told them.

Finally, a gray cat slunk around the corner and approached Mr. Gray. It rubbed against his legs, claiming him as its Cat Lord. To the world, the title "Lord" implies authority. But Robert Gray knew the truth: it was the other way around—he was a servant to his cats. And this one would need canned food later.

"Follow this girl," Mr. Gray said while sending a mental image of Norma Bellows to the cat. "Rub tracer dust on her." He pulled a small bottle from his coat, put some tracer on his hand, and stroked the cat, coating his fur in a fine powder. The dust was made from the dried petals of the Nosy Daisy—a particularly voyeuristic flower that grew only in Detritus. It was a favorite among the nosier neighbors. Mayzell had a garden full of them.

"Now, go," Mr. Gray instructed the cat. "I'll have some tuna for you when you're finished."

The cat sauntered off. And the Cat Lord returned to his classroom. He had a section of Advanced Placement Biology to teach. Today, they were dissecting roaches that he found in the cafeteria. Might as well use the resources you have.

* * *

Old Randolph the Wise but Ungrateful grumbled as he prepared his potion. "None of you appreciated my work last time. I don't see why I should bother trying to help you again."

"I'm sorry the Cat Lord was such a . . ." Artie paused and glanced at his mother. "Bad person. But he isn't here, and we really need your help."

Belinda smiled at the wizard. It was her prettiest smile. Old Randolph's frown melted a little. "Well, all I'm saying is, a little gratitude would be nice," he continued.

"Yes, gratitude is a very nice thing," Belinda agreed.

"And we are very grateful for your service," Lanora added.

"Humph," Old Randolph said, but his frown was nearly gone. He threw a handful of nettles into his cauldron, then squinted at his recipe card. It was an old, handwritten, lined, three-by-five card that had a green smudge on one corner.

"I don't understand how this is going to work," Belinda said. "I mean, I trust you. But it doesn't make sense to me that a potion would help forge a link between Lanora and Meridian, especially since Meridian isn't here to drink it. It feels like we're using chemistry when what we need is physics."

Lanora raised her eyebrows, which Artie thought was really attractive—almost sexy. But his mom was standing near him, so he worked hard to keep his brain in G-rated mode. "What's physics?" Lanora asked.

"You know, like gravity and light and energy," Artie explained. "And movement and matter. That sort of thing." Lanora blinked at him, which he *definitely* found sexy.

"Anyway, Mom," Artie continued, "you're thinking about it wrong. The way magic works here is it's basically about faith and imagination. Like, think about it from the perspective of a child. Meridian was young when she made all this up. And, from what I understand from being inside the Cat Lord's head—a scary place, by the way—what she makes up has gotten more sophisticated, but not a lot. Not a lot because Meridian isn't really concerned about the details of how the magic works. It just does. It's colorful and comes out of the air, but really, using magic is about pretending you know *how* to use magic. To be a great wizard, you just need a lot of imagination. Essentially, we're all just characters in a story."

"So, we just need to believe in this potion?" Belinda asked.

"Yes," Artie confirmed.

Belinda looked skeptical, then realized what her face was saying. She struggled to remove all traces of skepticism from her expression. Artie gave his mom two thumbs up. The potion bubbled in the cauldron. It was brown and slightly chunky. "Is Lanora going to have to drink that?" Belinda asked.

"Yes, ma'am," said the old wizard.

Lanora looked slightly pale, but she pretended to be very brave about it. Artie smiled at her reassuringly.

The wizard dipped a ladle in the potion and scooped up fluid, careful to avoid the chunks, for which Lanora truly was grateful. He poured the liquid into a mug and handed it to the princess. She closed her eyes and drank it. She wrinkled her nose, and Artie's heart melted.

"Oh, gross!" Lanora exclaimed. "What *was* that?" Her eyes widened. "Artie? Mrs. McClintock?"

"Meridian?" Artie asked, fully aware that his best friend was now inside the body of the girl he thought maybe he loved. *Life is about to get awkward*, he realized.

Meridian looked around, eyes wide. "I'm really here," she whispered.

"Well, kind of," Artie replied. "Your soul is here, in Lanora's body. Kinda like the Cat Lord is sometimes here in mine, but not really. We made a connection between you two. A stronger one."

Meridian looked at Artie through Lanora's eyes. She raised an eyebrow, and Artie blushed. "Well, I'm glad to see that you're okay, Mr.

Jedi-Wizard. So, what happens next?"

"We're going to use the connection to go home," Artie explained.

"Okay."

"Like it's a highway or something."

"It's more like an internet connection."

"Whatever, Lanora. Er . . . Meridian."

Old Randolph cleared his throat. Lanora, who felt crowded sharing her mind with Meridian, pulled out her purse and handed him a gold coin. "Thank you for your service, good sir," she said. The wizard looked at the group expectantly.

"So, I guess we'll go now," Artie said. "We can finish this at the Cat Lord's cottage. I assume Meridian would like to see it anyway."

"I would very much like to see it. I wish we had time to go to the Roanoke Market."

"We could make time."

"Carl and Cheese Fry and a whole bunch of other people are in danger. There are zombies and ghosts and a tank on Main Street. And the Shadow King tried to strangle me. I don't think we have time for a market."

"Remember when Ms. Gershwin said you always use present tense when writing about books because they always exist in the now? Like that one chick in *The Crucible* is always sticking a pin in her belly any time you turn to that page? Maybe Detritus works like that."

Meridian thought about it. She could remember how the Shadow King's claws felt on her skin, crushing the life out of her. She wasn't in a hurry to go back. Besides, she could still see what was happening there. She was, strangely, present in both places. "That still seems like it would be irresponsible," she felt. "But we're really just sitting around waiting for the Cat Lord."

"He went back in time to track Norma Bellows," Artie informed Meridian.

Meridian blinked a couple of times while she processed that sentence. “Why?” she finally asked.

“That new girl, Bird, is evil. She’s the one opening and closing all the doors. She has a key, and the key is . . . or was . . . Norma Bellows. Like, the new girl literally turned her into a key.”

“Ha! I knew there was something off about that girl.”

“Of course, we have a key, too,” Belinda said, holding up the key Lanora had given her for safekeeping.

“Right. Hang on to it,” Artie told his mother. “I think you may need it later.”

“I think a trip to the Roanoke Market sounds like a lovely idea,” Lanora interjected, smiling shyly at Artie.

“*You like him*,” Meridian’s words echoed in Lanora’s head.

“*And you don’t?*”

“*Not like that.*”

“*He’s very good and very, very brave. I think you just haven’t looked at him the right way.*”

“Okay. Let’s go to the market,” Meridian finally agreed. “But if the forces of darkness suddenly attack Galactic Books, we’ll have to leave immediately.”

* * *

The forces of darkness were, in fact, in the process of gathering around Galactic Books. The Shadow King stood at the intersection of worlds, a place that exists outside of space and time. The place was a drain where the dregs of each world—the twisted, the forgotten, the lost, the irredeemably violent or insane, and others—sometimes slipped through into nowhere.

The drain was a place known only to monsters and the damned. And the Shadow King now called to them. He invited them to join his army.

He promised them power.

He promised them food.

He promised them a really good time.
They believed his promises and came to his call.

Chapter 30

THE CAT LAY in the sunshine outside Biddleborn High School, waiting. Cats are good at waiting, but only while on the hunt. If it's dinner time, then cats don't wait if they can help it. But this cat was hunting.

The cat's prey was inside the building, sitting at a table with a girl who smelled like death and darkness. The cat was afraid of the other girl. She didn't seem to be a human at all.

Suddenly, there was a noise like a thousand jingle balls rolling, and the humans got up and left the rooms they were in. The noise happened all over the building, all at once. The cat wondered if the humans had heard the jingle balls and were running to play with them.

The cat slipped in through an open window and followed the girl—not the one who smelled like death and darkness but the other one. The one who smelled of loneliness with a faint undertone of peanut butter. The cat hated peanut butter.

The girl turned down a hallway that had far fewer bodies pressing through it. The cat was grateful. The girl stopped and looked around. Cats recognize sneakiness, and that's clearly what she was up to.

The cat rubbed up against the girl. "Ew. Get away from me!" she scolded it.

The cat saw the foot coming in time to duck. He ran. But his mission of planting the tracer dust was accomplished. Now to find the Cat Lord and demand to be fed.

* * *

Lanora didn't need a map to lead the others to the Roanoke Market. The market consisted of a collection of brightly-colored tents joined by dusty paths worn by Detritusian shoppers going from stall to stall. It reminded Artie of the Renaissance Fair he and Meridian had once attended in Darmstadt.

"Here's Surjay, one of my favorite merchants," Lanora announced while entering a blue and purple tent.

The merchant inside the tent was the most frightening man Artie had ever seen. He was exceptionally tall, very, very thin, and strangely lumpy. His teeth were yellow when he smiled, and his eyes were ringed with purple. His skin was a mottled gray.

"Come in, dear Princess!" the merchant called out. "Bring your friends! I have many wonderful new things that I'm sure will make your heart go pitter-pat!"

The tent was, indeed, full of many things, although Artie wasn't sure all of them were wonderful. There were items he recognized, some of which he suspected came from his world: lamps, a vacuum cleaner, a Coca-Cola tray, and a set of dishes like the ones his grandma used to collect. Then, there were items he suspected would have a *Made in Detritus* stamp on them somewhere: swords with jeweled handles, knives that glowed, leather bags, earthenware pots, and bottles and jars of herbs and slimy-looking things Artie didn't want to contemplate too deeply.

"*It's just as I imagined it,*" Meridian said inside Lanora's head. "*I can't believe I'm really here.*"

"*Is there anything you'd like to purchase?*" Lanora asked. "*I could send it with Artie.*"

"*A knife. A knife would be useful.*"

Lanora started looking through the knives.

The creepy merchant smiled an oily smile at Artie. "Would the young man like a sword? We have the sharpest in town. Perhaps a sentient sword? One with battle experience?" He held out a sword for Artie to examine.

Artie reached out and took the sword. "You will not find a finer sword in all of Detritus," the sword said to him.

Artie turned the sword over and tested the blade. He handed the sword back to the merchant. "I suspect this guy would rather belong to a swordsman. I'm a Jedi-Wizard, so, you know, I prefer a lightsaber." Artie hurried away to stand near Lanora and his mother.

Lanora was inspecting knives while Artie's mother looked at a jewelry display. "Be careful buying anything sentient," Lanora said softly. "Sometimes, they're fake—their souls, I mean. It's hard to tell until later, when it's trying to kill you."

"How do you fake a soul?" Belinda asked.

"The fake ones have been shadow-touched. They have, at one time or another, served as a vessel for a shadow wight. They never quite lose the memory," Lanora explained. "How about this one?" she asked, holding up a knife.

"It's nice," Artie said.

"Oh, sorry. I was talking to Meridian." Lanora tilted her head, clearly having an internal conversation with Artie's best friend.

It was still weird to Artie how much Lanora looked like Meridian but also how different she was. Was it possible he had just never really looked at his friend? Were Meridian's fingers as long and delicate? Artie tried to picture them and couldn't.

"I'll take this one, Surjay," Lanora said to the merchant. She was holding a knife that was made of a metal that was almost white. The blade was six inches long and looked very sharp. The handle was the same pale color as the blade.

"Oh, my princess will be most pleased with this one!" the merchant asserted. "The blade is magic-infused—perfect for either ordinary use or the killing of monsters. This knife once belonged to Sir Monty the

Slayer of Evil. With it, he killed many vampires!" The merchant smiled.

"One never knows when she might be assaulted by vampires. I'll take it. And this necklace, too." Lanora pointed to the bronze cameo Belinda was admiring.

"Oh, you don't have to—"

"I want to, Belinda. Please."

Surjay smiled. "Perhaps the young wizard needs a new hat?"

* * *

Something heavy thumped on the roof. The people and dragon congregated inside Galactic Books looked up. They could hear something scuttling across the roof—something that sounded too big to be a squirrel or a raccoon.

"Did we relock the door?" Cheese Fry asked Ross.

"Nope."

Something was coming down the stairs. "It's moving too fast to be a zombie," Elijah said.

Carl checked his clip. "Whatever it is, I'm ready for it."

"Make sure it isn't human before you shoot," Carolyn reminded him.

"Make sure it's not a friendly monster, either," Zelda said.

"And make sure it's not a cartoon bear," Ross said. Everyone looked at him. He shifted uncomfortably.

Calvin drew his sword. He and Carl stood on either side of the door marked *Employees Only*. "Please do let me know if you need me," Sir Walter said. He was browsing the shelves.

The door opened, and a man stepped into the store. He was old and neatly dressed in a dark blue suit. His white hair was cut close to his head. And he wore glasses.

Calvin lowered his sword, and Carl lowered his gun, but neither man put his weapon away. "Who are you, and what do you want?" Carl asked, a little rudely.

The man smiled. His teeth looked very sharp. And there was something off about his eyes.

"Vampire!" Meridian yelled.

Calvin raised his sword as the vampire threw himself at Carl. The gun went off, the bullet ripping through a vintage copy of *Alice in Wonderland*. Meridian jumped over the counter and ran at the vampire. She had a knife made of light, and she stabbed it into the creature's back. The vampire fell. He exploded into dust before hitting the floor.

"Dadgum consorn rock salt filly," Carl said.

"Language!" cried Mayzell.

"Did he bite you?" Meridian asked.

"No, but he drooled on me." Carl shuddered. His shirt was soaked.

"Where'd you get that knife?" Calvin asked.

"I bought it."

"In Roanoke?"

Meridian smiled. "Isn't it lovely?" The light had faded, revealing the blade to be a pale metal of some kind not found on earth.

"Magic-infused?"

"Indeed."

There was another thump on the roof.

"We need to lock that door," Carl said.

"I'll go," Sir Walter volunteered.

"I'm not sure you'll fit in the stairwell," Elijah warned him.

"Oh, posh. I'll fit if I want to."

"Do you need backup?" Carl asked.

"Of course not." The dragon squeezed through the Employees Only door and disappeared into the back of the store.

There were more thumps. "Look!" Isaac and Orson yelled. They pointed at the window. Shapes were pressed against the glass.

"What in tar—" Carl began.

"Those aren't zombies," Ross pointed out.

"Those are blood moles," the Salt Boy said. "We're all going to die."

* * *

The Cat Lord followed the tracer dust to the school library. Norma Bellows's body lay on the floor. Her soul was gone, having been turned into a key.

The Cat Lord could have followed Norma there an hour earlier, before she was dead and her soul had been turned. But it was the soul-turned-key that he was after. Besides, he was trying very hard not to create a time paradox.

The Cat Lord pulled a pair of gloves from the inside pocket of his feathered cloak. The last thing he wanted to do was leave fingerprints for the sheriff to find. "Hello, Norma," he greeted her soulless body. "Let's get you out of here. We need to have a chat."

The Cat Lord picked up the girl's body. Now, it was time to join the others at Galactic Books.

* * *

Sir Walter squeezed back through the door into the bookstore proper. "The door has been relocked," he announced.

"Cool," Ross said. "I was afraid maybe I broke the lock."

"Oh. You may have. But I don't trust flimsy human-made locks anyway. So, I used magic. Works much better. Hooligans of all kinds can pick locks, but they can't very well pick magic."

Calvin smirked. *He* could pick magic.

"I have a magic butter knife," Ross said. "Betcha it could pick magic."

Sonny Rogers raised an eyebrow and made a mental note.

"This place is under attack," Carl said. "Anybody got a plan?" His cell phone dinged, announcing a text. It was from Franklin.

Franklin: *Hey, u got monsters outside.*

Carl: *Seen em.*

Sir Walter cleaned his glasses as he said, "I hate fighting monsters. They have no finesse. But I suppose we must. You'll need better weapons, however." He looked at Carl's gun.

Carl saw the look and said, "This'll put holes in any monster."

"Not *any* monster. But some monsters, certainly. Meridian, dear, how did you come by your blade?" Sir Walter asked.

Meridian blushed. "I got it from the Roanoke Market."

Carl looked at her. "When did you do that?"

"Earlier. After the Shadow King tried to choke me but before the vampire came down the stairs."

"While you was sitting there?"

"Yes. Through Lanora. She's a princess in Detritus. Artie's with her, and they forged a connection between us—between Lanora and me. So, I'm sort of . . . in two places at once."

"That's wonderful," said the dragon. "Are you still in the market?"

Meridian nodded. "Artie's trying on hats."

"Good. I have a shopping list for you. In the meantime, Mr. Cheese Fry, will you gather your frogs? I need to speak with them. We're going to need them to lead the attack."

Cheese Fry frowned. "That sounds dangerous."

"Life is dangerous."

"And we got a dadgum poop mill of monsters outside," Carl pointed out.

"Yeah, okay. The frogs can lead the attack," Cheese Fry agreed.

The frogs were scattered all across the bookstore: clinging to shelves, hopping across the floor, looking for bugs. Now, sensing their leader wanted them, they gathered around Cheese Fry. Plop plop plop plop plop.

"Very good," the dragon said. "Now, listen closely." And Sir Walter shared his plan.

Chapter 31

OUTSIDE ON MAIN STREET, monsters came from nowhere. They suddenly just were, and their focus seemed to be on the bookstore. They crawled along the sidewalk in front, scaled the walls, and jumped onto the roof. They covered Galactic Books like flies on dog poop.

"That ain't good," Chip said.

"No. No, that can't be good," Sheriff Amory agreed. "Hey, Franklin! We might need your assistance, but don't forget there are people in that building. Including your brother."

Franklin Davis, who had climbed down from his tank to help the officers reload their weapons, sized up the situation. "This is the weirdest apocalypse I've ever seen."

"I think you need more lawnmowers," Mowey suggested.

Franklin blinked at him. "Did that lawnmower just talk?"

As tempted as Amory was to say no, this wasn't the time for it. "He did," the sheriff confirmed. "This is Mowey."

"Hi," Mowey said.

"Well, if that don't beat all," Franklin said.

"What's your plan?" the sheriff asked Mowey.

"Well, I was just thinking that lawnmowers are harder to kill than people. And we have wicked sharp blades, mostly. So, we could probably kill a lot of monsters. If you wanted us to?"

"What about weed eaters?" Franklin asked. "Can they get in on the action?" His face was serious.

"Weed eaters would just annoy the monsters—get 'em mad, like swinging at a bee," Mike said.

"Chainsaws?" Chip asked.

"Sure," Mowey replied. "Any kind of saw. They like a good fight."

"Maybe a wood chipper, too," Mike suggested.

"Do they need to be special lawnmowers and things, Mowey?" the sheriff asked. "Like you? Or can they be just ordinary, non-talking lawnmowers?"

"There's probably enough magic inside to give them souls," Mowey replied. "That boy with the hurt leg, he seems to have a lot of magic."

"Ross Jacoby? Oh, geez." The sheriff rolled his eyes.

"Well, what do you think?" Franklin asked.

"Sure," Amory agreed reluctantly. "What do we have to lose? Only, we don't have a lot of time, so we might want to . . . commandeer some equipment . . . from Bucky's Hardware & Garden Center."

"All right!" Franklin said, with a little more enthusiasm than the sheriff thought strictly necessary.

"Chip, you and Franklin gather the lawnmowers and whatever else you find that has a good, sharp blade. Mowey and I are going to fight our way through to Ross Jacoby."

"Can't Ross just do it over the phone?" Franklin asked.

The sheriff thought about it. "Maybe?"

"I think so," Mowey said.

Franklin called his brother. "Hey, Carl. Sheriff needs to talk to that drug dealer kid."

* * *

The Cat Lord reached out to Artie. "*You drive cars, right?*"

"*I don't have a car, thanks for asking. But I sometimes use my mom's.*"

"I have never driven a car, but I find it necessary to do so. Your assistance would be greatly appreciated."

"Is that a dead body you're carrying?"

"Yes. That's why I need a car."

"I'll take this one and maybe that blue hat."

"What?"

"Sorry. I was talking to Surjay."

"You're at the Roanoke Market?"

"Don't worry. We're helping the fight. Lanora's buying a bunch of weapons for the people at Galactic Books, which is being attacked by monsters, incidentally. The people there are all wondering where you are."

"I'm on my way. This girl is the key. Well, not the key per se, but she's the key to the key."

"So, whose car are you going to drive?"

"Oh, I think this one here will do."

Artie could see through the Cat Lord's eyes. The Biddleborn High School science teacher had been jiggling door handles along Cherry Street, near the high school. He had finally found an unlocked door. It was attached to a lavender Chevy Spark.

"Why don't you just use a map and walk?" Artie suggested. *"She can't be that heavy."*

"Shut up and help me drive."

The Cat Lord attempted to lay Norma in the tiny back seat, but rigor mortis made it difficult to fold her legs so she'd fit. *"Okay, scratch that. I need a truck."*

"Lanora was able to send Meridian a knife. Can I send you a . . . horse?"

"Artie, you're brilliant. Bonus points on your next assignment. Send me a Pegasus."

"Do they sell those in Roanoke?"

"They sell everything at the Roanoke Market."

* * *

The frogs had their assignment. Only one assignment because frogs are very single-minded.

The people inside Galactic Books only needed the door opened a little. But the hulking creature that was currently shaking the door made opening it at all seem a bad idea. In fact, the people inside Galactic Books weren't certain it was going to hold.

Zelda had her laptop open. Rose Marie read over her shoulder as she typed: *The door to Galactic Books was made of steel and warded with an ancient magic. The creature outside, whose arms were now very weak and tired, couldn't budge the door. He got tired and wandered away, in search of . . .*

Zelda paused. She didn't want to terrorize the people of Biddleborn. She hoped they were sleeping through all of this—somehow. *Ice cream*, she wrote. No, that would take the creature to a store or someone's freezer. She deleted it. *A flower.*

Sir Walter walked among the frogs carefully. "Are we ready? Mr. Cheese Fry, are you ready?"

"Yessir. Ross?"

Ross was stationed at the window. He had Carl's cell phone and was in communication with Sheriff Amory. Sonny Rogers stood near him. "Ready," Ross said.

Sir Walter pushed open the door of Galactic Books and stepped outside. He unfurled his wings and breathed fire at the monsters crowded near the front of the store. The frogs hopped out, using the dragon as cover. Plop plop plop plop plop.

A blood mole threw itself at the dragon while another scrambled toward the open door. The battle had begun. Carl pulled the door shut, and Elijah locked it.

Zelda typed: *Magic sealed the door—magic no blood mole could stand to touch.*

Outside, the frogs attacked. Inside, Ross Jacoby said to Sonny Rogers, "You see, the frogs have piranha teeth. They can eat a monster down to the bones in a matter of minutes."

"Is that so?"

Cheese Fry stood just outside the doorway, more terrified than he had ever been in his life. He held a sword that had been forged in another world. He took a step forward. A blood mole jumped at him, but his frogs were faster. Their one assignment: protect the king. Like piranhas, the frogs ate the monster down to the bones.

"This is going to be an epic story," a voice said. It came from the ghost of Jazz Miller, standing next to Cheese Fry.

* * *

Mayzell was knitting as those who could wove their magic. The Salt Boy was pulling light and salt out of his hat. Calvin had rolled magic into a ball, and Mayzell used it as yarn.

"Open the door!" screamed a voice outside.

"That sounds like Robert!" Zelda said.

"It is Robert," Carl said. He unlocked the door, and the Cat Lord fumbled to open it. Elijah pushed it open for him.

The Cat Lord carried a dead girl into Galactic Books. Carl relocked the door as a blood mole and two vampires rushed at him. Through the glass, he could see a dozen frogs eating something that looked like it had a giant squid attached to its face. One of the vampires pressed its face against the glass. He and Carl stared at each other.

"Mr. Davis, I'm pretty sure you're not supposed to look into their eyes," Sonny said. Elijah shoved Carl away from the door. And the Cat Lord placed the girl on the counter. She was a little bit stiff.

Carolyn gathered her children and pulled them into the break room. "We're going to go read."

"That's Norma Bellows," Meridian realized.

"She's going to help us," the Cat Lord said. "But first, we need to put her in a dungeon for a thousand years."

"I don't think we can wait a thousand years," Meridian said.

"She's dead!" Zelda said. "What happened?"

"That's a long story," the Cat Lord replied. "But the short version is that she trusted the wrong person. I think she's the one responsible for all of this. The darkness used her."

"And why do we need to put her in a dungeon?'

"So she can rot and grow wise."

"Like me!" Calvin said.

"Precisely. Norma's ghost has been turned into a key, and we can't get her to help us in that form. What we need is an approximation of Norma. We need a Norma skeleton or something very much like that. Do you know how Calvin became Calvin?"

"By sitting in a dungeon for a thousand years?" Zelda suggested.

"Yes, but more accurately, he became Calvin in a matter of moments when a certain girl mourned the death of her friend and invented a skeleton to stand in for him, as it were."

"Oh. Yeah, I guess that happened," Meridian remembered. "I mean, technically, Calvin was already part of the story. He just . . . took on some new personality traits."

"Right. So, we need you to reach deep inside and find some part of you that is sad about Norma's death."

"Could I reach inside and be sad about her life instead? Maybe sad about how we stopped being friends?"

"Sure. That'll work."

* * *

Outside, the night sky tore, leaking dark on dark. Inky blackness spilled from one world to the next. As Mowey prepared the lawnmowers for battle and as the firefighters put out the blaze that ate Biddleborn's post office, a cloud of evil descended. Hundreds of shadow wights joined the fray.

* * *

Meridian failed to turn Norma into a proper skeleton. It had been a rough night. She was tired.

Meridian honestly didn't know why she had decided Calvin was going to be a skeleton. It just happened that way. She didn't plan the story out. Detritus just *was* sometimes. It seemed so long ago, but Calvin had only existed in Meridian's imagination for a few days.

Unfortunately, Norma turned out to be more zombie than skeleton. The flesh dried and clung. It was not what Meridian had intended.

"I am so, so, so sorry," Meridian said to the thing that was Norma Bellows. Or maybe Norma was now the thing. Meridian's head hurt.

"You're the one who's going to have to look at me," Norma replied.

"I think you look lovely," Calvin said.

"Okay," the Cat Lord interrupted, "enough banter. Are you three ready? You know what to do?"

Meridian repeated the instructions he had given them: "Close the doors that are circled in green. Open the doors marked with a red X."

Norma had recreated Bird's map. Meridian, Calvin, and Norma were going to retrace the steps she had taken with Bird earlier in the evening.

"I don't like this," Carl said. "Why can't I go with them?"

"Because there's no room for you on the Pegasus," the Cat Lord informed him. "I named him Spencer, by the way. Be good to him, Meridian."

Meridian had her knife and a sword that Lanora had purchased at the Roanoke Market. She wore chain mail over her T-shirt. Norma had a sword and battle-ax. And Calvin had his sword and a series of knives.

"Hey. Take this with you," Ross said. He handed Meridian his butter knife. "Remember that time I threw dirt on you? I'm really sorry. Turns out, you're pretty cool."

"Okay. I mean, thanks."

Ross smiled at her.

"Okay. Well, we're going to go . . . save the world or something," Meridian said.

"Be careful," Elijah told her.

"Yep." Meridian sensed that hugs were coming. So, she grabbed her two dead companions and steered them toward the back of the store before the hugs could manifest. Spencer was waiting on the roof.

Meridian, Norma, and Calvin climbed the stairs, with Calvin leading the way. He used his magic-lock-picking skills to remove enough of Sir Walter's magic to open the door.

"I have a butter knife if you need it," Meridian reminded Calvin.

Calvin scowled. He pushed the door open, and the three of them stepped onto the roof.

"Greetings," Sir Walter said. He stood guard over Spencer.

Now that she was about to climb onto a Pegasus, fly through a monster-filled night, and help two very decayed corpses open and close portals to other worlds, Meridian was nervous. Spencer nudged her shoulder. She stroked his neck. "Hey, fella."

Meridian, Norma, and Calvin climbed onto Spencer's back, which only worked because two of them were excessively thin. "Imagine you're in a saddle, that you have reins to hold onto, and that you're a very skilled horseman," Sir Walter said. "You'll be fine."

What Meridian imagined instead was that she was on a ride at Universal Studios. She was very securely strapped in, she convinced herself. She couldn't *really* fall to her death—it wasn't possible.

Spencer ran across the roof and leaped into the sky.

Chapter 32

IN ROOM SEVEN of the Paradise Motel, Holmes Peabody was acquiring superpowers. He now had the strength of the Hulk, and he could fly. His arms could turn into blades to slice through any monster.

"And give him some kinda laser eyes," Rose Marie suggested, reading over Zelda's shoulder.

Holmes Peabody's eyes could see evil, Zelda wrote.

"That ain't what I meant, but I guess that's pretty good."

"He can punch through steel," Zelda informed Rose Marie. "He doesn't need lasers."

"Does he have a mustache?"

"No. He's clean-shaven."

"I think he needs a mustache."

"Why?"

"I like men with mustaches."

Zelda sighed. *Holmes Peabody's mustache offered him magical protection.*

"That's more like it," Rose Marie said.

Holmes Peabody awoke. He had to get to Main Street. Biddleborn needed him. He pulled his Glock—

"Give him a machine gun."

He pulled his machine gun out of the closet and loaded it in his car. His laser-powered, magic-infused eyes could see the glow of evil even in the darkness. He sped toward it.

* * *

In his new blue hat, Artie tilted his head and listened to the voice inside his mind. "The Cat Lord is sending us a guide to help us get home," Artie told his mother. "You don't have to come with us if you don't want to," he said to Lanora, hoping she would ignore that suggestion.

To Artie's relief, Lanora replied, "You might need me. Even though you're a powerful Jedi-Wizard, I know Detritus better than you do. You're strong, but this is not your world. And besides, I'm not ready to say goodbye." She blinked at Artie with her big, beautiful eyes.

Belinda stared hard at the ground and bit back a smile. "Oh, hey!" she said. "It's my kitten!"

Pineapple rubbed against Belinda's feet. "Meow. Mrrr," said the kitten. "Did you miss me?"

"*She's your guide*," the Cat Lord informed Artie.

"*Really? We're supposed to follow a kitten?*" Artie sighed, picturing how often they were going to have to stop so she could groom herself or pounce on a leaf. But maybe that was okay. He wasn't in a hurry to leave. He loved Detritus.

Pineapple took off running. "Oh, shoot!" Artie cried.

The three of them—Artie, Belinda, and Lanora—hurried after the cat. Pineapple slowed down. But she kept a steady pace as she led them through the market and into a dense forest of strangely fat trees.

"This can't be the way," Lanora said. "These are the Shadow Woods."

"Tell that to the cat," Artie said.

"I'm too old for this," Belinda said. "And I'm wearing the wrong shoes."

Artie and Lanora looked at the little black flats Belinda was wearing. "We'll soon be home," Artie assured his mother.

"Pretty sure the apocalypse is going on at home."

Artie stopped walking, causing his mother to bump into him. "You're right, Mom. Maybe you should stay here with Lanora. I can come back and get you later."

"Are you out of your ever-loving mind? Let you go face monsters without me?"

"I really am a wizard now."

"You think you're still going to be a wizard when we get home?"

Artie looked at Lanora. "Will I? Do you know?"

"I don't know. That's a question for the Cat Lord, I think."

"I guess it doesn't matter." Artie started walking again. "Only, it's cool to have power. Like, I can actually help people. I can save them. It's like being a superhero."

"Mrrrr!" said Pineapple.

"Okay, okay. We're coming," Artie said.

* * *

The Shadow King stepped out of the night and onto Main Street. His forces were hard at work, crawling over the bookstore and fighting . . . lawnmowers. The Shadow King frowned, then sighed.

Now, it was time to remove the magic warding from the enemies' fortress. He whistled a low, mournful sound. His shadows drew close, lending him their strength. As one powerful beam of darkness, they punched through the front window of Galactic Books. Glass shattered, and shadows poured in.

* * *

Jazz Miller called, and the ghosts assembled. "If these shadows win, we'll have nowhere left to haunt," he told them.

The soldiers lifted ghost weapons. The children picked up ghost rocks. The women shouted a war cry. And the ghost of Clyde J. Anderson tugged at his mustache. "I propose—" he began, but no one cared to hear a speech. The ghosts were ready for violence!

* * *

Monsters and shadows poured into Galactic Books. The Salt Boy attacked the nearest blood mole. He hacked it with a sword, then threw salt on it. Its skin flamed where the salt touched.

Zelda's computer started typing on its own: *And then, everyone inside Galactic Books died terrible, terrifying deaths.* Zelda screamed. Rose Marie grabbed her baseball bat and beat the computer until the screen shattered and the casing cracked open.

Zelda took the bat from Rose Marie and continued beating the computer. Then, she turned the bat on a vampire who was trying to sneak up on her. Rose Marie made a fist and began pounding on the vampire's back. But the vampire had no idea she was even there.

Mayzell pulled Rose Marie out of the way. "Here, Lovely, let me." She stabbed the vampire with a knitting needle. He exploded.

A Bandersnatch had Elijah cornered. He swung his sword furiously, but the monster was fast. It lunged, wrapping itself around him. Elijah could hear its teeth clicking together.

Across the room, the Cat Lord reached into his pocket and pulled out a small, pewter object he had been carrying around for days. He threw it at the Bandersnatch. It was the Han Solo chess piece! Han's blaster was firing as he hit the Bandersnatch and rolled off.

The Bandersnatch screamed and recoiled. Elijah ducked and ran to the back of the store. He needed to get his family out of there.

* * *

Holmes Peabody parked his car on a residential street. He could hear the battle going on inside Galactic Books.

A monster stood in the front yard of a tiny bungalow. He seemed to be admiring the flowers. Holmes's arms transformed into machetes. He sliced the creature in two. Blood spatter rained down on the flowers.

As Holmes flew toward Main Street, a purple pansy opened its eyes.

* * *

A round creature with too many legs ran toward the Cat Lord, its mouth open, revealing blackened teeth. It was uncoordinated, as if it hadn't yet learned how to walk with so many appendages. The legs were mismatched. Most of the legs looked human, but like they were stolen from humans of varying sizes. Two of the legs were insectile. And the creature's head was at waist height.

"Have you ever noticed that monsters are almost always ugly?" the Cat Lord mused aloud as he sliced off one of the monster's legs. "And the heroes tend to be attractive?" He threw magic in the monster's face. The magic clung and spread, turning the creature into a hundred yellow kittens. The kittens scampered off in the direction of Mayzell.

"It's unrealistic, I think," Carl said.

A vampire fell from the ceiling. "But *I'm* attractive," it said.

"That's true," the Cat Lord agreed. "Vampires are often the exception, depending on the storyteller."

The vampire swung its fist. The Cat Lord ducked, but not quite fast enough. The vampire's fist connected with his ear.

"Ow! Of course, our primary storyteller is a seventeen-year-old girl," the Cat Lord continued. He swung his sword at the vampire. It parried and produced a sword of its own from the air.

"Impressive," Carl noted. "Anyway, of course Meridian went with pretty vampires."

"Thank you," the vampire said. His blade collided with the Cat Lord's.

"You probably glitter all over the place when no one's watching," the Cat Lord told the vampire.

"Everyone needs a hobby," the vampire responded.

Three more vampires, as lovely as the first, joined the battle against the Cat Lord.

* * *

The first door that Meridian, Norma, and Calvin reached had blood moles crawling out of it. Calvin slid to the ground as Spencer flew low over the monsters. Calvin decapitated the first mole on his way to the ground.

"I want wings," Norma said to Meridian.

"What?"

"I want you to give me wings. Not stupid little fairy wings, either. "

"More like a Victoria's Secret model?"

"Bigger. I want an impressive wingspan."

"Won't wearing clothes be difficult?"

"That's what string bikinis are for."

Meridian clung to the Pegasus with her eyes closed, imaging zombie Norma with wings. And a bikini top—a red one.

Norma jumped off Spencer's back and spread her own wings. She swung her sword and battle-ax, twirling as she fell. Zombie Norma was more graceful than human Norma had ever been.

"Okay, Spencer. Let's go kill some blood moles," Meridian said.

Spencer flew low, zigzagging through the crowd of monsters while Meridian swung her sword. But she wasn't strong enough to do more than annoy them, really. A blood mole swatted at her, almost knocking her sword from her hand.

"This isn't working," Meridian realized. "I'm just . . . I'm not Lanora." When she imagined battles, she imagined swords slicing through bodies, which was maybe unrealistic. She had created Lanora to be strong—stronger than any seventeen-year-old girl in the real world. But that's all Meridian was. She was a normal teenager. And not even an athletic one.

Spencer neighed and huffed.

"Darn right, Spencer. I can't fight, but I can imagine."

Meridian closed her eyes and pictured the battle. She imagined Norma weaving like a dancer—a winged, superhero dancer—through the monsters, blood spouting as she cut off heads and sliced through bellies. Calvin jumped and spun, running up one monster's back to leap upon another.

And then, because characters sometimes do what they want without waiting for the storyteller's say so, a blood mole wandered away from the group. He sat on the ground and looked up at the girl on the flying horse.

Blood moles, like regular, yard-destroying moles, don't see that well. This blood mole saw white and wings and a girl. He wasn't smart—his mind clicked along slowly, like a clock with dying batteries—but he knew an angel when he saw one.

"What are you looking at?" the angel said.

"Oof oof oooooh," the blood mole said.

The angel landed. She made a soft sound, like a horse's whinny.

"Oooooffffff," the blood mole purred.

"Go kill your brothers."

"Ooop?"

"Yes. Oop. Go oop. Kill them all."

The blood mole, taking Meridian's orders, pushed himself to his feet. He wandered back to the group and started gnawing on another blood mole's head. The other moles saw what he was doing and followed his example because blood moles have a herd mentality. They began to eat each other.

"Time to lock the door?" Calvin asked.

By way of answering, Meridian nudged Spencer toward the door that was really just a swirling blackness hovering in the night. She pulled out the butter knife Ross Jacoby had given her. Like a child pretending to lock a door, Meridian held the knife in front of her and gave it a turn. The swirling blackness disappeared with a slam and a bang.

"Okay. On to the next one," Meridian said.

* * *

Elijah and his family were surrounded by monsters. Most of them were big and slimy, a few were hairy, and one seemed to have feathers. There were some smaller monsters thrown into the mix as well, like muppets with teeth.

Madeleine was crying. Orson was trying hard not to. And Isaac was being quiet in a way that suggested years of therapy in his future. Carolyn pushed her children behind her. She and Elijah stood shoulder to shoulder between the monsters and their offspring.

The puppy, Sasha, wiggled free from Isaac's arms. She hit the floor and started growing. She ran at the nearest monster, still growing as she ran. Her teeth were huge, and her mouth stretched. She looked like a shark was stuck to her face.

Sasha roared and attacked. The monster, a hairy giant, shrank back a bit, then lunged. The dog jumped at his throat and latched on. Sasha shook the monster like a toy.

A slimy, toad-shaped monster wrapped its tongue around Elijah.

Chapter 33

BIRD TOUCHED DOWN on the roof of Bucky's Hardware & Garden Center, across the street and down from Galactic Books. Folding her wings, she laughed at seeing the post office in flames as firemen turned their hoses on monsters instead of the fire. The Shadow King had done well.

There was chaos below. A police officer was being pummeled by a reptilian creature with long, muscled arms like an ape. A lawnmower came to his rescue, slicing through the creature's legs. Blood spewed, and Bird laughed seeing it. She hadn't had this much fun in a thousand years.

The ghosts were fighting the shadow wights. It was a quiet battle. And there was a dragon in the midst of it all. Bird watched as he picked up a blood mole and stuffed it in his mouth like it was a jelly doughnut someone had left in the break room. Then, he looked up and saw Bird watching him.

The dragon cocked his head to one side. His pince-nez made him look like a scholar. He turned around and squeezed through the doorway of Galactic Books.

* * *

Elijah screamed as a tongue wrapped around him. His wife screamed. His children screamed. But his dog, Sasha, lunged at the tongue, grabbing it in her teeth and shaking.

Galactic Books frowned. It loved Elijah. A fist made of bricks flew out of the wall, punching a hole where the monster's head used to be.

After a brief silence, the Schmidt family screamed again. The fist opened and scooped them up, including their puppy-turned-hellhound. It pulled them into the wall and wrapped itself around them protectively. "You'll be fine," the building murmured.

* * *

Sir Walter squeezed into the bookstore, which was a little easier now that all the front glass had been shattered. "Hey, Cat Lord," he said.

"I'm quite busy!" The Cat Lord was fighting a half dozen vampires. They circled him like a gang of bullies.

"I can see that. But I thought you might want to know about the creature on one of the buildings across the street. Some kind of winged demon."

"Does she have a magical key?" The Cat Lord ducked and rolled as a vampire lunged at him. The roll brought him close to a female vampire, who kicked him with her stylish boots. He grabbed her foot and pulled her down as he jumped to his feet. He stabbed her with his sword, then parried as another vampire took a swing at him.

"You know, you're pretty spry for a middle-aged human, Robert," Sir Walter noted. "I'll go see if she has a key. I didn't notice one."

Sir Walter squeezed out of the bookstore. As he left, a monster latched onto his foot. He pulled it off and ate it. He was starting to get full.

Outside once again, Sir Walter looked at the demon again. He closed his right eye and looked at her through his left eye only—the magic eye, with the glowing astigmatism. The demon looked to be pure evil, made up of colors, including red, black, and . . . gold; there it is. She had a key—a magic one that was forged from a soul. Forged from the zombie girl's soul.

Sir Walter squeezed back through the doorway. "She has the key, Cat Lord," he announced. He plucked a vampire from the fight and tossed it. "Speaking of keys, when Artie fetched me for you, he said you needed me to forge a key?"

"Not anymore," the Cat Lord replied. "Gonna steal one instead." He threw his sword at the nearest vampire as his cloak turned into a thousand crows. The Cat Lord was gone.

* * *

Pineapple led Artie, Belinda, and Lanora to the Shadow King's lair. It was a castle that made Artie think of the Castle Grayskull play set his dad had found at a yard sale when Artie was a kid. His dad had been more excited than he was.

"We're not going in there, are we?" Artie asked.

"No, surely not," Belinda agreed.

"We shouldn't even be this close to it," Lanora said. The trio were crouched behind trees at the edge of the Shadow Woods.

"Mrrrr," the kitten said, pacing in front of them. She headed toward the castle, weaving in its general direction until she abruptly stopped and rolled onto her back.

"Okay. Let's be smart about this," Artie said. But his eyes were closed, so it wasn't clear whether he was talking to Lanora and his mother or to the Cat Lord.

"Should we turn around and go back to the Cat Lord's Cottage?" Belinda asked.

"No," Artie replied. "The Cat Lord needs us to do this. Apparently, so does Meridian. She's meeting us on the other side of the door. But the door is in the Shadow King's throne room."

"If we're going, and I think we must, then I have a request," Lanora said. "I want Belinda to stay here."

"But this is it. This is the door to our world," Artie pleaded.

"She will almost certainly be killed en route."

"That's a good point," Artie said. "Mom. You stay here."

"That's ridiculous, and you know it," Belinda said, with her hands on her hips.

Artie sighed. "Okay. Let me think." He stared at the ground, thinking. *Why did I bring my mom here? And how? The uncle . . . they traded places. What if . . .?* "Got it. We're sending her home the same way she got here."

"No," both women said.

"I'm going with you into that creepy castle, and you just deal with it," Belinda asserted.

"And I don't want my uncle back. Ever!" Lanora chimed in.

Artie shrugged. "Okay, but Mom, you need some kind of weapon or power or shield or something. A force field."

"I'm your mom. I *am* a force field."

"I believe her," Lanora said.

"Well. Okay then," Artie finally agreed. "Let's storm a castle and go home."

* * *

Sheriff John Amory was in trouble. He was out of ammunition. Even Franklin Davis seemed to be out of ammunition, reduced to running over monsters with his tank. But the sheriff didn't have a tank. He had one fellow officer, who was out of commission. Sonny Rogers had been pummeled by a giant, beefy-armed lizard. He was unconscious but safe, tucked inside the tank with Franklin.

The sheriff had a chainsaw in his hands. He was flanked by a young Bandersnatch and a couple of lawnmowers. But the monsters just kept coming in a never-ending flood.

"RRRah!" said the baby Bandersnatch.

Amory glanced at the Bandersnatch, surprised. "Good job, buddy! I don't know what that meant, but I'm sure it scared the Dickens outta someone."

"RRRRgh."

A fuzzy, blue monster ran at the sheriff. "He's fuzzy and blue,"

Amory noted aloud, feeling just a twinge of guilt as he cut into the monster with a chainsaw. It was like killing Grover. He half expected cotton stuffing to fly everywhere, but it was just blood and guts instead. "From head to bottom of shoe," the sheriff sang.

"RRRREEEE!"

"You're probably too young to know that one." And that's when Sheriff Amory saw the teenage girl standing in the street. "Aw, geez," he remarked. The Bandersnatch growled at her.

"Officer!" the girl yelled. Her shirt was torn and covered in blood. "Help me!"

Chip Harding ran to the girl. And the sheriff started to follow. They had to get her out of there.

The Bandersnatch grabbed the sheriff's pant leg with its teeth. "Let go," the sheriff demanded.

"Rrrr."

"Seriously. Let go."

The Bandersnatch looked up at Amory. Both eyes were as huge as they could get, which meant the big eye was enormous and the small one really unimpressive.

The girl clung to Chip's arm. He put a hand on her back and began guiding her toward the tank. But she tore his arm off. Black wings sprouted from her back and horns from her head. She was black leather all over. She smiled at the sheriff. "Won't you please help me, Mr. Sheriff?"

"I'll help you," the Cat Lord said, stepping through the battle toward her. He was carrying a sword and wearing a cloak that looked like it was made of dead birds.

"Ah, the famous Cat Lord," the girl said. "I'm going to enjoy killing you." Chip Harding used his dying breath to stab the girl's foot. "Ow!" she yelled. She kicked him, but he was already dead.

The Cat Lord dove at the girl with his sword. She suddenly produced a sword of her own and parried. The Cat Lord's sword shattered into dust. The girl reached out to grab him, but he turned into birds and scattered. He reassembled ten feet away.

"Cheater," the girl said.

An old woman with a knitting basket full of kittens and a teenage boy in a top hat stepped through the broken window of Galactic books and walked toward the confrontation. The old woman set her basket down next to the sheriff. "Be a good lad and watch this for an old Betsy, eh?"

"Ma'am, I don't think you should be here," Amory replied. "And these kittens *definitely* shouldn't be here."

The battle went on all around them. Ghosts fought shadows. A heavily-armed child ghost launched a very real grenade at a line of shadow wights. A car exploded.

"You're the one who shouldn't be here," the teenage boy said to the sheriff while pulling a sword from his hat.

"That chainsaw needs a wee bit more magic, I'd say, hey wot," the old woman said. She pulled a strand of light from her basket, twisted it in the air, and threw it at the sheriff. He and his chainsaw both sparkled alarmingly.

A winged monster flew at Amory. He slashed through it with renewed energy. Electricity sparked, singeing the monster as it fell.

"Can you do that for the others?" the sheriff asked, nodding toward Mike and the firemen. They were stuffing a monster into a wood chipper while the lawnmowers around them fought creatures of varying sizes and physiques.

"Oh, those are lovely laddies." The woman patted her hair, pulled out her knitting needles and a ball of magic, and slipped through the battle to go weave some magic.

* * *

Cheese Fry stood in the battle, in a sea of calm, protected by frogs. It was amazing how quickly they could reduce a body to bones.

* * *

The Cat Lord sized up his opponent. "Who are you?" he asked.

"Just a bird, like you," the girl replied.

"I'm a cat, actually."

"You're a contradiction. I like it." The girl winked at him.

"You're not from Detritus."

"I was. Once. But then, someone forgot about me, and I slipped through to another story. A darker one."

"Ah. A forgotten character. What a pity."

"You're the one who needs pity."

The Cat Lord smiled and nodded at someone behind the girl. She took a step back and risked a glance. Cats—five of them, just sitting and watching.

"I'm not intimidated by your cats," the girl spat.

"If you're a bird, you probably should be."

"I'm so much more than a bird."

"I can see that. And you have a pretty key."

"And you have nothing at all." The girl pulled magic and began to weave a net made of darkness.

The Cat Lord reached into his cloak and pulled out light. "*Let's see what kind of weapon you got for me*," he said to Artie.

"*I think you're really going to like it*," Artie told him.

The light became a lightsaber. "*Nerd.*"

Bird threw the darkness. The Cat Lord ran to meet it, swinging his blade.

"*Now YOU'RE a Jedi, too!*" Artie said.

* * *

Blackbird Lane was full of shadows. "You worry about the door; let us worry about the shadow wights," Calvin said to Meridian. He and Norma slipped off Spencer's back.

"*Lanora? Are you in place yet?*" Meridian asked. "*Lanora?*"

* * *

Even with so many shadow wights having slipped through the door to cause trouble in Biddleborn, the Shadow King's fortress was heavily guarded. "They'll know we're here before they even see us," Lanora warned Artie and Belinda. "The magic will alert them."

"And where is this door that we're looking for?" Belinda asked.

"In the throne room, at the heart of the castle."

"Of course," Artie said.

The Shadow Woods ended abruptly one hundred feet from the castle. It was all the clearing the Shadow King felt he needed to ensure no one sneaked up on him.

"So, what's our plan, Artie?" Belinda asked.

"Meridian can get us right inside the throne room. Do you still have the key?"

"I do."

"We'll need it for this door. It has to be opened from both sides."

"How's Meridian going to—"

Before Belinda could finish, they were in a vast room, before a throne. The Shadow King was in Biddleborn, so no one was sitting upon the throne. A shadow wight screamed. It was a high-pitched sound that reverberated throughout the castle.

"I don't see a magical-looking door," Belinda noted. Artie waved a hand through the magic-laden air, like pulling back a curtain. "Oh, I see it now." It looked like an ordinary door—like the sort of door that might enter into a child's bedroom.

Shadows poured into the room. They were accompanied by an old woman in enormous glasses. Belinda pulled out the key. "You two fight. I'll get the door unlocked."

Lanora and Artie ran into battle. Artie screamed, "Cowabunga!"

Artie's mother rolled her eyes. "That boy."

Chapter 34

THE SHADOW KING STEPPED OUT of the air and onto Blackbird Lane, where the dead girl, Norma Bellows, and her friends fought shadows. He stood before the door.

Meridian attempted to slip gracefully from her winged horse's back, but her foot hit a rock. Her ankle twisted, and she fell to her knees. "Dadgummit!" The Shadow King moved toward her. "Norma! We forgot to finish the story!"

Norma swung her ax at one shadow while ducking the claws of another. "What story?"

"The Shadow King. Remember? At our sleepover."

"Ah yes, *that* story! You go first."

The Shadow King reached out to put his hands around Norma's throat. Meridian swung her sword, clumsily but with rage. She took a step back. "Everyone feared the Shadow King, but they didn't know he had a fear, too—a secret fear . . ."

"No!" the Shadow King shouted as he threw himself at Meridian. Meridian stabbed him. But he dissolved, then reformed behind her with his hands around her throat.

"His fear was of the undead," Norma said, continuing the story, "because of the prophecy that he would one day be slain by one who was neither living nor dead."

Meridian kicked. Her fingers scrambled to free her throat. Norma ran at the Shadow King with her ax. He dropped Meridian and turned to face her, but it was too late.

The zombie girl's ax split open the Shadow King's head. "Oh, look. The prophecy came true," Norma said.

Meridian threw up on the grass.

* * *

The Cat Lord cut through Bird's net of dark magic. Twirling in an athletic way that he would deeply regret in the morning, he attacked her. She parried and spun with all the energy of youth.

"I don't believe you," the Cat Lord said.

"You don't believe what?"

"That you're just a girl. I think you're a thousand years old if you're a day."

Bird laughed.

Shadow wights screamed around them. They could feel the Shadow King die. The ghost of Jazz Miller whooped in triumph.

"She's definitely just a really old crone," Ross Jacoby said, running by. He was being chased by a giant hellhound.

Holmes Peabody landed in front of Ross. He punched the hound. And the hound flew away.

The Cat Lord turned his attention back to Bird, who was starting to look old around the eyes and mouth. "You're both wrong," she said. "I am young and carefree. I am chaos. I am youth. I am beauty."

"Now that's an obvious lie," Ross said.

"Look around," the Cat Lord told Bird. "You're losing this battle."

"Am I? It was never about winning or losing. It was about chaos and oblivion."

"Oh, well, in that case . . ." The Cat Lord pounced on Bird, turning into a large black and white cat in mid-jump.

Bird tried to stab the Cat Lord but found she had no arms. Her sword fell as she turned into a bird. The cat fell on her, pinning her. He ate her, key and all.

* * *

In a child's bedroom, on the other side of Biddleborn, a group of five pajama-clad seven-year-old girls sat in a circle. One held a flashlight. "And then, the brave child defeated the monsters," she said. She handed the flashlight to the girl next to her.

"The battle was over," the next girl continued. "The doors were opened and closed."

The next child held the flashlight. "The monsters all died or went home."

"Well, *almost* all the monsters," said the last child.

* * *

The shadow wights fled from the castle. The Shadow King's emissary glared at Artie, Belinda, and Lanora, with her eyes magnified behind her glasses. "You think you've won, but you're wrong," she told them. "This night marks the end of your world as you know it."

"That is probably true," Artie said.

Lanora raised her sword and ran at the old woman. The emissary hesitated, then ran from the throne room. Lanora watched her go. "Coward," Lanora muttered.

"Okay, let's do this thing," Artie said.

Belinda put the key in the door. On the other side, Meridian picked the lock with a butter knife. The door crumbled to dust.

"Is that what was supposed to happen?" Belinda asked. "Because that seems like a bad thing."

"We'll need to secure this fortress so that the shadows don't return," Lanora said. "We'll keep this doorway safe. We cannot let the Shadow King have free access to your world."

Meridian stepped through the doorway into Biddleborn. "The Shadow King is dead," she announced.

Artie smiled at Meridian. But Meridian was focused on the throne room. Then, she looked at Lanora. “It’s you!” she exclaimed.

“Indeed,” Lanora replied.

The two girls stared at each other, each one a filtered, perfected image of the other.

“That can’t be mentally healthy,” Artie stage whispered to his mother.

Calvin and Norma Bellows stepped through the open doorway. “My lady! It’s good to be home!” Calvin said. “Although Biddleborn is a nice place to visit, I assume, on a normal, monster-free day.”

Norma had been in the Shadow King’s throne room once before. It seemed a lifetime ago, but it had been, what . . . the day before? She wasn’t the same person as that girl had been, though. Zombie Norma was as much a product of Meridian’s imagination as Calvin was. She was no more Norma Bellows than he was Jazz Miller.

“So, what happens now?” Artie asked. “Is the battle over?” Meridian shrugged, and Artie closed his eyes. “Ew,” he said. “The Cat Lord’s eating . . . a bird.” He looked at Meridian. “Dude. I have so much to tell you. Also, I can’t believe you made all this up and never told me about it.”

Meridian shrugged again. “I never intended to share it with anyone.”

“Would you like to explore Detritus?” Lanora asked.

“I would. But not tonight. I need to make sure Carl’s okay.”

“And you have school tomorrow,” Belinda pointed out.

Meridian and Artie looked at her. “You can’t be serious,” Artie said. “I didn’t even finish my homework.”

Chapter 35

SHERIFF AMORY AND MOWEY organized the cleanup on Main Street. Mowey convinced the now-sentient lawnmowers, saws, and wood chipper to return to Bucky's and to refrain from talking when humans were around.

The fire department declared the post office fire an accident. The firemen helped pile up the zombies that weren't destroyed in the fire. Sir Walter burned the zombies, as he was far too finicky to eat zombie flesh. But he took the rest of the monsters' bodies home with him. He froze most of them, wrapped in butcher paper with the date neatly written on, thinking he could have a barbecue. Maybe he'd invite his new friends from Biddleborn.

Franklin Davis removed his tank from Main Street. The ghosts faded away. And Sonny Rogers was taken to the hospital. "He fell down a flight of really mean stairs," was the excuse Franklin gave to the emergency room staff.

Ross Jacoby was also taken to the emergency room, driven there by Zelda and Rose Marie. "You can take tomorrow off," Zelda told him. "But I expect to see you in class on Monday."

"Yes, ma'am," Ross agreed.

Zelda hugged him.

Rose Marie told the ER staff that Ross had been bitten by a really mean dog. "A little one," Ross added. "And it's probably not mean anymore. Just scared. But someone'll find it and give it a good home."

Rose Marie ruffled the boy's hair. "That was a good story," she said.

The Salt Boy stole an entire *Star Wars* chess set from Galactic Books before returning to Biddleborn. And the bookstore opened its wall and let its owner and his family out. It patted Elijah on the head and went back to sleep.

When the Schmidt family returned home, their house was devoid of monsters. Mr. Fred was in the living room, watching an infomercial about a three-in-one exercise machine.

* * *

The chickens were in the coop when Carl and Meridian arrived home. The sun was just beginning to rise. The sky showed pale through the trees that encircled their property.

"You're not making me go to school tomorrow, are you?" Meridian asked.

"No. I may never let you out of my sight again, in fact," Carl replied. The rooster was patrolling the yard. He crowed. Carl pulled out his sword. "You stay away. I don't feel like fighting with you."

The rooster plucked a spider from the ground and ate it. "That should be the last of 'em," the rooster said. "Don't be such an ingrate."

Carl sighed and put his sword away. "Sorry. Thanks."

The rooster nodded.

Carl and Meridian went into the house. The ghost of Carl's mother was gone, having drunk all the Pepsi. Meridian went up to her room and sat by her window.

Detritus was real. Lanora and the Cat Lord and Calvin were real. Mayzell was real. It felt weird and wrong to Meridian to continue making up stories about them, but what if those stories were necessary? What if the characters only existed as long as she made up adventures for them?

Besides, Meridian had made a promise to the Salt Boy. She didn't want to keep it, but . . . it would make for a really good storyline for him to ascend the throne as the King of Detritus.

* * *

Artie tried to talk Cheese Fry and Meridian into moving forward with the prayer vigil for his safe return, but they voted him down. He wanted to make up an exciting story about where he had been for the past couple of days, but they voted him down on that, too. "It needs to be a boring story," Meridian said.

"But maybe it involves Artie finding a treasure?" Ross Jacoby suggested.

"But if I found a treasure, would I want to tell everyone?" Artie pointed out.

"No. Definitely not," Ross agreed.

In the end, the story they agreed on was that Artie got turned around in the woods and wandered for a couple of days before he found his way back to the highway. Sheriff Amory said the story was good enough for the *Biddleborn Daily News* to believe and boring enough for the news outlet not to pursue it any further.

Artie bought a journal so he could write about the adventure he had—he didn't want to forget any of it. He stuck mainly to the truth, but Ross had made a really good point. So, Artie added a paragraph about the treasure he had found.

* * *

Holmes Peabody decided that this little town he found himself in wasn't such a bad place. Its inhabitants certainly seemed as though they could use a resident superhero. And it was time for him to start over anyway. Why not there? No one would ever think to look for him in Biddleborn.

Holmes would need a secret identity, of course. There was a vacancy on the police force, such as it was. That seemed like the perfect cover.

* * *

On Monday, Meridian and Artie were surprised to see the Cat Lord was still teaching science at Biddleborn High School. “I thought you’d be home by now,” Meridian said.

“With the door between worlds gone, it’s so easy to come and go,” Robert Gray replied.

“You like teaching us?”

“I mean, it’s not terrible. And it’s only five more weeks, right? It wouldn’t be easy for them to find someone else.” Mr. Gray shrugged. “Besides, there may be some lingering . . . *effects* that need to be dealt with.” He looked at Artie.

“So, what are we learning about today?” Artie asked.

“Uh . . .” Mr. Gray looked at his notes. “Blood and stuff, mostly.”

From the Publisher

Thank You from the Publisher

Van Rye Publishing, LLC ("VRP") sincerely thanks you for your interest in and purchase of this book.

VRP hopes you will please consider taking a moment to help other readers like you by leaving a rating or review of this book at your favorite online book retailer. You can do so by visiting the book's product page and locating the button for leaving a rating or review.

Thank you!

Resources from the Publisher

Van Rye Publishing, LLC ("VRP") offers the following resources to readers and to writers.

For *readers* who enjoyed this book or found it useful, please consider receiving updates from VRP about new and discounted books like this one. You can do so by following VRP on Facebook (at www.facebook.com/vanryepub), Twitter (at www.twitter.com/vanryepub), or Instagram (at www.instagram.com/vanryepub).

For *writers* who enjoyed this book or found it useful, please consider having VRP edit, format, or fully publish your book manuscript. You can find out more and submit your manuscript at VRP's website (at www.vanryepublishing.com).

Thank you again!

About the Author

SHEILA STOWERS was born and raised in Southern Illinois, where she taught high school English for a long time. She now lives in Northeast Arkansas, where she shares a small cabin with an awful lot of cats and a solitary tortoise. She also has a small herd of goats and a flock of chickens, including a rooster who regards her with suspicion. Some of Sheila's animals helped inspire the characters in her debut young adult fantasy novel titled *Biddleborn: A Fantasy World Attacks*. When she isn't caring for animals or writing, Sheila works at a local university, where she stares at data and writes reports.

www.ingramcontent.com/pod-product-compliance
Lightning Source LLC
Chambersburg PA
CBHW070855250626
47159CB00003B/1072

* 9 7 8 1 9 5 7 9 0 6 0 2 7 *